THE MYSTERY OF
THE *SEMPIONE*

BLACKIE & SON LIMITED
  16/18 William IV Street,
    Charing Cross, London, W C.2
  17 Stanhope Street, Glasgow

BLACKIE & SON (INDIA) LIMITED
  103/5 Fort Street, Bombay

BLACKIE & SON (CANADA) LIMITED
  Toronto

Also by Percy F. Westerman

HELD IN THE FROZEN NORTH
THE WESTOW TALISMAN
CAPTAIN STARLIGHT
DAVENTRY'S QUEST
THE LURE OF THE LAGOON
CADET ALAN CARR
WINGED MIGHT
MIDSHIPMAN OF THE FLEET
THE MISSING DIPLOMAT
"SEA SCOUTS, ALERT!"
etc.

A challenge for Captain Corbière

Page 192

THE MYSTERY OF
THE SEMPIONE

PERCY F. WESTERMAN

Illustrated by P. B. Batchelor

BLACKIE & SON LIMITED

LONDON AND GLASGOW

First published 1957

Printed in Great Britain by Blackie & Son, Ltd., Glasgow

Contents

Illustrations

I

THE SCHEME

'BOMBARDO'S given permission, Brian,' exclaimed Ambrose Steele, tenant of the Estancia Miraflores on the outskirts of the town of Camata in the republic of Bolomaya.

'That's grand news, Dad,' exclaimed his son. 'That means it's quite all right for the three of us?'

Mr. Steele shook his head. 'Unfortunately no,' he replied. 'But we must, I suppose, be thankful for small mercies. He writes that he is now willing to give permission for Ted and you to leave the country, but before you do he insists upon a personal interview with both of you.'

'I can't clear out back to England and leave you here alone,' declared Brian explosively. 'What do you say, Ted?'

'Can't be done,' rejoined Ted Evans. 'I'll stick it with you, Bags! This tin-pot war can't last much longer. When it's over, who's to stop us clearing out?'

'Bags' was the name by which Brian Antony George Steele was commonly called when he was at school in England. Actually he owed that nickname to his parents and his godparents at his baptism since the initials, plus that of his surname, made up a word that according to the dictionary means in the singular a pouch or a sack. Brian would have it that it was schoolboy slang meaning 'claim' or 'choose', although his fellows asserted that it had something to do with an article of apparel. In any case Brian accepted Bags much in the same way as he received 'impots'—and he used to have more than a fair share of these!

Two years previously Mr. Steele had taken over the Estancia Miraflores from his uncle, who had settled in Bolomaya some years earlier. Under Bolomayan laws no foreigner can own property although he can rent it, under a complicated system, and not be dispossessed except for treason or rebellion or failure to pay rent and government taxes. With these exceptions his tenure was secure. On the other hand he could only quit when his liabilities to the republic were liquidated. If, for example, a life-tenant got into debt with the government his goods could be seized, but he must remain and work until his commitments were liquidated. During that period all his earnings went direct to the authorities, who, however, allowed the unfortunate tenant a small monthly sum for the bare necessities of life.

Obviously the Republic of Bolomaya had it both ways!

For the first twelve months of his occupation of the Estancia Miraflores, Ambrose Steele had done remarkably well, even exceeding his expectations in view of his ignorance of the ways and means of the country. So much so that he had sent for his son, who had just left school, in order to give him what promised to be a good start in life.

With Brian came his school friend Ted Evans, for the more or less plausible reason that he wanted to learn Spanish as spoken in South America before taking up an appointment with a shipping firm whose interests lay chiefly in the Pacific ports.

Then came the war with Grossaguay. Most of the *peons* left the Estancia Miraflores, though greatly against their inclinations. Mr. Steele was invited to take an active part, since he had held a commission in the Royal Engineers. Most justifiably he had refused.

President Hermandez Bombardo had taken the Englishman's refusal with ill-grace. Every petty annoyance he could think of he put into operation against Ambrose Steele. While hostilities lasted, the occupier of the Estancia Miraflores had no means of obtaining redress. Communications with outside were practically cut off. Correspondence was strictly censored and in many cases letters were not allowed to go through. There was a British Consul in Ligna Salta, the capital of Bolomaya, but he, like many of his confrères in smaller countries, was a native of the country. Señor Limones, although he sported the arms of Great Britain over his door, took very good care not to fall foul of the arrogant President Bombardo!

Very soon after the declaration of hostilities Ambrose Steele was almost on his beam-ends. His capital was 'locked up' by the Bolomayan Government. No currency was allowed to be sent out of the country. It had to be held by the government against a 'paper' guarantee. Things came to such a pass that Steele decided to cut his losses and return home until conditions in Bolomaya improved—if ever they did. Now hitherto unsuspected difficulties arose; he was informed that he could not give up the estancia until certain financial conditions had been observed—conditions that, in the circumstances, were beyond his means to carry out.

Then Steele made an application to the Government for permission to be given to his son and Ted Evans to leave for England. Again Bombardo refused. But now, when the boys were reconciling themselves to an enforced detention, came the President's letter giving the required permission in the case of the two youths, subject to an interview with Bombardo at the Presidency at Ligna Salta.

'It will have to be done, boys,' said Mr. Steele quietly, in answer to their protests. 'The sooner you two get away from here the better! I wish I could too! I'm practically on my beam-ends. Alone, I can jog along until there's a change for the better. I don't mind telling you that I've just about enough ready cash to pay your fares as far as Panama. Then you'll be all right, as I know of someone there who will advance your passage money. I'll give you a letter for him.'

'What's the bright idea of having an interview with Bombardo, Dad?' asked Brian.

'I don't know,' confessed his parent. 'It seems—well—unusual.'

'Perhaps he wants us to promise we'll say nothing about your plight when we get out of the country, Mr. Steele,' suggested Ted.

'If that's what it is, he's wasting his time,' asserted Brian stoutly. 'Are you coming with us for the interview?'

'Bombardo particularly stressed the point that I was not required,' replied Mr. Steele. 'However, I am riding into Ligna Salta with you. Then, if his conditions—I fancy there are conditions!—aren't straight and above board, we'll abandon all present attempts to leave the country and stick it out! All the same, I want you both to return to England, so if there's nothing unusual about Bombardo's terms you'd better agree.'

'Well, gentlemen, that is the present position,' declared President Hermandez Bombardo, giving a swift comprehensive glance at the faces of his colleagues seated on both sides of the long table. 'We are more than holding our own, as the reports I have just read to you from various commanders in the field tend to prove. It wants but a sortie by General Sandano, timed to coincide with our advance northwards, to get the Grossaguayan forces into a trap from which they will not be able to extricate themselves. Our present difficulty is to get into direct communication with Sandano. But how? Has anyone any suggestion to make on that matter?'

For some moments there was silence broken only by the buzzing of insects as they flew in and out from the *patio*.

No one present believed the President's assertion. He himself did not, but that hardly mattered. If, as seemed likely to happen, the Grossaguayans won the war—and they had been forced into it by the Republic of Bolomaya's acts of aggression extending over a number of years—this Bombardo would take care to make a speedy exit, together with all the available cash upon which he could lay his hands!

At best, the war between Grossaguay and Bolomaya was a miserable affair. The opposing powers had commenced with tolerably well-equipped armies. A few weeks of desultory engagements had deprived both sides of their aircraft; an arms embargo by the United States and most of the European countries had crippled their supplies. Mechanical transport had broken down owing to lack of oil; medical supplies were almost at vanishing point. Yet in spite of these deficiencies, the rival armies were still at it, with every prospect of success going to the Grossaguayans.

It was not as an effort to retrieve the fortunes of the day that President Bombardo had suggested co-operation with General Sandano, whose army was at that moment practically surrounded. Far from it! General Sandano had been Bombardo's rival, although the breach was supposed to have been healed when the war with Grossaguay was begun. He was holding his own, and if circumstances made it necessary, he could retreat with his men and be interned in the neighbouring republic of Catamarca.

This was precisely what Bombardo did not want.
His chief interest, apart from making a safe exit himself, was to see Sandano out of the way. Sandano
might well be the next President of Bolomaya—he was
far more fitted for that position than the present ruler.
To Bombardo such a position was unthinkable. Rather
in his downfall he would drag his rival down. Yet at
the conference the double-faced President was sug-
gesting co-operative action with Sandano against the
enemy!

'We can send an aircraft,' suggested one of the
assembly.

Bombardo shrugged his shoulders. 'Where is there
one fit for service? Even if there should be, it would
be better employed in dropping bombs. And, fortunately for us, the enemy machines are worn out.
Otherwise we might not be sitting here in comfort!'

'By radio, then.'

Again Bombardo shrugged his shoulders. 'That is
not to be thought of, Major Ramon. You, as well as
all of us, know that General Sandano cannot decode
messages since his cipher-key was lost during the
retreat to Carabaya.'

'Not lost, but deliberately destroyed, Excellency,'
corrected Ramon. 'We had it on unimpeachable
authority.'

'That does not affect my point,' returned Bombardo
coldly. 'The fact remains that we cannot communicate
with the brave Sandano by air or by radio. As you
know, no *peon* will dare attempt to make his way
through the enemy lines, bearing in mind what happened to those who tried and failed. Well, gentlemen,
since no one seems to be ready to suggest a feasible
plan, it falls upon me, your President, to expound
one—one which I think will meet with your entire
approval.'

There was a prolonged murmur of applause.

Actually it meant little. The President's sycophants were probably thinking that they were about to listen to yet another of his ill-considered schemes. Goodness knows, they had listened to several of Bombardo's plans that invariably had come to naught.

The President fairly beamed. Like many another arrogant, self-opinionated person he almost existed on adulation. 'I have received another application from the Englishman Steele, on behalf of his son and of the other youth, also an Englishman, who lives with them,' he proceeded. 'He again asks permission for them to leave Bolomaya. This time I am prepared to grant his request—at a price!'

The assembly began to sit up and take notice. What connection was there between Señor Ambrose Steele, now resident in Camata, and General Sandano?

'At a price?' echoed Ramon. 'Why, the Englishman isn't worth a thousand dollars! His estancia was searched for hidden wealth. Since then, part of it was burned—accidentally, of course. Your Excellency, do you hope to get money out of him?'

'I do not,' replied Bombardo. 'Here is my plan: I propose letting these two English youths leave the country on condition that one of them carries a letter to General Sandano arranging for the sortie. The ship in which they will sail from Santa Teresa puts in at La Serena, since she is under the neutral flag of Catamarca. At La Serena they will hand the dispatch to one of our trusted agents who will arrange for it to be sent to Sandano at Carabaya.'

'But the Grossaguayan warships?' demurred another of the assembly. 'They search every vessel leaving and entering our seaports.'

'Exactly,' agreed Bombardo. 'That is why I have decided to employ these English youths. Because they are English they will not be subjected to search. None of our nationals would dare venture himself at sea

2

on account of risk of capture and imprisonment by the enemy.'

'Your plan seems good, Excellency!'

'Of course it is good,' rejoined Bombardo complacently. 'At the end of this meeting I will see that the necessary letter be sent to Señor Steele. And now to other matters.'

II

THE AMBUSH

EARLY next morning the three Englishmen set
out on their twenty miles' ride to the capital.
To those accustomed to easy locomotion on modern
roads twenty miles seem a mere nothing. In Bolomaya
roads were never good, while a year of hostilities had
allowed them to deteriorate. There was very little
motor traffic. Petrol for private use had long been
exhausted; even the mechanical transport of the
Bolomayan armies could scarcely be kept running
owing to scarcity of fuel, quite apart from the fact
that most of the vehicles had been worn out, chiefly
through ignorance or neglect on the part of the drivers.
The railways, too, were mainly restricted to the use
of the government. Coal- and oil-fed locomotives had
been reduced to burning wood in the furnaces and
even wood was scarce. Even if there were room for
three civilians—and *Americanos*, as Englishmen are
frequently termed in many parts of Latin America,
at that—the almost prohibitive cost combined with
the slow and erratic speed of the train made them
decide to go on horseback.

Riding, too, was not an easy matter, although in
the country districts even the *peons* were frequently
to be seen mounted. Recently conditions in that respect
had changed. Almost every well-conditioned horse
had been requisitioned by the Government. At the
Estancia Miraflores only three miserable 'screws' had

been left in the long range of stables, and it was on these three animals that Mr. Steele and the two lads started on their arduous ride to Ligna Salta.

Arduous! It was positively dangerous.

Even before the war with Grossaguay, Bolomaya was remarkable for the lawlessness of its mixed population. Now conditions were worse. Bandits, recruited from deserters from the rabble that for the most part composed the armies, roamed in bands. Hitherto poor travellers had been left alone; now no wayfarer was safe, since the robbers were as much in need of food and clothing as they were of money. The only safeguard was to be well-armed and resolute. It was even difficult for travellers to be well-armed, since good rifles had gone the way of good horses. Mr. Steele carried a Remington rifle slung over his right shoulder. Brian and Ted each sported a large revolver of ancient vintage. What these weapons lost in accuracy they made up for in noise. Among the three horsemen they mustered twenty-five rounds of ammunition.

For the first five or six miles their journey was uneventful except for the difficulties of the bad road. Several groups of doubtful characters were met but since these gentry rarely possess courage unless backed by long odds, the sight of three armed men was sufficient to restrain their nefarious ardour.

Then came a defile called by an Indian name which means 'the twists of a snake'. It was an ideal place for an ambush—one of the bandits' favourite methods of attack, although they usually made the mistake of opening fire at ranges that gave them a chance of missing their victims, especially as their rifles and ammunition were not reliable.

For the first time since they left the Estancia Mira-flores, Mr. Steele unslung his rifle. He didn't like the look of the place and wished he and his youthful companions were safely through the narrow pass. 'I'm keeping twenty yards ahead, boys,' he announced. 'Ted, you'd better drop back until you're the same distance behind Brian. Keep your pistols handy and if you see a suspicious movement, fire a couple of rounds.'

The lads took up the desired intervals. So thick was the cloud of dust thrown up that Brian could not see his father, while Ted could discern neither. This was an advantage, since, if there were bandits lying in wait, they would be unable to make out the number of the approaching horsemen.

Nothing happened until Ambrose Steele was within a hundred yards of the end of the pass. Then a regular fusillade rang out. Bullets whizzed overhead, some ricocheting against the rocky walls of the miniature canyon. Above the crack of the rifles came the deeper sound of an explosion, followed by groans and shrieks.

Brian spurred on his horse. He could hear the sharp crack of his father's Remington. A moment later he caught sight of his parent through the dust. Ambrose Steele had dismounted and was keeping his rifle trained upon the clump of cacti from which the shots had come. There was still a lot of shrieking and groans. Men were running for dear life towards the place where they had hobbled their horses.

For some reason or other the ambush had failed, unless the flight and the groans were part of a ruse to lure the travellers to their destruction.

'You all right?' asked Mr. Steele without turning his head, and keeping his rifle levelled at the sound of the attack.

'Yes,' replied Brian.

'Where's Ted?'

Brian couldn't say.

'I'm not wasting cartridges on them,' continued his father, indicating the fugitives. 'There's the little mob that may give trouble—behind that scrub. Ted here yet?'

'Here he comes!'

Ted's sorry steed at first had shown a tendency to bolt at the noise of the firing; now it went to the opposite extreme. In spite of its rider's effort to pull it up, the animal dashed forward, narrowly missing a collision with Brian's mount. Mr. Steele had to leap sideways to avoid being run down. Hampered as he was by holding his rifle he could not clutch at the runaway's bridle. The maddened brute had actually reached the end of the pass before Ted managed to get it under control. He had now placed the suspected clump of cacti between him and his friends, but no shots were fired either by the bandits who were supposed to be in ambush or by those who had fled.

In a minute or so, Brian heard the hoofs of Ted's mount. Then Ted emerged from the heavy, stifling cloud of dust. 'What's up over there?' he exclaimed breathlessly. 'It looks as if the bandits have been shooting a batch of prisoners!'

Such a thing was by no means uncommon. Murder is quite a frequent occurrence in Bolomaya, and robbers often shot their victims in cold blood when the amount of the booty fell short of their expectations.

But that did not account for the fusillade directed at the Steeles and young Evans. With their weapons ready for instant use, they rode along the narrow road towards the clump of thorns. It proved to be an unnecessary precaution, for the four men lying on the ground were beyond being capable of resistance. Brian and his father dismounted and gave the reins to Ted whose mount had now regained its normal state of docility.

It was a nasty sight that met their eyes. One man had both arms shattered above the elbow; two men were writhing and holding their hands to their faces;

the fourth, groaning dismally, had his groin pierced by the barrel of a rifle. He was trying, though ineffectually, to pull the metal tube from his wound.

Taking one of the wounded men's gaudy scarves, Mr. Steele began to apply a rough and ready tourniquet. He was too late. The man died even as his intended victim attempted to aid him.

It was the same with the bandit who had been transfixed by the gun-barrel. Even as Ambrose Steele gently applied force to the piece of bent metal, the victim, giving a hideous shriek, kicked convulsively and died.

For the two blinded bandits they could do little beyond tying wet bandages over their scarred faces. No doubt their villainous comrades would return to the scene after the coast was clear.

Out of curiosity, Mr. Steele extracted one of the unused cartridges from the bandolier of the bandit whose arms had been blown off. A brief examination told him how the tragedy—fortunate as far as he and his companions were concerned—had foiled the robbers in their cowardly attempt.

Owing to the scarcity of ammunition the bandits had hoarded their spent cartridge cases, refilling them in many instances with common gunpowder and recapping them with detonating powder of a doubtful quality. The victim had gone one further. Ignorant of its peculiarly deadly properties he had filled his cartridges with dynamite, with the inevitable result. Instead of expelling the bullet, the dynamite had shattered the rifle at the breech and had killed or blinded the owner and three others nearest to him. No wonder, then, that their companions, terror-stricken at the seemingly inexplicable blow, had jumped to the erroneous conclusion that their intended victims had hurled a bomb into their midst. That explained their headlong flight.

This was the only adventure that the Steeles and Evans had on their journey to Ligna Salta. Quite possibly the surviving bandits, on their flight, had communicated the news of their discomfiture to other bands of marauders, and, filled with superstitious fear, the Bolomayan 'gentlemen of the road' had decided to suspend business for that day.

III

THE INTERVIEW WITH BOMBARDO

THREE hours later the travellers arrived at the capital. Stabling their horses, they entered the *fonda* for a much-wanted meal.

'I'll wait here until you have seen Bombardo,' said Mr. Steele. 'If it is quite satisfactory I'll go on to Santa Teresa and see you safely on board.'

'But how about getting back to Miraflores?' asked Brian

'That will be all right. I'm selling the horses in any case. They'll fetch a fair price here and then I think I can run to the expense of a railway ticket.'

At four in the afternoon, the time-honoured South American custom of *siesta* being over, Brian and Ted presented themselves at the main entrance to the buildings.

A sentry, who was lolling in the shade and smoking an enormous cigar, lazily picked up his rifle and demanded their business.

'We wish to see President Bombardo,' declared Brian.

The soldier shook his head and ordered arms—he did this by dropping the butt of his rifle on the ground, and letting the fixed bayonet rest against his left shoulder.

'We have an appointment with President Bombardo,' announced Brian.

The sentry was unconvinced. '*Americanos?*' he asked.

'*Si!*' Brian knew that it was a waste of time to reply that he and his companion were English. The soldier would not understand the difference. 'Where is *el capitan?*' he demanded.

The sentry shrugged his shoulders. He did not know where the captain of the guard was. What he did know was that he was not in his quarters attached to the main-guard. After some delay he went off to fetch the sergeant. In the meanwhile Brian and Ted could have slipped through. They didn't. If they were late for the appointment they could get a bit of their own back upon the impudent sentry.

The sergeant, although annoyed at being disturbed in the middle of a game of cards, was impressed. All the same, he demanded to see the letter of appointment, which he held upside down and solemnly pretended to read.

'Our appointment with President Bombardo is at a quarter past four,' announced Brian firmly. 'It is nearly that now. If we are late his Excellency will ask why. I should regret to have to explain that, Sergeant —what is your name, Sergeant?'

That had the desired effect. They were escorted by a couple of soldiers to the portico of the main building. Here they were received by a gaudily uniformed official who, on being presented with their credentials, ushered them into an ante-room.

It was now four-fifteen.

Actually the clock had struck five before they were shown into the President's room and another twenty minutes elapsed before Bombardo arrived.

In spite of his tardiness Bombardo got down to business. 'You know, Señores, that I am making a great concession when I give you permission to leave Bolomaya? Already I have refused at least twenty such applications from foreigners.'

'We appreciate your condecenssion, Excellency,' replied Brian.

'That is well,' continued Bombardo with an oily smile. 'Of course, there are conditions.'

'Of course, Excellency!' echoed young Steele. 'Naturally, for instance, we would not give information likely to be of use to the enemies of the Republic.'

The President paused. He wasn't at all certain whether this young Englishman was not 'pulling his leg'. 'Supposing one of the conditions is that you render a service to the Republic?' he asked suavely.

'That depends,' replied Brian guardedly.

'It does; it depends upon this: if you refuse, then permission to leave Bolomaya is refused.'

'That's splendid!' declared Brian, to Bombardo's unconcealed astonishment. 'We don't want to go. It was only to fall in with my father's wishes that we agreed. If you say "no" that's final, I take it, Excellency?'

'I do not say "no",' declared the President. 'I give permission, but only upon a condition—one condition. It is a simple one, and you will not transgress the neutrality laws of your country if you give me your promise to carry it out. Now, this is the situation: I have arranged passages for you on board the Catamarcan ship *Sempione*, which is now loading in Santa Teresa harbour. She calls at La Serena, which is a Catamarcan port, on her way to Panama. Your passages to Panama will be provided free by the Bolomayan Government.'

'Free—why, Excellency?'

'I happen to know the financial condition of your esteemed father. Therefore it is within order that you two can be repatriated as distressed aliens. Now for the condition——'

'One moment, Excellency,' interrupted Ted, speaking for the first time during the interview. 'Knowing

Mr. Steele's financial difficulties, why cannot you give him permission to leave the Estancia Miraflores and go with us?'

Bombardo frowned. 'It is for purposes of diplomacy that I keep Mr. Steele here in Bolomaya!' he exclaimed angrily. Being angry, he threw away his sense of caution. 'I keep him in order that you carry out my instructions faithfully and well! Now listen: you go by the *Sempione*. You understand? I give you a letter. See, here it is——' He brought his clenched fist down upon the table. 'It is addressed to Señor Madeira in the Calle Huerta, La Serena, with an enclosure for my very dear friend and trusted colleague, General Sandano. The *Sempione* will remain in that port for a whole day; so you will land and deliver this letter personally to Señor Madeira. You will take great care of it, not show it to anyone except to the person addressed.'

'Why could you not give it to one of your fellow-countrymen to deliver?' asked Brian. 'That seems far the easier way.'

'For reasons that I prefer not to explain, I have decided to appoint you as my messenger, Señor Brian Steele,' replied Bombardo coldly. 'If this business is carried out to my entire satisfaction perhaps I can arrange for your father to follow you in the next ship leaving for Panama.'

'That's all right, Bags!' prompted Ted in English.

'What does this gentleman observe?' demanded the President suspiciously.

'Only that he's willing and so am I,' replied Brian, stretching out his hand for the sealed envelope.

'Not yet,' declared Bombardo. 'It would not be safe for you to carry that letter about here, in Ligna Salta, especially as you do not embark before noon tomorrow. When you arrive at Santa Teresa this envelope will be handed to you by one of the officers of my bodyguard. *Adios, señores!* Do not fail to be on board the *Sempione* before noon!'

He rang a bell. A manservant entered and escorted Brian and Ted from the President's room.

Bombardo waited until the sound of their footsteps died away along the marble-floored corridor. Then he rubbed his hands in utter self-satisfaction. His deep-laid plans were going well.

IV

FAREWELL TO BOLOMAYA

BRIAN and Ted lost no time in returning to the *fonda*.

'Well, lads?' inquired Mr. Steele.

They described the interview in detail.

'H'm! As far as I can see there's nothing against your becoming a sort of courier, Brian. Of course you don't know the contents of the letter and if anything should happen—we have to take possible happenings into account—you can honestly declare that you have no idea of what is inside the envelope. All the same, I'd like to know what is at the back of Bombardo's mind! And I'm to be a sort of hostage for your integrity and good behaviour!'

'What have you done about the horses, Dad?'

'Sold all three,' was the reply. 'And at quite good prices, too! I also got rid of one of the revolvers— I think I'm doing right by holding on to one. You won't want to handle a firearm again, I hope, once you are safely on board. Now, what about a meal? We'll have to turn in early as the train for Santa Teresa leaves at six—or, at least, it's supposed to start at that hour.'

A few minutes later they sat down to an unappetizing meal. Food was scarce and expensive, the bread consisting of a dull grey, stodgy substance. There was also soup—a fishy mixture, in which swam morsels of leathery meat the origin of which the chums debated

upon with the utmost candour. They were certainly
better off, from a gastronomic point of view, at the
Estancia Miraflores. There the home-produce was
good even though it erred on the side of monotony.
Then followed wine, and maize-cake and cheese.

Mainly for reasons of economy Mr. Steele had
engaged one fairly large bedroom on the second floor
of the inn. It was plainly furnished in the Bolomayan
style. Next morning they washed and dressed hurriedly
in the dim light of the kerosene lamp. The reek of
charcoal fumes and the chattering of voices proclaimed
the fact that the *fonda's* kitchen staff were preparing
the morning meal.

After a decidedly unsatisfying breakfast of coffee
and maize-cakes, Ted and Brian, accompanied by
Mr. Steele, made their way to the railway station.
They arrived there at five minutes to six. There was
no sign of the train, although a corpulent official
remarked that he thought it would soon be in.

Actually the train panted into the station at five
minutes to nine. Without any attempt at haste the
mob of passengers climbed the three steps to the
corridor carriages, taking their belongings, including
several dozens of live fowls and a couple of scraggy
goats, with them.

Then Ambrose Steele and his party boarded the
train and were fortunate enough to find themselves
with only about twenty fellow-passengers, including
half a dozen soldiers of the Presidential guard. Evidently Bombardo meant to make sure that his two
English envoys didn't back out at the last moment.

Still the train made no effort to start. The conductor, a gorgeously, though shabbily uniformed individual, was talking with the top-hatted station-
master. The driver, armed with a revolver and a
machete, had left his cab and was arguing angrily
with a wrinkled old woman.

Then another passenger arrived—a thin side-whiskered individual in sombre black clothes. The station master saluted him, as did the conductor. The driver, breaking off the argument, of which he obviously was getting the worse, climbed heavily into his cab. The conductor blew a blast upon his horn and with a wheezing grinding sound the train jerked itself into motion.

'Off at last!' exclaimed Ted.

The distance from the capital to Santa Teresa is eighteen miles. The journey took exactly an hour and five minutes. It wasn't the driver's fault. He, unlucky man, did his best to make up for lost time, but fate in the shape of neglected tracks was too much for him. At several places the line was so worn that the rims of the wheels rattled on the chairs; while at a trestle bridge the passengers were told to alight and walk across while the engine cautiously drew two carriages at a time across the rotting structure.

'Here at last!' declared Mr. Steele, as the train drew up with a bump as if reluctant to stop now that the journey was completed.

'You seem pleased to see the last of us, Dad!' remarked Brian.

'Pleased to see you out of this benighted hole,' confessed his father candidly. 'I only wish I was in the same boat, figuratively and literally. Suppose you try to get on board and see what happens. You'd better get a move on, it's nearly half past eleven!'

There were no taxis available, so the boys had to hire a couple of Indian porters to carry their belongings down to the harbour, a distance of about half a mile.

They found the *Sempione* lying alongside the inner mole. Cranes were still moving slowly, lifting goods from the quay and depositing them in the ship's holds. Nearly a hundred *peons*, gesticulating and shouting, were hindering the work in their languid efforts to assist. Near the gangway stood a group of shore officials and some of the *Sempione's* officers.

'*Halte!*'

A soldier with rifle and fixed bayonet came from behind a large crate. Brian and Ted stopped. An official detached himself from his fellows and demanded passports.

'Ahé! Señor Brian Steela and Señor Edouard Evanez! Bueno! His Excellency the Presidente has provided passages, I understand. Wait one moment.'

He beckoned and the black-coated, side-whiskered individual who had been the last to board the train at Ligna Salta came up, and was rewarded by the shipping official with an elaborate salute.

The two conversed in an undertone, and then the civilian produced a small green envelope. This he showed to the official and then handed it to Brian.

'You understand, Señor?' he asked in a stage whisper. 'The address, that of Señor Madeira, is here. Do not fail his Excellency, at your peril. You will please sign this receipt.'

Brian did so. The black-coated one replaced his certificate of delivery in his pocket and waved the two lads up the brow.

'Must we go on board now, Señor?' asked Brian. 'The ship isn't sailing yet. My father——'

'My orders are to see you on board directly you have been given the letter, Señores.'

'All right, then,' agreed Brian, who had no option in the matter, especially when the official had armed men at his disposal. 'But cannot my father come with us until just before the *Sempione* sails?'

'I regret, Señor, that it is not permitted. My orders are that you proceed on board and hold no further communication with anyone on shore.'

'You had better go, lads,' said Mr. Steele in Spanish, as he invariably spoke that language to them when

3   (H 60)

in the presence of Bolomayans. '*Adios*, Brian; *adios*, Ted!'

Hurried handshakes—but what a lot they meant!—and Brian and Ted ran up the gangplank. When they gained the upper deck and looked shorewards they caught a glimpse of Ambrose Steele's broad back as he strode towards the railway station.

The President's emissary remained until the *Sempione*, having completed taking in cargo, cast off from the mole and stood seaward. Then he, too, hurried off to the post office, whence he dispatched a message to Bombardo declaring that the two English señores had sailed with the important letter in their possession.

V

BLACK TREACHERY

A GRIM smile spread over President Bombardo's olivine features when he read the telegram from Santa Teresa. Locking up his desk, he went to another room in which was installed his private telephone.

Internal and inter-state communication was in a very bad way in Bolomaya. Most of the telegraph and telephone lines were hopelessly out of order. The state wireless was by no means efficient and when in use, messages, even in code, were frequently intercepted and made use of by the Grossaguayans.

There was, however, one method of communication which remained at Bombardo's disposal. The telephone lines to La Passena, across the Catamarcan frontier, were in working order and from thence communication could be made to the neighbouring republics, including Bolomaya's enemy, Grossaguay.

Had any of his followers been in a position to overhear his conversation the President's life would not have been worth a moment's purchase. More than likely the justly infuriated Bolomayans would have broken into the Palace and torn him limb from limb and he would have well deserved that fate.

Disguising his voice, he asked the exchange to put him through to La Passena. When the connection was made he asked La Passena to ring up Avanata 445, which was the number of his rival, President Paulo Vega of Grossaguay!

The call was answered by one of Vega's secretaries who declared that the President of Grossaguay was paying a visit to his troops in the field and followed up this information by asking who it was that was speaking.

'A friend of Grossaguay speaking from Ligna Salta!' replied Bombardo. 'In my own interests I cannot give you my name but my message is most important and in the highest interests of Grossaguay. Listen! Are you there? You can hear well what I say? Today a vessel under Catamarcan colours has left Santa Teresa for La Serena. Her name is the *Sempione*. She is not a Catamarcan ship but has been chartered by the Bolomayans as a commerce-raider. I know that there are rifled cannon in her hold ready to be mounted and used against Grossaguayan shipping. I leave it to President Vega to take all necessary action. Is that all? No, this is most important. There are two English youths on board the *Sempione*. The father of one—Steele is his name, Steele, spelt Es, tay, ay, ay, el, ay—is the agent who sold thousands of rounds of defective ammunition to your troops! These boys have a letter addressed to Señor Madeira at La Serena. Enclosed is an order supposed to be signed by President Bombardo that General Sandano make a sortie from Carabaya on the morning of the 14th by El Lopez Pass. This sortie is to be in conjunction with a covering attack by the main Bolomayan army. Is that perfectly clear? Excellent! Now President Vega must let that order go through to Sandano, but there will be no co-operation by the Bolomayan main forces. You will be able to cut off and annihilate General Sandano and his men. No, do not use radio. Send the order to him by an Indian runner, but bribe the man to make it seem that he comes from the south. That is all!'

Bombardo switched off. He knew that he ran a

risk—a slight one—of this doubly treacherous message being overheard by operators in the three exchanges. If inquiries were made the author of the message would be taken to be a traitor amongst his own followers—certainly not the President of Bolomaya!

In any case he would have to flee the country before very long, and he had arranged for the defeat and probable death of his rival, General Sandano, who would fight to the death and disdain offers to surrender. More than that, should the Grossaguayans capture the *Sempione* on the strength of his statement that she was a disguised Bolomayan commerce raider—that is why he had sent two obsolete guns as cargo to a fictitious address in Panama—there would be a prompt declaration of war by Catamarca against Grossaguay, although he, Bombardo, would not be in a position to benefit by it.

Hermandez Bombardo placed a very high value on the satisfaction of revenge even though his position as head of the Bolomayan Republic was already as good as lost!

VI

THE FRACTURED MAIN SHAFT

THE S.S. *Sempione* was a vessel of 2300 tons built on the Clyde. Originally launched as the *Cumbrae Star*, she was later sold to Sweden, her new owners replacing her triple-expansion steam engines with a heavy oil motor. After two years under the Swedish flag she went out of Lloyd's Register until—and no one seems to know what happened to her during the interval—she appeared under Catamarcan ownership with her name, thrice-changed, now the *Sempione*. She was still motor-driven, having the original engine that had been installed by her former Swedish owners. She was now engaged in the inter-port trade on the west coast of South America.

Brian Steele and Ted Evans were not sorry when they found that they were the only passengers, although more were expected at La Serena. There was only limited accommodation and only one class at that.

The captain and officers of the ship were most genial towards the sole passengers. Their attitude might have been influenced by the mistaken idea that Brian and Ted were personal friends of President Bombardo. The boys were told that they could go wherever they liked while they were on board and they took full advantage of the privilege—so distinct from the strict regulations in force in the Royal Mail vessel that had brought them from England.

Brian was particularly keen upon spending a good deal of time on the bridge. Navigation and seamanship intrigued him. He was very keen on picking up hints on these subjects even if they were conveyed through the medium of the pompous and yet condescending Captain Esmeraldas.

Ted, on the other hand, did not share Brian's enthusiasm on these matters. Engineering was his hobby, particularly with regard to internal combustion motors; but Brian looked upon machinery merely as a sort of side-show—a means to an end when it came to going from one port to another. The massive though somewhat antiquated heavy oil engines of the *Sempione* fascinated Ted, greatly to the delight of the fat, perspiring Chief Engineer, Juan Santos by name, who took more than ordinary pride in the still efficient propelling machinery.

The ties of friendship were too strong to allow the lads to separate; otherwise Brian would have spent most of the day and part of the night on the bridge, while Ted would have made himself scarce, in the bowels of the ship, where the half-caste greasers had a comparatively easy existence compared with that of the firemen and trimmers in a coal-burning ship.

So they arrived at a compromise. During Chief Engineer Santos' watch they spent the time in the engine-room, listening to the Catamarcan's whole-hearted explanations of this and that pertaining to the machinery under his charge. During the afternoon they were on deck, either on the navigating bridge or else right in the eyes of the ship, watching the dolphins skim across the bows and the white foam falling from the ship's bluff stem as she lifted to the long Pacific rollers.

They had a common interest in the wireless cabin adjoining the Captain's quarters on the lower bridge. It fascinated them to see the tall, thin, dark-eyed operator tapping the key with his long slender fingers. They wondered how he could pick out from a seemingly confused jangle of dots and dashes sent out at high speed a message from, perhaps, a Japanese vessel a thousand miles or more away and distinguish the call of a British liner bound from Auckland to Liverpool, from the shore-signal station at Valpo. More than that, the operator, who could speak no language but the Spanish as spoken in South America, was able to take down the messages and render them in English—thanks to the universal language of the Seven Seas as expressed in the International Code of Signals.

On the second day out and while Ted and Brian were at lunch with the officers in the saloon—the ship was rolling heavily in a strong beam wind—there was a sudden jar that shook the *Sempione* from stem to stern. This was followed by a sinister racing of the motors until the engineer on duty cut off the fuel supply.

Captain Esmeraldas jumped from his swing chair at the head of the table and made a hurried dash for the companion ladder, ejaculating: 'It is a catastrophe.'

There was a general exodus. Officers and passengers, their meal half-finished, hurried on deck.

The *Sempione* had almost lost way and was wallowing in the trough of the long rollers. Most of the watch below had turned out and were standing as helpless as a flock of bewildered sheep.

At the fidley hatch Chief Engineer Santos was shouting to his subordinate on duty, but without attempting to go below to see for himself what had happened. Santos was something of a dandy and even a serious mishap to his beloved engines was not sufficient for him to overcome his scruples and go below in his white duck uniform.

'It is the main shaft, Capitan!' he reported at the

end of the discussion with the Second Engineer. 'It is completely fractured. Nothing can be done!'

Directly Santos went off to report, Brian and Ted nipped down the slippery steel ladder to the engine-room, curious to see what had occurred.

The motors were now silent. The heaving engine-room was filled with the fumes of hot oil. A couple of greasers, holding on to a handrail, were arguing in high-pitched voices. A sliding door in the after bulk-head was open. Beyond and between two large ballast tanks was the tunnel in which the main shaft ran—or was supposed to run; it was now motionless. The Second Engineer was examining the fracture by the aid of a smoky oil lamp.

'Let's go and have a look,' suggested Ted.

'He'll hoof us out,' objected Brian.

'Not he! Santos wouldn't mind.'

They crept through the doorway and groped their way along the narrow space, guided by the glimmer of the oil-lamp.

The Second Engineer looked up and recognized them. 'It's a bad business, Señores,' he declared. 'See; the fracture is close to the stern gland. Impossible to repair it without going into dry dock and the nearest dry dock is eight hundred miles away. The only thing to be done is to radio for a tug.'

The word 'radio' suggested other attractions. For the time being the lads lost interest in the fractured main shaft. It would be most enthralling to see the operator get to work to summon assistance.

Regardless of the rust and oil stains on their clothes, they regained the upper deck via the motor room and thence hurried to the wireless cabin.

The operator gave them an encouraging smile. He had discarded his headphones and was reaching for his white patrol jacket—a sign that his watch was over, although the second operator had not relieved him.

'Are you sending for a tug, Pedro?' asked Brian.

'Not until el Capitan orders me,' replied the operator. 'There is a Guavilian cargo-boat to the south'ard and she is following our track. If he can strike a bargain with her for a tow it will be cheaper than a tug from Punta Negro.'

'When should she come in sight?' asked Ted.

'I do not know. And I would advise you not to worry el Capitan with questions.'

'We don't mean to,' rejoined Brian with a mental picture of the formerly urbane Esmeraldas now almost beside himself with excitement. 'All I hope is that there's plenty of grub on board!'

They went on deck, but for once they avoided the bridge. It seemed very different on board. The *Sempione*, instead of being a thing of life, was motionless. Her officers and crew seemed listless, now that the first moments of excitement were over. No orders were being given; no one appeared to be doing anything even though the glass was falling and a hard blow, probably a gale, was imminent.

'Why don't they set a staysail and keep her out of the trough of the seas?' thought Brian. 'She'll shake her masts and funnel out of her if she rolls much more.'

They went on deck again.

This time something was happening. The officers on the bridge were levelling binoculars upon some object well away on the starboard beam—a blur of smoke beaten down almost horizontally by the strong breeze.

In a few minutes they could distinguish a fairly large grey-painted vessel approaching bows on. She was travelling at high speed, judging by the enormous 'bone in her teeth'.

'A warship—a Grossaguayan one!' declared the bo'sun, who was standing close to Brian. 'She must be the *Chacal*.'

When about a cable's distance from the *Sempione* the light cruiser—for such she was—turned rapidly under full starboard helm. Then she reversed her engines. From her signal yard-arm a two-flag hoist stood out board-hard in the wind.

Brian and Ted had not the slightest knowledge of what the message meant; but Captain Esmeraldas and most of the officers had.

It was brief and peremptory: 'Heave-to instantly or I will fire into you!'

VII

UNDER ARREST

PART of the signal was unnecessary. The *Sempione* was already hove-to; she had been for the last two hours. It was the latter part that took Captain Esmeraldas and his officers by surprise. It was one of the last things to expect. The *Sempione* was on 'her lawful occasions' and not even within territorial waters. She was flying the ensign of the Catamarcan Republic, which she had perfect right to do, and she was bound from, not to, a Bolomayan port, so she could not be carrying contraband of war for Grossaguay's enemies.

On the other hand she was challenged by a Grossaguayan cruiser and threatened with dire penalties if she refused to surrender. Captain Esmeraldas knew perfectly well that refusal would be met by instant and drastic action.

'She has made a mistake!' he declared, addressing the white-lipped Chief Officer. 'Make our number!'

The four-flag hoist, indicating the *Sempione's* name —which the cruiser must have seen painted on her bow—was hardly 'close-up' when the *Chacal* signalled: 'Strike your colours!'

'We had better do as they wish, Capitan!' quavered the Chief Officer. 'They are training a quick-firer on our bridge—where we are standing!'

For an instant Captain Esmeraldas hesitated. He was proud of the flag under which he sailed. To strike his colours to a warship belonging to a friendly republic seemed insufferable; and yet the sinister muzzle of the gun on the *Chacal's* fo'c'sle sent a shiver down his spine.

'Lower the ensign!' he ordered.

A seaman doubled aft, uncleeted the halliards and lowered the yellow and green bunting level with the taffrail.

By this time the *Chacal* had closed to within half a cable's length. From her bridge an officer hailed the *Sempione* through a megaphone. Down wind the words came clear and distinct, leaving no doubt as to their meaning.

'*Sempione* ahoy! The master is to repair on board us, bringing with him his ship's papers. There are two English passengers. They must also be brought on board us, together with the dispatch they are carrying from President Bombardo. We hold the captain of the *Sempione* personally responsible that this document be delivered intact. You will comply immediately.'

'That's torn it, Bags!' exclaimed Ted. 'We're the cause of this; but how did those blighters know we had that letter?'

'Goodness knows.'

'What are you going to do about it?' continued Ted. 'You don't know what's in the envelope, do you?'

'Haven't the foggiest notion.'

'You'd better heave it overboard while you've the chance.'

'Not I,' replied Brian. 'I'm freezing on to it. If those blighters——'

'Señor Steele!' Captain Esmeraldas was calling from the bridge.

'*Si, Capitan?*'

'Come here, please.'

'Come along too, Ted,' exclaimed Brian, as he began to ascend the bridge-ladder.

'You heard?' inquired the Captain.

'Yes, sir!'

'You have that letter? Give it to me.'

Resolutely Brian shook his head. 'It was entrusted to me,' he expostulated. 'I'm not giving it up except under compulsion. You had better let someone in the *Chacal* take that responsibility.'

'*Sempione* ahoy!' hailed the *Chacal*. 'Hasten and lower that boat! Obey our orders promptly or we fire!'

For a moment Captain Esmeraldas stood irresolute. Then he raised a megaphone to his lips. 'Too big a sea running for us to lower a boat,' he protested. 'If you will stand by until the weather moderates I will comply with your demands. Meanwhile I take responsibility over the matter of the two English passengers and the despatch they bear.'

For some minutes no reply came from the Grossaguayan cruiser. A group of officers could be seen conferring on the bridge. Meanwhile the quick-firer on her fo'c'sle remained trained upon the *Sempione*. It wanted but a slight pressure upon the trigger of the firing-pistol to send a shell to burst with devastating effect.

Brian realized the nerve-racking position. Somehow, while he was standing on the upper deck, the menace did not seem so imminent. Here on the exposed bridge the full significance of that loaded and trained weapon left little to the imagination!

Then the *Chacal*'s megaphone boomed again: 'You are to follow us to Punta Negro. Speed ten knots, distance two cables!'

Evidently the Grossaguayans were unaware of the *Sempione*'s disabled state. They had jumped to the erroneous conclusion that she had stopped her engines —an indication that the vessel flying Catamarcan colours was the disguised Bolomayan commerce-raider they had been ordered to intercept and capture —because she realized that 'the game was up'.

Captain Esmeraldas was beginning to take the situation more cheerfully. The *Chacal* hadn't opened fire as she had threatened. She had accepted the excuse that the sea was too rough for a boat to be lowered. If the *Sempione* was to be taken into a Grossaguayan port—there her case could be investigated— then it was up to the *Chacal* to take her there! It would save the otherwise heavy costs of a tow!

'I regret I cannot comply with your orders,' declared Captain Esmeraldas. 'Our main shaft is broken.'

Again there was a conference on board the cruiser. Apparently the statement of the surrendered vessel's master was accepted. Then——

'Stand by to take our hawser!'

This time the skipper of the *Sempione* rubbed his hands together gleefully. He was having his revenge in a mild sort of way. He also made up his mind to give his captors more trouble over the despatch that the two English youths were carrying.

He shouted an order.

The crew, who had been thoroughly scared during the last few minutes, had taken heart when they heard that the ship was not to be sunk but was to be taken in tow. Half a dozen of them ran to the fo'c'sle in preparation for this operation.

They were about to range a shackle of cable when the Captain ordered them to stand fast. The *Chacal*, instead of taking the *Sempione's* hawser, was passing the merchant craft her own! He could see the hands aft unreeling a three-inch flexible steel wire.

A motor launch was then swung out. Half a dozen men clambered into her as she hung from the davits. Just as she was about to be lowered an order was given for her to be turned in and secured again. The Grossaguayan captain had evidently come to a similar conclusion as that of the master of the *Sempione*: that the state of the sea was too disturbed to risk the lowering of a boat.

The *Chacal* then forged ahead. Having twin screws she expected to be able to manœuvre with little difficulty. Men stationed aft stood ready with heaving lines.

At the first attempt the ropes fell short. At the second —the cruiser had to make a complete circle before she was again in a favourable position—the scend of the sea threw her so close to the *Sempione's* bows that it looked as if a collision was inevitable. In that case even the heavier steel side-plating of the cruiser would not have withstood the shock; the *Sempione's* stem would have been shattered by the impact and both vessels would be in great danger of foundering.

Cries of alarm came from the crews of both ships. The *Chacal's* port engine was put full astern and the cruiser drew clear with barely ten feet between her and the Catamarcan craft.

Again the cruiser made a complete circle; but this time she approached head to wind and sea. A couple of heaving lines were thrown, but the demoralized seamen on the *Sempione's* foredeck failed to catch them.

'If you do not secure the lines at my next attempt, I will sink you!' roared the now angry captain of the cruiser, who thought that the *Sempione's* crew were deliberately 'muffing' the operation.

The threat had its effect. The *Chacal* established communication, lost way and commenced to pay out the steel hawser to which one of the heaving-lines had been bent.

It was no easy task. The two vessels were constantly altering the intervening distance, with the result that the men engaged on hauling in were again and again thrown on the deck. Foot by foot, fathom by fathom

Taken in tow by the enemy

Page 48

the bight of the heavy hawser was brought nearer and nearer until it was secured to a pair of massive bollards.

Then the cruiser forged ahead, slowly lest the jerk should either snap the wire or tear the bollards from the deck.

Round swung the *Sempione* until she was head on to sea and wind. Gradually she increased her way in the wake of the powerfully-engined *Chacal*. Into the teeth of the rising gale she pitched and pounded on her way towards the Grossaguayan harbour of Punta Negro.

Brian and Ted did not relish the prospect of being carried willy-nilly into a port in the Republic now at war with Bolomaya. Much as they disliked President Bombardo they felt in honour bound to carry out their part of the bargain in return for the free passage to Panama. It seemed, however, that before very long the letter containing the dispatch must fall into the hands of the Grossaguayans.

It was now six o'clock. In another forty minutes it would be dark. It was too exposed for comfort on the bridge, even if the Captain now permitted them to go there. The engine-room no longer was an attraction, since the motors were silent. The wireless cabin was locked, following a signal from the *Chacal* forbidding the *Sempione* to use radio communication.

They retreated to the saloon. It wanted another forty minutes to dinner—unless the cooks and stewards in their highly strung state had neglected their duties.

Presently Captain Esmeraldas came in. It was the first time he had left the bridge since the accident to the main shaft. He was fairly cheerful. He was confident that the Grossaguayan authorities would release his ship with profuse apologies, since the incident might result in diplomatic relations being broken off between the Republic and her more powerful neigh-

4

bour Catamarca. As for the matter of the dispatch, that was of small consequence. How was he to know that these two English boys were President Bombardo's emissaries?

Brian promptly broached that subject. 'Do you think I'd better destroy the letter to prevent Bombardo's enemies gaining possession of it?' he asked.

Esmeraldas jumped up as if he had been shot. 'Caramba! A thousand times, no!' he exclaimed excitedly. 'You come on board under false pretences. You are Secret Service agents. You compromise me!'

'We're not Secret Service agents and we weren't given our passages under false pretences, Captain!' protested Brian warmly.

'You carry secret correspondence from Bombardo. You yourself admit it, Señor Steele! That pig of a Grossaguayan holds me responsible for the surrender of that letter. You refused to give it to me.'

'I did,' agreed Brian doggedly. 'And I'm not going to give it to anyone. I won't heave it overboard because I don't want to get you into an awkward fix; but it will have to be taken from me by force!'

Somewhat to Brian's surprise Esmeraldas' attitude underwent a complete change. 'You will not be compelled to surrender that document,' he declared. 'Listen! We are being towed into Punta Negro, a Grossaguayan port. There I will rehoist my country's flag. In effect the *Sempione* is Catamarcan territory, although she is a ship. I claim protection from my country and the Grossaguayan Republic will not dare to insult her.'

'But she has already done so,' Brian reminded him. 'The *Chacal* is a Grossaguayan warship.'

'You need not remind me of that!' exclaimed Esmeraldas hotly. 'She would not have stopped us except on the High Seas. There she could sink us without a trace.'

'But she didn't,' said Ted. 'Perhaps she mistook the *Sempione* for some other craft.'

Such a suggestion, that wasn't far from being correct, hadn't occurred to Esmeraldas. He shrugged his shoulders. 'You will be safe under the Catamarcan flag!' he declared.

Then came an interruption.

The Second Officer, white-faced with apprehension, appeared in the saloon doorway. 'Come quickly, Capitan!' he said excitedly. 'The hawser has parted. The cruiser has signalled to us to abandon ship!'

VIII

THE SEA-COCK

BRIAN and Ted lost no time in following the
Captain and the Second Officer to the upper
deck. Then, noticing that Esmeraldas was too pre-
occupied to trouble about them, they swarmed up
the bridge ladder in his wake.

For some moments they could see nothing but their
immediate surroundings. The darkness of the night
seemed intense. Overhead, black clouds hid the stars.
The surface of the water was invisible except for the
menacing wave crests.

On the fo'c'sle a group of men under the orders of
the Chief Officer were heaving in their part of the
broken cable. The *Sempione* was still carrying way
although her bows were beginning to swing. Seas
were pouring over the fore-deck and drenching the
cable-working party. Of the *Chacal* the only sign was
her white stern light, which Brian judged to be about
a quarter of a mile away.

Even as he looked the cruiser commenced to turn
until her port and masthead lights were visible. There
were a few lamps showing through the windows of her
chartroom. Otherwise she was in darkness. Not a
glimmer showed through her double line of scuttles.

Then a Morse lamp resumed its long and short
dashes: 'Acknowledge and comply instantly!'

'How can we abandon ship in this storm?' asked
Esmeraldas, addressing the frightened Second Officer.

'We cannot, Capitan! No boat could live in this sea!'

'Signalman! Acknowledge the signal and say that we cannot comply owing to the state of the waves!'

The *Sempione's* lamp flashed out the Captain's objection.

For half a minute the *Chacal* gave no sign. Then a searchlight was unmasked from a platform in her mainmast. It swept the angry sea inquiringly until the beam picked up the *Sempione*. Then it held her in the dazzling rays, temporarily blinding everyone on the bridge and in its vicinity.

The cruiser's commanding officer was both angry and impatient. He was unwilling to close and pass another hawser owing to the darkness and the confused sea; but he still considered it practicable for the *Sempione* to lower her boats and abandon ship.

The searchlight was switched off. Again the *Chacal's* signalling-lamp began to speak.

'I give you ten minutes to lower your boats and abandon ship. You will open the sea-cocks before so doing. Signify your intention to comply or I will open fire and send you to the bottom!'

This ultimatum left Captain Esmeraldas with no option but to carry out these drastic instructions. The boats might be swamped or they might not. The *Sempione* with one or two shells pumped into her would sink within a few minutes, taking all on board down with her.

'Under protest I will comply within the stipulated time!' replied Esmeraldas. 'Signal that message! Santos! Where's Chief Engineer Santos? Bring him here, you!'

In the darkness and labouring with tense excitement the Captain did not realize that he was addressing Ted Evans.

Without replying, Ted touched Brian on the arm. 'Better hook it, Bags!' he whispered.

They scuttled down the bridge-ladder, found Santos in his cabin—he was on the point of turning in—and gave him the Captain's message.

'What does he want?' asked the Chief Engineer.

'The cruiser has ordered him to lower boats and to sink the ship.'

'Sink the *Sempione*?' exclaimed Santos in horrified tones. 'Impossible! It is a massacre!'

'The sea-cocks have to be opened or they'll sink her by shell-fire!' announced Brian. 'You'd better hurry. They've given us only ten minutes and two have gone already!'

Santos, coatless and without his shoes, ran towards the bridge-ladder. The chums remained in the alley-way.

'Look here!' began Brian, speaking hurriedly. 'I'm not going in one of those boats. I vote we stop here. Are you game?'

'What's the idea, Bags? I don't want to drown!'

'Neither do I. Now listen.' He proceeded to outline his plan.

'Risky!' decided Ted.

'So it will be in the boats. We've a sporting chance.'

'Right, then!'

'Then we'll make ourselves scarce, in case Esmeraldas spots us. Watch when Santos comes up from the engine-room.'

They dodged behind the engine-room fidley. They had not long to wait, for in less than a minute the Chief Engineer ran to the engine-room hatchway and descended the ladder. Meanwhile the *Chacal* had turned on two searchlights that flooded the exposed parts of the *Sempione* until they looked as if they were made of polished silver and threw correspondingly dark shadows across the deck on which the chums were waiting.

From below came a peculiar metallic sound. Santos

was operating the worm gear of the sea-cocks. Tons of the Pacific Ocean were pouring into the ship.

Up came the Chief Engineer, perspiring and breathless, to join the other officers and crew, who were feverishly swinging out a couple of boats.

The first was let go with a run. The lads, from their hiding-place, could hear the crash as it surged against the ship's side, and the shouts of the terrified boat's crew. Apparently she got away all right, for the thud of the lower blocks of the falls could be heard, followed by the irregular plashing of oars.

Then the second boat in charge of Captain Esmeraldas was lowered. Evidently it was taken for granted that every one of the passengers and crew had taken to one or other of the boats. There was too much confusion for anyone to be missed. Within limitations, it was each man for himself.

Once clear of the now listing *Sempione* the boats' crews pulled their hardest, realizing that the sooner they made the *Chacal* the less would be their chance of being swamped. It was a pull dead to wind'ard and in the teeth of a nasty sea and every man not straining at the oars had to bale furiously to keep down the water that constantly broke over the boats.

Suddenly the *Chacal's* searchlights were masked. Her captain, having satisfied himself that the *Sempione* was listing and would soon make her last plunge, had ordered the searchlights to be switched off so as not to blind the men in the boats. This was not from any humanitarian motive. The boats with the supposed hostile raider's crew could be swamped for all he cared except that he had strict injunctions to secure the dispatch from President Bombardo. That had to be given to President Paulo Vega at all costs.

Safe from the risk of detection, Ted and Brian staggered up the sloping, heaving deck and looked in the direction of the cruiser. She was no longer to be seen. A heavy rain-squall had blotted out everything. Even if she again used her searchlights the rays would be unable to pierce that veil of falling moisture.

'Now for it!' exclaimed Brian. 'We may just do it!'

They scuttled down the slippery ladder to the engine-room which was now in complete darkness. In fact, all the ship's lights had been switched off before her crew abandoned her.

Well it was that Ted Evans had taken such an interest in the engine-room. He knew exactly where the sea-cocks were. Apart from that he was guided by the noisy inrush of water.

Santos had opened only one sea-cock and had not damaged the mechanism. Being a skilled engineer who loved his work he could not bring himself to damage his charge.

Knee-deep in swirling water, the lads groped their way to the big pipe in the ship's wings through which the torrent was surging. Rapidly they turned the cranked handle. Exasperatingly slowly, so it seemed, the valve moved until the inrush diminished. They could not see it; only by the noise did they know their task was being accomplished.

Then the handle brought up with a jerk. The sea-cock was closed.

Hurriedly they returned to the deck, anxious to know what the *Chacal* was doing. She had switched on her searchlights, but owing to the tropical downpour the rays stopped far short of the *Sempione*. They reminded Brian of the headlights of a still distant car approaching on a foggy night—an ill-defined blur that failed to penetrate with any clearness the semi-opaque curtain of rain.

For nearly ten minutes Ted and Brian waited, hanging on to one of the empty davits and peering in the direction of the cruiser. Would she close the supposedly abandoned ship and assure herself that she was sinking? If she did, the peril would be desperate, for the *Chacal*, impatient at the time taken by her prey to disappear, would hasten the order of her going by a few well-directed shells.

Then, suddenly, the feeble glare vanished.

The cruiser, unable to locate the *Sempione*, had come to the conclusion that she had 'dipped', and having failed to pick up the boats, was steaming towards Punta Negro—her captain foiled in his attempt to secure the much-wanted document and yet to learn that he and his government had been deliberately misled as to the genuine nationality of the vessel that he had, as he thought, sent to the bottom of the Pacific.

IX

BRIAN'S FIRST COMMAND

'NOW what's to be done?' asked Ted, who fully realized that in matters of seamanship Brian was his master, although in things mechanical he could give Bags points and win easily.

'We can't do much till daybreak,' replied Brian. 'I wonder if we could set the staysail? That would pay her head off and would take us farther from the coast. I don't want the *Chacal* or any other Grossaguayan vessel to fall in with us.'

'How far are we from land, do you think?'

'Haven't any idea. May be twenty miles or it may be a hundred. Sea-room's what we want. Come along and see if we can coax the sail up.'

'How about the water?'

'Can wait. It will act as ballast. No need to swot at the hand-pumps. She's not making any more.'

The *Sempione* was lying broadside on to wind and sea. The list was decidedly pronounced though by no means dangerous. Waves were occasionally sweeping across both the after and the fore well-decks. It was a disconcerting motion and the sooner a bit of canvas could be set for'ard the more chance there would be of the ship riding easier.

Watching their opportunity, for their eyes were now quite accustomed to the darkness, the boys hurried along the well-deck and gained the ladder leading to the fo'c'sle before the next comber poured inboard.

The fore-deck was in a state of confusion. The hands, interrupted in their task of getting the hawser aboard, had left several fathoms of the springy steel rope still trailing over the bows. The coils, rolling with each movement of the ship, constituted a very real source of danger.

The staysail was already hanked on to the forestay, but was stowed in a pyramid-shaped bundle under a tarpaulin. The halliards, too, were bent to the sail.

Going to the fife rail, Brian uncleated and tried a couple of ropes before he found the one he wanted. Next he shouted to Ted to cast off the tarpaulined sail cover. The now loosely stowed canvas shivered ominously in the hard wind.

'Stand clear and bear a hand here!' yelled Brian.

They heaved and sweated at the halliard. The canvas was stout and heavy but slowly it travelled up the forestay, flogging violently in the wind and threatening to flap itself into rags.

Then ensued a terrific struggle to get the staysail sheeted home, until, breathless and well-nigh exhausted, the amateur sailors succeeded in taking a couple of turns round a stout cleat.

In a very short while the effect of the headsail became apparent. Instead of lying helplessly in the trough, the ship was now making way, with the wind and sea on her starboard quarter.

Making his way to the bridge, Brian switched on the binnacle lamp. The course by compass was roughly west-by-north, enough to take them more and more from the Grossaguayan coast.

'How about the masthead and sidelights?' asked Ted.

'We won't switch them on yet,' replied Brian. 'In any case, we don't use the masthead light since we're under sail, although we should show something to indicate that we are a "steamship" with her engines stopped. I'll have to look it up in that book in the chartroom. And it's not much use trying to steer her. She'll run all right without that.'

'Then what's to be done next?'

'Nothing except to shove on some dry clothes, have grub and then turn in,' replied Brian, with a cheerful grin. 'There's no need for us to keep watch.'

'Yes, but we simply must switch on the sidelights,' declared Ted. 'Even at the risk of being spotted by that beastly cruiser! We aren't far off the steamer track on the West coast, and if a vessel ran into us and we weren't showing lights it wouldn't be fair on her, would it?'

'S'pose not. All right then,' conceded Brian. 'Switch them on and let's go below. It's about time we shed these wet togs.'

It was a weird sensation being alone in the relatively large vessel. They turned on the light in the saloon and having changed their clothes they contrived to cook a satisfying meal in the galley.

Just before midnight they went on deck to have a final look round. The rain had ceased. Overhead the stars shone brightly. The wind had eased slightly, but was still blowing strongly in the same direction as before. Visibility was good; but not another light was to be seen on any bearing.

Dog-tired, both boys slept soundly in spite of the excitement of the previous day. They were in happy ignorance of the fact that a north-bound British tramp, the S.S. *Getaway*, had passed within two cables' lengths of the *Sempione*, and had to alter course in order to pass under her stern. But for Ted's insistence the otherwise lightless ship might easily have come into collision, with fatal results.

The slanting rays of the newly-risen sun roused them from their slumbers. They dressed after a fashion and went on deck. Again the horizon was clear.

They were not labouring under any misapprehension. On the contrary, they looked upon the situation as a sort of huge joke. They felt exhilarated, especially at the thought that they had 'done the *Chacal* in the eye' over the matter of Bombardo's commission.

'I shouldn't mind a week of this,' declared Brian.

'Neither should I, Bags,' agreed Ted. 'Only your Dad will be in a tear when he hears that this old tub is supposed to have been sunk.'

'He won't know anything about it for at least ten days,' observed Brian. 'So why worry?'

'I'm not,' rejoined Ted. 'But what's the programme?'

'We'll hoist signals of distress to the first ship we sight, unless she's a Grossaguayan vessel. It seems to me that we ought to get a tidy bit for saving the old *Sempione*.'

'The vessel that picks us up will get that, never you fear. She'll want to tow us into port and put in a claim for salvage. But what if we don't sight another ship?'

Brian pondered. That suggestion had never occurred to him. 'We're bound to fetch up somewhere, sooner or later, if we don't fall in with a vessel,' he replied. 'We've plenty of grub—enough to last us a twelve-month, I should say—and the old tub's already weathered one gale. So why worry?'

'I've already told you I'm not worrying,' reiterated Ted. 'Now, what about some scoff? After that, we can start getting rid of some of the water down below.'

Because it was a novelty, they both went to the galley and cooked a satisfying meal. Later the task would become an irksome—a hateful one!

Having fed, they climbed to the bridge. A glance at the steering compass told them that the course was now due west, although the ship yawed alternately a point and a half. They judged her speed through the water to be three knots. Actually it was barely one; but there was another factor that they had not taken into account, for the simple reason that they had never heard of it.

The *Sempione* was in the grip of the relatively cold Peruvian current that, skirting the west coast of South America, eventually describes a quarter circle and merges into the west-going Equatorial Current. The ship was also influenced by the 'south-east Trades', so that under these combined natural forces she was being urged 'over the ground' at a steady four knots —equivalent to a hundred and twelve statute miles in every twenty-four hours.

Then the lads made a discovery that took them down a peg; they were not so smart as they thought they were in the management of the ship.

They had left the sidelights burning!

'That won't do!' declared Brian. 'We'll soon run the batteries down at that rate, and I don't know how long they'll go before discharging themselves.'

'We needn't worry about that,' remarked Ted.

'Why not? There are oil lamps, I admit; but they're a nuisance.'

'We can recharge the batteries, Bags. What are the auxiliary engines for? I tell you what: we'll start one up now and see if it will work the bilge pumps. It'll save swotting with the hand pumps.'

In the engine-room and on a bench above the flooded floor, Ted tackled a petrol motor. It was not of a type he knew, being of Swedish make, but after half a dozen attempts—at one of them he narrowly escaped a broken wrist through a vicious back-fire—the engine awoke into intense activity.

Presently a two-inch suction hose was doing its bit, while a delivery hose of similar capacity was expelling the bilge water over the side.

They left the pump working and it took more than

a couple of hours to get rid of the quantity of water let in through the sea-cock in a little less than fifteen minutes.

During that interval the chums made an exploration of parts of the ship with which they were not previously acquainted. After a while they happened upon the sail-room. Amongst the bundles of awnings and bolts of spare canvas they discovered a large squaresail. Judging by the dirt and dust, it had not been disturbed for several years.

'We'll set this,' declared Brian. 'There's bound to be a yard somewhere.'

'It doesn't look as big as the trysail, so why worry?' asked Ted.

'It is; and she'll run better with it,' Brian explained. 'The staysail's all right for a steadying sail, but there isn't much pull in it. Bear a hand!'

Actually it required four hands assisted by a tackle and a couple of handspikes to get the heavy sail from its locker to the fo'c'sle. Then came the hunt for the necessary spar, which they eventually found on the boat deck. By the time they had hauled it into position, adjusted the slings and bent the head of the squaresail to it the clock in the chartroom told them it was noon.

'*Siesta!*' exclaimed Ted breathlessly.

Brian laughed. 'We've finished with Bolomayan customs! This sail's going to be set before either of us knocks off!'

'Brutal slave-driver!' rejoined Ted. 'All right! Have it your own way, then!'

They had to bring the halliard to one of the winches before they could raise the heavy spar and sail to the required position. Then they sheeted it home and stowed the now unnecessary staysail.

And what a difference! The *Sempione*, now riding lightly, since she was free of an excess of water ballast, no longer rolled sullenly. With the canvas bellying out before the stiff breeze, she ran with quite a respectable turn of speed—nearly two knots—and no longer yawed on her course. Since it did not matter where they went, provided the ship was not cast upon the South American coast—a very unlikely chance—they could let her run before the breeze without having to touch the wheel.

After a light lunch they rested until four—their first 'stand easy' since they had turned out that morning. Then they slung out the Captain's gear, scrubbed his cabin and transferred their own things to it.

'It's more like being on the spot if anything happens,' observed Brian. 'After all, we are no longer passengers; we're running this old tub!'

Although he spoke disparagingly of the *Sempione*, he was beginning to be proud of her. To all intents and purposes she was no longer a Catamarcan ship. He and Ted had saved her by their own resource and determination. He had one regret: there was no British Red Ensign in the locker amongst the weird assortment of flags.

Towards sunset Ted happened to glance aft over the starboard quarter. There was a peculiar red line, well down on the eastern horizon. It puzzled him. 'What's that?' he asked.

Brian fetched a pair of binoculars. 'Sunset in the Andes,' he explained. 'I reckon they are sixty miles away.'

Actually the snow-covered peaks were not less than ninety miles off.

It was their last sight of land for many a day!

X

'MAN OVERBOARD'

IT was a novel experience to wake up next morning in new surroundings and be able to sit up on their respective bunks and look through the for'ard scuttles of the Captain's cabin under the bridge.

They could see most of the well-deck and the break of the fo'c'sle. Above it was the stumpy foremast with the almost board-hard squaresail intercepting a generous expanse of sea and sky.

It was difficult to realize that throughout those eleven hours of darkness that sail had been urging the *Sempione* onwards without a hand at the wheel. The ship was making her way farther and farther into the wide Pacific and so far not another sail had been sighted although one passing craft had caught a glimpse of her during the hours of darkness.

By common consent they both kept hard at it during their waking hours. Although the novelty of the situation had not yet worn off they realized that inaction was the forerunner of discontent and frequently of dejection. If work were not forthcoming they would have to make it!

There were the two pairs of empty davits to be swung in. Ted and Brian found themselves wondering what had happened to the crews of the two boats.

In point of fact neither had survived the attempt to make the *Chacal*. Both were swamped by the heavy breaking seas and there were no survivors. This disaster made things rather difficult for the captain of the Grossaguayan cruiser. He had failed to gain possession of President Bombardo's secret dispatch. However, he put a bold face on the matter. Mustering his officers and men, the captain of the *Chacal* swore them to secrecy with the promise of a big reward from the Republic. They were to back him up in his story; how that the *Chacal* had fallen in with the Bolomayan disguised commerce raider, which had refused to surrender. Instead, she had opened fire, but fortunately none of the shells took effect. In the engagement the *Chacal* sank her opponent, which went down with all hands and with colours flying. In spite of a search extending over an hour the victors failed to find any survivors.

The *Chacal* returned to Punta Negro at daybreak. The news of the glorious victory quickly spread. Flags were hoisted and bells rung. The town went mad with excitement. President Paulo Vega flew from Avanata to Punta Negro to congratulate the *Chacal's* crew and to bestow decorations upon her captain and officers; but he expressed regret that he had not been put in possession of the much-wanted dispatch.

Two days later the Catamarcan S.S. *Sempione*, bound from La Serena, Panama and intermediate ports, was stated by the authorities at La Serena to be overdue. Radio messages were sent from the wireless station requesting all ships in the vicinity to keep a sharp look-out for her. Unfortunately the wireless operator of the S.S. *Getaway*, the only vessel that had sighted the missing ship, was off-duty and so a great opportunity was missed.

During the forenoon of the second day following the partial abandonment of the *Sempione*, Ted and Brian thought they would have a look round the wireless cabin. The door was locked, but that presented little difficulty. A hammer and a cold chisel soon settled the problem. They entered and contemplated the now silent set.

'Going to try to call up some ship?' asked Ted.

Brian shook his head. 'No,' he replied. 'What's the use? We're all right as we are. And I don't think you could transmit if you tried?'

'I'd make a better fist at it than you could,' retorted Ted. 'I'm not going to try, though. As you say, we don't want assistance, but there's no harm in seeing if we can pick up signals.'

After some experimenting at the risk of wrecking the installation, they succeeded in getting a lot of Morse; but, although they knew that mode of signalling, the messages came in at such a rate that they were quite unable to read them.

'Not much sense in that,' remarked Ted. 'Come on! Let's get out of here. I'll race you three times round the well-deck!'

'Right-o; and the loser gets the grub ready?'

This suggestion took Ted slightly aback. It was the first indication that Brian's interest in the galley was waning. 'I'll take you!' he replied.

They descended the ladder to the deck, on which the contest was to be held. One complete circuit was equal to about a hundred yards, with a few obstacles to avoid. Neither youth was in anything like training. Three days ago they had been riding along a rough road in high-pommelled uncomfortable saddles; but they were quite used to that. During their stay at the Estancia Miraflores they had done no long walks—no one in Bolomaya did—and as for running, they had rarely sprinted fifty yards since they first set foot on republican soil. During their brief acquaintance with the *Sempione* their walking exercise had been strictly limited and consisted chiefly of ascending and descending ladders and traversing the intervening distance between each; but they had become used to the motion of the ship as the deck rose and fell under their feet.

'Ready?' asked Brian. Then: 'Go!'

At the end of the first lap they were about equal although Ted had taken up a position known in horse-racing circles as 'next the rails'. The second round found Brian leading by about a yard with both runners labouring heavily. At the finish they were floundering and almost abreast again as they threw themselves across the rope that represented the tape.

Almost exhausted, Ted leant against the low bulwark. It was at that moment that the ship rolled more than usual. He lost his balance. There was a muffled scream, followed by a heavy splash.

Brian realized that he was alone. Ted had fallen overboard!

His first impulse was to jump in to the rescue. Fortunately he did not, or both of them would have been in much the same position as a couple of mice swimming round and round the inside of a bucket, only in their case they would be outside the ship with no means of hauling themselves back again.

The *Sempione* was now doing about one and a half knots or considerably less than a leisurely walking pace, and Ted had fallen from the well-deck within ten feet of the break of the fo'c'sle.

His temporary exhaustion forgotten in his determination, Brian, resisting the temptation to see what his unfortunate friend was doing, ran aft. Then snatching up a coil of rope—how fortunate it was that they had made a good job of the falls of the empty davits! —he made a loop in the free end—it wasn't a bowline but it might serve its intended purpose—and dangled it over the side.

He was in plenty of time. The shock of the immersion had made Ted put out his remaining energies, and he was swimming with the slowly moving ship.

'This way, Ted!' shouted Brian, holding the rope at arm's length.

Ted saw his last chance. He stopped his unequal swimming contest and, treading water, allowed the looped rope to bear down upon him. He grasped it and slipped the bight over his head and under his shoulders.

Then Brian took a turn round the belaying-pin of the davit. It was well that he did so, for the jerk as the rope took up the strain was surprisingly strong!

For the present Ted was safe, but the problem was how to get him up the side. He had not much strength left to help himself and it was evident that Brian could not haul him up bodily owing to the friction of the rope over the capping of the rail. That was as much as a couple of hefty men could accomplish.

'You all right for a bit?' Brian hailed.

'Yes; I think so,' replied Ted none too confidently.

'I'll be as quick as I can; I'm bringing a ladder!'

Brian had remembered that close to the starboard entry port he had noticed a rolled Jacob's ladder. It was still there and it required the work of about a couple of minutes to carry it aft and unroll it. At one end a short length of rope spliced into a cringle. This he bent to a pin in the fife-rail and hastily dumped the rest of the ladder over-board. In so doing he narrowly missed stunning Ted with the stout ash treads of the ladder, though he didn't realize it until that danger was past.

Then it was a fairly easy matter to tow Ted for'ard until he was able to grasp the ladder. There Ted clung, too exhausted to climb unassisted, and it was not until Brian took most of the strain on the looped rope that he ascended, flopped aimlessly over the rail and dropped unconscious in the scuppers.

And no wonder! Both he and Brian had seen how narrowly he had escaped the culminating peril, for hardly had the rescued youth's feet drawn clear of the surface when an enormous shark glided past, belly uppermost and displaying the wide open maw with the triple row of teeth ready to seize its victim.

Thoroughly alarmed at Ted's condition and hardly knowing whether he was alive, Brian set to work to revive the senseless lad. Although his methods were not orthodox they had the desired effect, for presently Ted opened his eyes and attempted to raise his head.

'Ugh!' he ejaculated feebly. 'Did you see that?'

Brian nodded. He, too, knew what 'that' meant.

'Don't know how I came to overbalance,' continued Ted. 'I was a silly ass to do it!'

'It doesn't much matter now,' rejoined Brian. 'Lie still for a bit.'

He fetched a cushion from one of the cabins and put it under Ted's head. Then he began to haul in the Jacob's ladder, hoping that it would never again have to be put to a similar use. To his surprise it was little more than half of its original length. Both ropes had been severed, leaving the strands splayed like Irishman's pennants.

The shark, baulked of its living prey, had made off with a dozen stout ash rungs of the ladder!

XI

A NIGHT OF DREAD

IT was a couple of hours before Ted recovered his strength and spirits. The shock of his narrow escape had jolted him pretty badly; but after a meal —which Brian prepared without reference to their compact—he was almost his usual self.

Just before sunset Brian stopped the auxiliary motor of his charging plant—and how quiet the ship seemed after the pulsations had ceased—and switched on the navigation lamps.

Then they went to the wireless room. There was plenty 'on the air'.

'See if you can get La Serena or Santa Teresa,' said Brian.

The Bolomayan station was turning out its usual crop of war lies under the heading of propaganda; that of the Catamarcan port was just finishing a concert of national music. Then the announcer gave out:

'No news has been received of the missing *Sempione*. Again we send out an appeal to all ships off our coast and between the parallels 10 and 30 south to keep an alert watch for this overdue vessel. . . . This morning Guzman Vaquillo, a barber employed in this town, discovered that he——'

Ted switched off. They weren't interested in the unknown Guzman. The previous paragraph was quite a different proposition.

'I say: oughtn't we to do something about it?' asked Ted.

'What can we do? You notice it doesn't say anything about Captain Esmeraldas and the crew. If they got to the *Chacal* the *Sempione* would be reported as a derelict. It seems as if the boats were not picked up.'

'Couldn't we send a message. We could tap it out in Morse—it would be very slow, I know—but ships are bound to be on the look-out for messages.'

'You can try,' agreed Brian dubiously. 'I don't think you'll have any luck!'

'I've seen Pedro at work . . . I think this is the knob!'

Confidently Ted depressed the ebonite handle. There was a vivid flash accompanied by a fierce crackling sound. A thin haze of bluish smoke issued from the transmitter. Instantly he switched off.

It was too late. The *Sempione's* wireless was permanently out of action.

'That's done it!' Ted exclaimed ruefully.

'That's a fact,' agreed Brian. 'No more reception either. We're cut off from the civilized world! But don't worry; we can do without it.'

'Must,' added Ted, conscious of the fact that his over-confidence had been solely responsible for the mishap.

Because they had deprived themselves of the boon of being able to receive messages they had missed by a matter of only a few minutes a gale warning issued from La Serena—a hurricane was expected from a westerly point and would probably turn in a south-easterly direction before blowing itself out.

Unprepared, although they could have done nothing beyond stowing the squaresail and setting a storm staysail, they turned in, in happy ignorance of forthcoming events. They hadn't even looked at the barometer in the chartroom!

About two a.m. they were awakened by the sound of very heavy rain thudding on the deck-head. The wind had dropped, leaving the *Sempione* rolling sluggishly in the long sullen swell. The air was unpleasantly close, even the downpour failing to give relief. The yard of the now idle squaresail was banging dismally against the foremast.

'Thank goodness the roof doesn't leak!' remarked Ted.

'No; we're all right here,' added Brian. 'Hello! There's lightning!'

A vivid flash lit up the interior of the cabin and then left the two lads blinking in a darkness so profound that it seemed to press upon their eyes.

'Think there's a chance of being struck?' asked Ted anxiously.

During their stay at the Estancia Miraflores they had learnt to have a great respect for thunderstorms. Those in England were nothing to be compared with the awe-inspiring displays in that part of South America. They had seen twenty head of cattle killed within a radius of as many yards; they had seen a huge rock not far from the house split from a cliff by lightning. The *peons* on the estate had related strange and wonderful tales of the appalling effects of thunderstorms—tales, that, although undoubtedly exaggerated, lost little or nothing in their telling.

'The ship being struck? Very little chance, thank goodness!' replied Brian. 'I was speaking to Santos about it. He pointed out that there are lightning conductors on both masts and if they were hit the current would pass harmlessly into the sea.'

'I hope he's right,' observed Ted. 'Hello! There's another. Nearer this time!'

Soon the flashes succeeded one another in an almost continuous blaze of light, accompanied by deafening peals of thunder. So dazzling were the flashes that the two lads pulled their blankets over their heads in an ineffectual attempt to shield their eyes from the painful glare.

About an hour later the lightning ceased and the noise of the thunder rolled away in the distance. There was a marked fall in temperature, accompanied— though they were unaware of it—by a further and rapid drop of the barometer.

'That's over at last!' exclaimed Brian drowsily. 'And we can stop in as long as we jolly well like. We're our own masters here.'

That was where Nature chipped in as a reminder that no human being can have absolute control.

With a vicious shriek the white squall hurled itself upon the helpless, almost stationary vessel. She reeled under the blow. The superstructure, including the cabin the lads had appropriated, groaned and quivered under the impact. The squaresail, taken aback, burst from its bolt-ropes. The jagged canvas flogged furiously, emitting whip-like cracks that out-voiced the whine of the wind.

Brian, who was in the wind'ard bunk, got out hastily; or rather he was forcibly ejected in spite of the pro-tective bunk-board. Ted, on the opposite bunk, was wedged between it and the bulkhead.

Scared stiff, Brian lurched across the steeply-inclined deck and switched on the light. Beyond enabling them to see within the limits of the cabin, it did not help them much. Of what was taking place outside they knew nothing except what their hearing told them.

Quickly a heavy sea had arisen. The *Sempione*, at first taken aback, had gathered sternway until the wind again hit her in the bows. Then she swung until she remained 'stern-rode' with wind and sea hammering on her starboard quarter.

Without speaking a word, Ted jumped out of his

bunk. The two lads commenced to dress hurriedly.
The storm was the worst they had experienced; the
night when the boats put off to the *Chacal* seemed
nothing in comparison. They quite imagined that the
Sempione would capsize and founder; so by some
unaccountable reason they were dressing themselves.
Perhaps it wasn't decorous to drown when clad in
striped pyjamas!

The ship no longer rolled from side to side. She
corkscrewed violently—a combination of rolling and
pitching to the accompaniment of a crescendo of
noises coming both from without and within.

As he was pulling on a shirt Brian sat down heavily
upon a suitcase that had been dislodged from a rack,
and finished off by banging the back of his head against
the chest of drawers. It was just at that moment that
a heavy sea broke inboard, smashing one of the scuttles,
bursting open the latched door and flooding the cabin
to a depth of six inches.

This aroused the chums to action. Better do something than wait mutely for the end. They secured the
deadlight, forced the door back and bolted it. Then
they set to work to bale out the water, not giving a
thought to the fact that should the ship make her last
plunge their task would be unnecessary!

After that they hardly knew what happened until
daylight. Then the awfulness of the seas became
apparent. Although the wind had eased and had backed
to the south'ard the waves were running mountains
high. At one time the ship, hit by the full blast of the
wind, was lying well over on the crest of a tall ridge;
at another she was lying in the trough and almost
entirely sheltered from the furious blasts. Through
the lee'ard scuttles nothing was to be seen but a
sloping wall of water. Then the disabled vessel began
to lift to the succeeding wave until the whole nerve-
racking performance was gone through again.

Curiosity prompted Ted to time the period of the undulations. It took three and a half minutes for the *Sempione* to ride from one crest to another, while, according to his estimate, the vertical height was not less than thirty feet.

This state of things continued throughout the forenoon and the greater part of the afternoon. Towards sunset the wind died down and although the seas still ran high, they lost most of their menacing appearance.

Then the pangs of hunger became pressingly apparent.

'How about grub?' asked Ted. 'It's eighteen hours since we had our last meal.'

'Seems like eighteen days,' replied Brian. 'We'll have to be jolly careful when we go out.'

They unbolted the cabin door and, watching their opportunity, made a rush for the guard-rail. Here they stopped and looked down upon the well-deck over which the seas swept almost uninterruptedly. And no wonder! About twenty feet of the bulwarks on the starboard side had been swept away and two large gaps appeared on the port side. The hatches had stood —otherwise the ship would have gone down—but except for a few strips held by the wedges, the tarpaulin covers had vanished.

The squaresail was no more, but the yard still remained aloft with one arm entangled in the foremast shrouds. A seaman would have said that the yard was 'a'cock-bill', but Brian, unversed in sea-terms, contented himself by remarking that it looked 'wonky'.

The funnel had disappeared but that was of no consequence. Although motor-driven, the *Sempione* had retained her original 'smokestack' not only as a ventilator, but to inspire confidence amongst her passengers.

Of the two boats that had been left when her crew

abandoned the ship, one had been shattered. Only the stem and stern ring-bolts, with fragments of wood adhering to them, remained attached to the davits.

Apparently the remaining boat had survived without damage, although the lads did not attempt to investigate. It was food they were after!

They found the galley flooded out and most of the utensils washed away—and all because in their inexperience they had neglected to secure the metal door. For the present a hot meal was out of the question; so they made a descent upon the officers' pantry, from which they took a large tin of turkey, a maize-cake and some salt butter. With this they satisfied the cravings of the inner man.

There seemed no chance of setting the staysail while the wind was still so high. The canvas would flog itself to bits before it could be sheeted home— a task beyond the united strength of the two boys.

When darkness fell they returned to their cabin, leaving the ship to drive before the wind, in which direction they knew not. For the present they were beyond caring even if the wind had chopped round completely and was bearing them towards the Grossaguayan coast!

Both of them were—to use their own expressions although they did not voice them—fed up with the sea!

XII

SAILS AND SHARKS

WITH morning came a complete change of their outlook.

The sun rose in a cloudless sky. The angry waves had subsided into a long gentle swell. The salt-laden air was pleasantly warm. The Pacific was in one of its kindliest moods.

It wasn't as if the perils of the previous day had vanished like a dream. There were forcible reminders of the vehemence of the storm. Brian had a lump on the back of his head that felt as if it was as large as an egg! Ted discovered that his knees and elbows had been barked and that there was a livid bruise on his left shoulder, but how and when he had sustained this damage he was unable to say.

The condition of the ship was a more serious matter. In addition to the loss of the funnel, the destruction of one of the two boats and the breaching of the bulwarks, it was found that the *Sempione* had made a lot of water. It was up to the bed-plates in the motor room, while in sounding the after well, the lads discovered that there was six feet of water instead of the usual six inches!

'She's either strained her hull or else the fractured end of the propeller shaft has drawn,' opined Ted.

'The sooner we start the power-pumps the better,' decided Brian. 'Brekker will have to wait.'

In a few minutes the auxiliary engines were running

and discharging copious streams of water through the delivery hoses.

They left the pumps working and tackled the demands of the inner man, for since they had been afloat their appetites were twice as great as they had been at the Estancia Miraflores. There they had mostly had fresh meat and vegetables; on board the *Sempione* the fare, though plentiful, consisted of hard tack and tinned stuff—but they did not mind that! It would have been a very different tale if they had had to subsist on the coarse food served out in the fo'c'sle!

Everything considered, the *Sempione* was fairly well equipped in all departments. There were the navigating instruments—several sextants in first-class condition, for example—charts quite up to date and everything necessary for a skilled navigator to determine his position either by night or by day.

Neither Brian nor Ted was a skilled navigator. Brian's knowledge of seamanship was rudimentary; of navigation sketchy. He knew more or less where the ship's head was pointing but variation and deviation were to him meaningless terms.

There they were, with means of knowing where they were and yet unable to use them. They were lost somewhere in the vast Pacific. But by the aid of the charts and by 'reading up' a *Directory of the Pacific* in Spanish, Brian had gained some knowledge of their present course; that, if maintained, would eventually bring the *Sempione* to one of the numerous groups of islands of Polynesia. Alternatively there was the possibility of the chums being picked up by a passing vessel, particularly when the *Sempione* cut the steamer track between Auckland and Panama.

'That sail isn't helping us much,' observed Brian, indicating the trysail, which they had set during the forenoon. 'I wonder if we could cut down another squaresail from the others in the locker?'

'We'll try, anyway,' said Ted. 'Hang on while I switch off those motors. The pumps are sucking air.'

It was a matter for congratulation that they had succeeded in again freeing the ship of water. The question still remained: was there a leak below the waterline?

Armed with a lantern, they explored the holds. There was a fair amount of general cargo, but they were unable to find out its nature. Some had been immersed but so far there was no sign of the water coming in again.

Then they examined the tunnel of the propeller shaft. The fractured after-end had not drawn, but there was a slight leak through the gland—certainly not enough to account for the amount the ship had taken in. Fore and aft the ship seemed as tight as when she had left the slipway in the Clyde.

'It must have come in through the decks,' declared Brian.

'Don't see how,' objected Ted. 'All the hatches were closed. Of course some might have got down when the funnel carried away. Our cabin was flooded out, you'll remember——'

'No need to remind me of that.'

' 'Course not, Bags! But the base of the funnel casing is in the same deck.'

'That might be,' admitted Brian. 'Yet somehow——'

They continued their investigations, this time along the well-deck. The hatches over Number one hold had stood, although a certain amount of water must have poured in when the tarpaulin covers were carried away. Probably more would have done so, but for the fact that the big gaps in the bulwarks had acted as very efficient scuppers.

When they came to the hatch of Number four hold there was no doubt as to the cause of the inrush. The

stout metal coaming had been forced inwards, leaving a
lozenge-shaped gap, measuring seven feet by one,
between it and the deck. In addition, the buckling
of the coaming had lifted two of the hatch-covers.
The damage was beyond their resources to make
good. The deck, being of iron, could not be replaced
into position; it would be a most difficult task to cover
the gap with planks unless they could drill holes through
the metal to fit the necessary bolts.

They could not leave things as they were. With
every roll in even a moderate sea the well decks were
flooded. Something had to be done!

Searching in the engineers' tool-chest, they found
drills and braces. It took them the best part of two
hours' hard work under a hot sun to drill a couple
of holes. Then they fitted a plank underneath the gap
and another on top, binding them down with bolts
and nuts and caulking the upper plank with strands
of rope soaked in oil.

Next, the hatch covers had to be cut down to fit
the bent coaming and by the time this task was accomplished and the tarpaulins secured by wedges it was
nearly sunset.

'We'll call it a day!' declared Brian, wiping the
perspiration from his eyes. 'And, botheration! there's
grub to get!'

Before turning in they lowered the staysail, secured
all doors and made all possible preparation for another
blow; but during the night nothing happened. The
Sempione continued to drift, urged westward by the
unseen influence of the great ocean current.

Next morning the weather was again perfect, with
the Trades still blowing steadily. After breakfast both
Brian and Ted set to work on the new squaresail.
This they shaped by ruthlessly cutting down two
triangular sails, sewing the longer sides together and
laboriously roping the four outer edges. It was a case

of 'practice makes perfect', although their ideas of perfection fell short of those held by professional sail-makers. Fortunately they found a tattered copy of a book on sail-making in the bosun's locker and although the technical directions in Spanish puzzled them considerably they managed to grasp the correct use of a 'palm'. Even then, by the end of the forenoon, their hands were raw as the result of the unaccustomed use of the sharkskin guard and their finger tips were sore through coaxing the triangular needle with its beeswaxed thread out of the stiff canvas.

Towards sunset the task was completed. The sail was bent to the yard and made ready to hoist.

'Think we'd better?' asked Brian.

'Why not?'

'If it comes on to blow hard during the night all our day's work will be wasted.'

'The glass is high and steady,' declared Ted, anxious to make prompt use of the result of their labours.

Eventually they compromised and, on the ground that it wouldn't matter much if it did carry away, they kept the staysail up.

After supper Brian went to the side to throw a bucket of rubbish overboard. 'Come and have a look!' he called.

Ted was engaged in the now hateful task of washing-up. Only too glad of a temporary respite, he dropped what he was doing and hurried on deck.

The sea alongside was a sheet of shimmering phosphorescence; while as the offal slowly drifted past the ship's side long dark shapes darted hither and thither, leaving a trail of bluish light.

'Ugh, the brutes!' ejaculated Ted.

There were about half a dozen big sharks attended, at a safe distance, by three pilot fish, all intent upon the bucketful of scraps that Brian had tossed overside.

None of the sharks attempted to close until the stuff had drifted well astern.

Curious to see what would happen, the boys hurried aft and leant over the taffrail.

Presently one brute, turning on its back, made a grab at what was to it a tempting morsel. It was a signal for the others and since there was not nearly enough offal to go round the result was a free fight on a large scale. The gently heaving water was churned into a maelstrom, above which a cloud of iridescent spray was flung high in the air. This continued until after the ship had left the disputants too far astern for the onlookers to see how the fight ended.

'Wouldn't give us much chance if we fell overboard,' said Brian with a shudder. 'They say that if a fellow in the water kicks violently a shark won't touch him. I wouldn't care to test the truth of that with that savage crowd about!'

'They've finished,' declared Ted. 'Look, they're coming after the ship again!'

Owing to her slow speed the *Sempione* was leaving hardly any perceptible wake. The sharks were supplying the deficiency. They were overhauling her rapidly and leaving a phosphorescent trail that gave the watchers the impression that it was the ship's movement through the water.

'If those brutes are there to-morrow I'll do something to them!' said Brian.

'What'll you do, Bags?'

'You wait!' rejoined Brian darkly.

Next morning the sharks were still there, swimming lazily astern and doubtless keeping watchful eyes on the ship for anything edible—from a man to a morsel of fat pork—that might come their way.

While rummaging in the paint store, Brian had discovered a large tin of carbide of calcium. From this he took enough to fill an empty bottle, which he tightly corked and then wrapped in strips of very dry and unappetizing beef from the harness cask. This he threw overboard.

The bait sank a good two fathoms before it came to the surface again. Hardly had the ripples subsided when the sharks, now numbering nearly a score, converged upon it. For a while they swam round in decreasing spirals, suspicious both of it and their companions.

'Hurry up!' shouted Ted excitedly. 'Or it'll be too far away for us to see!'

Suddenly the largest shark turned on its back, snapped viciously at another that looked like forestalling him and then swallowed the bait after giving one bite that broke the neck of the bottle.

For, perhaps, thirty seconds nothing apparently happened. Brian was beginning to think that the tiger of the deep had 'got away with it' when a cloud of white smoke broke surface. Then followed a really violent commotion as the carbide fizzed in the shark's stomach and escaped in increasing volumes of smoke.

For half an hour afterwards smoke was still issuing from the dead body of the shark as it floated now more than a quarter of a mile astern. This time there was no commotion. The other brutes had not followed their usual procedure of tearing the victim to pieces. They made off hurriedly and for several days the sharks kept well clear of the slowly moving ship.

'So that's that!' exclaimed Brian, as he and Ted left the taffrail and went for'ard. 'Now for our new sail!'

The squaresail was larger than the one that had been blown away. The canvas, too, was of heavier texture. It took them the best part of an hour to hoist it while in order to trim it better they had bent a couple of braces to each yard-arm.

The result was quickly evident. The *Sempione* had

a distinct increase of speed, although Ted opined that it was still 'nothing to write home about'. On the other hand, the increased height had brought the foot so close to the deck that it was not possible to get a direct view for'ard from the bridge.

'Do you know what today is?' suddenly inquired Ted.

Brian had to think. He had almost lost count of the days of the week and month. 'Thursday, the 10th, I think,' he replied.

'Full marks for that, Bags! Also it happens to be my birthday. I have now attained the great age of seventeen.'

'Gratters, old son!'

'Thanks; we must celebrate! Special four-course luncheon in the saloon, which *you* will prepare! After that we will slack for the rest of the day, since nothing's likely to happen.'

'Do you think I'm going to stew in the beastly galley so that you can blow yourself out?' asked Brian warmly.

'I'll condescend to cold tack,' rejoined Ted with his cheerful grin. 'After all, I'm asking you to share my birthday feast.'

XIII

TEMPERS!

THEY did not neglect their routine before turning in for the night. They had now made a habit of consulting the barometer. Then the direction of the wind had to be noted, although during settled weather it remained almost constant at about sou'west, which meant that, taking it in conjunction with the ocean current, the ship's progress was roughly a hundred miles every twenty-four hours.

With the prospect of a continuance of fair weather they lowered the square-sail just before sunset and set the triangular fore staysail. It meant a certain amount of hard work but they had the satisfaction of knowing that during the hours of darkness the ship was not merely drifting broadside on to the wind and waves, but running, though slowly, towards her final destination.

For Brian was now firmly convinced that the chances of falling in with another vessel were becoming more and more remote and that the *Sempione* would eventually reach one of the outlying groups of the Polynesian Islands.

'How long will it take before we get there?' asked Ted, as they were preparing to turn in.

'Another twenty days, I think.'

'Twenty days! I'll have forgotten what it feels like to have dry land under my feet!'

'All I hope is that we don't have to swim for the

last lap!' rejoined Brian. 'Switch the light off. . . .
Good night, old son!'

Nineteen more days and nights passed and the
lads' expectations of sighting land increased. Very
little had happened to vary the routine into which
they had almost automatically dropped. So far the
possible monotony had not made itself felt. They
were in fairly high spirits and were buoyed up with
the increasing prospect of soon setting foot on dry
land.

Towards the end of the period they made a point
of climbing to the standard compass platform above
the chartroom the first thing in the morning and the
last at night. Armed with binoculars, they swept the
horizon ahead in an effort to sight one or more of the
islands they expected to find. This ritual they performed before they hoisted the squaresail and again
before they lowered it for the night.

On the evening of the twenty-fifth day after the
Sempione had left Santa Teresa the long steady wind
suddenly dropped to a flat calm. Had they but known
it, the ship had reached the northern limit of the
Sou'-east Trades and was approaching that belt so
dreaded by the old-time sailing-ships—the Doldrums.

Beyond the usual slight diurnal movements of the
barometer there was nothing to indicate any change
in the weather. Everything looked so calm and peaceful
that the boys thought it would be quite safe to leave the
staysail set.

'It's not doing much good, though,' observed Ted,
eyeing the heavy canvas as it hung idly from the wire
stay with its leach flapping lazily with the gentle
movement of the ship.

'It's there if the breeze springs up again,' rejoined
Brian. He went to the side and tossed an empty
tin overboard. Instead of drifting aft it remained

alongside gently rubbing against the weed-covered bottom as the *Sempione* rolled to the now gentle undulations.

The ship was entirely without way, her head pointing almost nor'west. Yet the unseen, unfelt, South Equatorial Current—gaining in strength as the *Sempione* was carried westward—was urging her at a rate of at least four knots.

'It looks as if we're stuck!' remarked Ted, who had strolled over to where Brian was standing. 'And those weeds! They're spreading straight out from the waterline. They must be at least six feet long.'

'We've had quite a good crop for some days,' declared Brian. 'Only while the ship is moving, they keep close to her sides. And she had her bottom freshly painted when we joined her at Santa Teresa.'

The lads remained on deck for some time after sunset. There was no inducement to return to the artificially lighted saloon. The evening was perfect. Overhead, stars shone brilliantly in their myriads, their reflections scintillating on the calm surface of the tropical sea. Then in a few minutes the scene changed. A veil seemed to have been drawn across the sky. The reflections vanished and in their place the sea was covered by a weird phosphorescence that threw an uncanny upward light upon the ship's masts and superstructure. Again and again darts of this peculiar light leapt three or four feet above the surface as a fish, pursued by a larger one of its kind, made a spring into the air in a vain attempt to elude its pursuer.

Curious to see if they could discover the cause of this uncanny glow, Ted fetched an electric torch and flashed it down. Within the oval-shaped glare the phosphorescence vanished, but to their astonishment they discovered that the ship was floating in the midst of a vast field of jelly-fish of all sizes. Some were quite six feet across, while their long tentacles could be seen slowly distending and contracting as they engulfed their prey.

'How would you like to have a swim, Bags?' asked Ted facetiously.

'Not much,' replied Brian. 'I was badly stung once, when I was swimming at Cromer.'

'That was your fault entirely. If you had swum over them and not let their tentacles trail over you you wouldn't have been stung,' explained Ted. 'I've smashed dozens with my fist and have never been stung.'

'Let's see you try now, then,' suggested Brian. 'I'll stand by with the rope-ladder when you've had enough!'

It was a challenge, and Ted accepted it. He began to peel off his shirt.

'Don't be an ass!' expostulated Brian. 'You're not going overboard! There may be sharks!'

'There aren't any. We'd see their tracks if there were,' persisted Ted, kicking off his shoes and picking up the rolled Jacob's ladder.

'No, you don't,' exclaimed Brian, grasping the ladder.

'I am!'

'You're not!'

In a moment tempers had flared. Ted, because he thought that Brian considered him to be a mere boaster, was determined to prove that he was not; while Brian, knowing his friend's rash impulsiveness, was equally determined to stop him.

'Let go, I tell you!' shouted Ted, as he tried to grab the ladder.

Brian complied, but only to get a better grip. The result was that the bundle of rope and ash rungs flew back and hit Ted heavily in the chest.

Ted sat down unpleasantly hard upon the edge of

a grating. The next instant he was on his feet and
fiercely attacking his friend.

It was a scrap! They hadn't fought each other since
their one and only encounter in the Fives Court during
their first term as Bessingborough School, when they
had an audience of nearly a hundred of their wildly
enthusiastic school-fellows. Now there were no spec-
tators to yell encouragements to their respective
favourites.

They fought grimly, Ted in his temper doing most
of the attacking, while Brian, though also furious, did
his best to counter most of his opponent's blows. Each
time their fists got home their tempers increased. It
was a fight in the raw, with no one to call time and
give them a respite.

For nearly five minutes they went at it hammer and
tongs until Brian dropped his opponent by a straight
left to the point of the jaw. Then in a moment the
victor's anger vanished. Hastily he fetched a basin of
water and a sponge and bathed Ted's face until he
opened his eyes.

'My word!' Ted exclaimed, when full consciousness
returned. 'That was a beauty, Bags!'

'Sorry, old son!'

'Right-o. You got my rag out, though! Do you still
say I wouldn't?'

'No,' replied Brian hastily and conciliatorily. 'You
were quite ready to prove you were right and I believe
you. Jelly-fish are harmless if you tackle them in the
right way; like grasping a sting-nettle!'

A grin spread over Ted's painfully discoloured
features. 'Good enough!' he replied. 'Hello! That's a
nasty gash above your eye. Let me bathe it for you!'

Their tempers had subsided almost as quickly as
they had sprung up. A sense of shame succeeded their
former outburst.

'Let's turn in,' suggested Brian.

'I'm ready.'

With hardly another word beyond an exchange of good nights, they went to their bunks. Each resolved never to mention the matter again, although there was every likelihood of a reminder in the form of cuts and bruises in the morning! And the whole business had been so absurd—like a couple of young dogs scrapping over a worthless bone!

XIV

THE WONDERS OF THE DEEP

IT seemed to Brian that he had not been asleep more than five minutes when he was aroused by a low deep rumble. He sat up, listening intently.

To him it could mean only one thing: the approach of another white squall, the forerunner of a terrific tropical storm; and the recollections of the last were only too fresh in his memory!

'Ted!' he exclaimed. 'What's that?'

Lifting his aching face from the pillow, Ted listened, resentful at being aroused just as oblivion was claiming him. 'What's what?' he asked drowsily.

Then, before Brian could explain that he thought another storm was approaching, Ted sprang from his bunk and switched on the light. Snatching the binoculars from their case, he threw open the door and went out.

Puzzled by his actions and by the rapidly increasing noise, Brian followed. Out in the open air he had no doubt as to the source of that deep though still far-off roar. It was the sound of a powerful aircraft.

'There she is!' exclaimed Ted. 'See her light?' He tried, at first unsuccessfully, to pick up the 'plane through his glasses. They were x8's, with a comparatively small field.

Meanwhile Brian had gone one better. Darting back to the cabin he fetched a pair of night-glasses of smaller but more brilliant magnification. He was just in time.

With a terrific roar the aircraft passed almost over-head. At least it seemed to do so, though had there been an observer five miles away and also at right-angles to its track, he might have claimed to have seen it immediately overhead!

They had a brief glance of the windows on one side of the cabin—now a blaze of light—as the huge machine tilted in a cross-current. Then the coloured navigation lights seemed to vanish while the saloon lamps appeared to diminish in intensity. In about a minute the aircraft was lost to sight, but for more than twice that time the two lads remained silent and motionless gazing in the direction it had taken.

'They'll land somewhere in America before dawn,' remarked Brian. 'And we've been weeks——'

'I wish we were on board her,' said Ted.

'Do you? I don't!' rejoined Brian stoutly. 'Here we're running the whole show! We can do almost anything we want. Over there we'd be just passengers bound by a lot of rotten red-tape rules.'

'M'yes,' agreed Ted reluctantly. 'But it would be exciting if we were co-pilots of a bus like that.'

Brian was not to be persuaded. 'It's not much fun,' he asserted. 'I've been up twice—across to Paris and back—but it's a tame business. You're no sooner up than you're down—with no sensation of speed when you're cooped up—and the only thrill is when the 'bus takes off and comes down. No, give me the sea every time! Of course, if a fellow's in a hurry——'

'We aren't, anyway,' interposed Ted. 'I wonder if we are going to sight land tomorrow?'

They went back to their respective bunks and were soon asleep.

At daybreak they turned out just as they were and hurried to their look-out. A careful examination of the horizon resulted in no sign of land; but a remarkable thing, and one that puzzled them at first, was that the sun was rising over the bows of the ship! It was not until they had consulted the compass that they tumbled to it. In the windless air the *Sempione* had been drifting aimlessly, swinging through all the points of the compass.

This sort of thing continued throughout the forenoon and well on through the afternoon; no breeze to temper the sweltering heat. Yet it was hotter about three o'clock than it was at noon when the sun was almost overhead.

Although they were used to tropical conditions the boys felt the heat more than they remembered ever having done before. The decks were too warm for them to remain more than a few seconds in one spot. In spite of their rope-soled canvas shoes the soles of their feet could not stand the heat radiating from the decks. Even under the awnings they had spread the atmosphere was stifling.

They obtained temporary relief by stripping and throwing buckets of salt water over each other; but in a few minutes the heat seemed as bad as, or worse than, before. And with it was the feeling that the *Sempione* was motionless. There was not much satisfaction in knowing that she was being carried along by a strong current if they couldn't see her move.

'Look!' cried Ted suddenly. 'There's land over there!'

Forgetting all about the heat, both boys sprang to their feet and rushed to the side.

About three or four miles on the port bow, or in a westerly direction, could be seen two rugged peaks rising above the horizon. The higher ground was destitute of verdure, but the lower-lying parts of the island were covered with palm trees.

'There's no wind,' said Brian. 'We haven't steerage way. What if the current sweeps us clear of the island?'

'There'll be others. Swarms of them. Mind you, I hope we don't get carried past that one. It looks a good spot—fresh coconuts, fresh vegetables and fresh water, what?'

Armed with binoculars, they hurried to the bridge. By this time the island bore broad on their port side owing to the ship continuing her erratic turning movement.

And then an extraordinary thing happened!

Even as they levelled the glasses the twin peaks rose slowly yet surely into the air. Their tops began to shiver. Higher and higher they rose, like two pieces of glutinous toffee being pulled apart. Then the palm trees commenced to ascend, leaving a stretch of unbroken water beneath, until the whole of the island vanished into thin air!

The watchers knew what had happened. They had just seen a rare phenomenon at sea—a mirage. In desert regions they are fairly frequent and have often raised false hopes in the minds of travellers on the point of dying from thirst. It was with somewhat similar feelings that the lads saw their prospects of closing land collapse.

'But there must be land *somewhere* over there,' said Ted, giving a comprehensive sweep with one hand in the direction where the mirage had been.

'I suppose so,' admitted Brian. 'There's one thing; there doesn't seem any sign of a breeze. When the island faded it went straight up like smoke from a chimney on a calm day.'

'Let's have another bottle of soda water,' suggested Ted. 'I've a thirst on me like a bale of blotting-paper!'

The surprises of the first Dog Watch were not yet over, for shortly after five o'clock—or rather what the clock told them, since in their westward drift the timepiece was an hour ahead of the solar time— they noticed what they first took to be a cone-shaped cloud about two miles away on the starboard beam.

'What's that—another mirage?' asked Ted.

Brian did not reply, for the simple reason that he didn't know.

The cone grew higher and was certainly approaching in a direction that would cross the *Sempione's* bows. It looked uncanny, moving as it did without visible agency since there was still no sign of wind. Then the apex seemed to expand until the whole assumed the appearance of a diabolo or an old-time hour-glass. All the while the top-heavy column was revolving.

It was another phenomenon of the sea and one that owed its origin to similar conditions to those responsible for the mirage—a waterspout.

Half a mile off, it changed direction and seemed to be bearing straight down upon the motionless ship. The upper cone was now much larger than the lower or first formed one. Even to the inexperienced observers it was evident that before long the 'neck' would break and thousands of tons of water now whirling in the air would descend with terrific force.

'It's coming straight for us!' exclaimed Brian in an awe-struck voice. 'Let's get below out of it.'

It seemed a futile course to pursue. The uprushing water of the spout was fierce enough to lay the ship over on her beam ends even if it did not capsize her, while if its spinal column were severed, the weight of the falling water would crush the ship's decks like egg-shells.

It was a toss up whether to remain on deck and be washed overboard when the flood descended or to go below and run the risk of being trapped when the ship fell over on her beam ends.

They ran for it, seeking a doubtful shelter under the break of the poop. Standing just under the alley-way, they peered out like cowed dogs in a kennel, uncertain whether to venture or not.

Land on the port bow

Nearer and nearer came the whirling patter of water. The din and the rush of displaced air became deafening. Momentarily they expected to find the *Sempione* heeling under the effect of the uprush.

When about three hundred yards off—to the boys it seemed very much nearer—the spout seemed to hesitate; then it made off in a direction roughly at right angles to its former course, until the expected happened.

The narrow spiral that formed the connecting link between the upper and lower cones suddenly broke. The lower mass subsided amidst a smother of foam, while the upper, held aloft for some seconds longer, expanded until it resembled a gargantuan mushroom.

Then it, too, fell with a rush and roar, throwing up concentric rings of breaking swell that, when they reached her, made the *Sempione* stagger like a drunken man. For perhaps half a minute furious wind-eddies swept over the ship and lashed the disturbed sea into foam.

Five minutes later all signs of the waterspout had vanished, leaving the *Sempione* rolling sluggishly in the calm sea.

XV

APPROACHING THE REEFS

SUCH freaks of the atmosphere could mean but one thing—a sudden change in the weather. Before nightfall the glass had dropped an inch and one tenth. The long cloudless sky was overcast with greasy looking patches of dark clouds banking up above the eastern horizon.

With the fall of the barometer came a decided drop in temperature. Within an hour Ted and Brian, previously sweltering in the stifling heat, were glad to don thick clothes, even to the extent of putting on oilskins formerly the property of the *Sempione's* Second and Third Officers.

Down swept the wind—fortunately before the rain. Already the staysail had been double-reefed so that it seemed but a fragment of its former self. Yet even that small spread of canvas did its work. It kept the ship's head off the wind so that she drove through the water at a good five knots instead of lying broadside on and drifting like a barrel.

'I'm not turning in tonight,' declared Brian. 'Or if I do, I'll do so all standing!'

'What's the idea?'

'If we're as near to the islands as I think we are we'll have to keep a sharp look-out in case the ship's carried on to a reef.'

'I don't see how keeping a look-out will help,' protested Ted. 'She'd be smashed up in any case.'

'Not if we can spot a channel through the reef and can steer her through.'

Ted shrugged his shoulders. 'Precious fine chance that!' he rejoined. 'All I hope is we're miles from land until this storm's over! Just as you like, though! I'm turning in properly.'

He did; but not so Brian! Until daybreak he stood at the open scuttles facing for'ard, holding on to keep his balance, staring through the darkness and straining his ears to catch the sound of the thunder of surf upon a reef.

Through it all Ted slept like a log. Brian reviled his indifference in his thoughts, but envied him his ability to forget present conditions.

Dawn brought no sign of land. As far as the eye could see there was nothing but a welter of white-capped, menacing waves and a wind-torn cloudy sky.

Ted slowly opened his eyes. 'Hello! You might have saved yourself the trouble, Bags!' he exclaimed ungratefully. Then before Brian could make any reply he continued: 'My word! You do look bat-eyed! Look here! You turn in and I'll bring along some brekker.'

'You won't be able to get to the galley,' said Brian dubiously, though grateful for his pal's tardy solicitude. 'The waves are washing over the well-deck still.'

Ted grinned. 'Let 'em! Before I turned in last night I lugged an oil-stove and some grub up to the wireless room. So in you hop between the blankets. I'll be as sharp as I can.' Hastily washing and dressing he took himself off. Presently he came back laden with coffee-pot, two mugs and a plate of buttered biscuits.

Five minutes later Brian was sound asleep.

Left to himself, Ted fought his way to the bridge. Obviously the storm was abating. To wind'ard the sun, still only fifteen or twenty degrees above the horizon, was shining brightly in an unclouded sky. Overhead, the tail end of the storm-clouds was visibly decreasing both in density and velocity.

Then Ted scanned the skyline ahead. Sure enough, one point on the port bow was land—two rugged peaks that were exactly like those of the mirage, except that they were quite fifteen miles away. The palm-covered lower slopes were as yet invisible beneath the horizon.

'No doubt about it,' said Ted to himself. 'No phantom island in this wind! Thank goodness it's easing down and we won't reach land for another four hours. By that time the seas won't be anything to worry about.'

He was on the point of skipping down the ladder to inform Brian of the glad news when he decided to hang on. There was no immediate hurry and old Bags would be all the better for a few hour's sleep.

On that account he did not attempt to hoist the square-sail, relying upon the reefed canvas to keep the ship on her course for the still distant island.

An hour later the seas had moderated considerably. Only now and again did a comber break through the gap in the bulwarks and surge harmlessly over the well-deck. The wind, too, had dropped until the small spread of canvas was doing hardly any work.

Still Ted did not attempt to wake the sleeping Brian. At intervals he climbed to the standard compass platform and scanned the land ahead.

Slowly but surely the island was rising above the horizon. Now he could see the upper limits of the zone of palm trees. Half an hour later he could make out a white line between the island and the ship. He knew perfectly well what that was: the surf pounding upon the reef. So far, he could discern no break in that barrier. The *Sempione* was dead to wind'ard of it.

Unless there was an entrance to the lagoon she would either have to alter course and steer wide of the island or else she would strike hard upon the reef and be pounded to bits in a very short time.

Nor could he see any sign of human habitation, although the glistening sandy beach was now distinctly visible through his binoculars.

Everything was favourable for the lumbering, almost unmanageable *Sempione* to make the island but for one defect—the absence of a channel through the reefs into the lagoon.

Very soon, or it would be too late, the decision would have to be made whether to stand on or to stand past the much-desired land. Ted, usually so self-reliant, felt unable to cope with the situation. The decision was too momentous for him to make alone. He went down to the former captain's cabin and roused his companion. 'Land, Bags!' he announced. 'We're only about three miles off!'

Brian sprang out of bed, his sleepless night forgotten. 'Why didn't you wake me before?' he asked.

'No hurry. You wanted sleep badly enough! But it's time you turned out. It's like this——' While Brian was hurriedly dressing Ted explained his view of the situation.

Then both climbed to the platform above the charthouse and brought their binoculars into action.

It was Brian's first sight of a coral reef. He had read quite a lot about them, and how that surf when viewed from seaward always looks less formidable than it actually is. In this case, when seen through the powerful glasses, the breakers looked fearfully menacing. It left little to the imagination to guess what they appeared like when seen from the lee side.

The reef on the east side of the island was about two miles in length without any sign of a break. Ceaselessly the waves pounded upon it, throwing up clouds of spray. Even against the wind the chums could hear the sullen angry rumble of the surf.

The *Sempione* was now in comparatively smooth water. The waves were long and regular; but for nearly half a mile to wind'ard of this low-lying coral barrier they were in a state of dangerous agitation, while on the other side of the reef the surface of the lagoon appeared to be as placid as a mountain tarn on a summer's evening. Within the lagoon were safety and tranquillity, but that was scant consolation to the two lads as they watched the turmoil on the reef that lay between them and the haven they desired.

'It can't be done, Ted!' decided Brian. 'Up with the squaresail! We'll steer for the north side of the reef and keep in as close to it as we dare. There's bound to be another island within a few miles—one with a gap in the reef!'

Hurriedly they set and braced the squaresail. Experience had taught them that it was possible to steer to two points on either side of the following wind. They could clear the corner of the reef with a point to spare—provided the wind remained constant in direction if not also in force.

Meanwhile Brian took the wheel and Ted went for'ard with a maul ready to knock away the slip on the sheet anchor cable in case it became necessary to let go. If they had to do this outside the reef it meant that it would be touch and go!

Presently he returned to the bridge and again scanned the reef. 'No sign of a gap anywhere,' he reported. 'And I can see most of it on the north side. Is she clearing it all right?'

'Easily,' replied Brian. 'What a marvellous island! If only we could get the ship through!'

They were now within a mile of the north-eastern angle of the reef. As Ted had announced, the northern side was visible and also a portion of the western barrier; and although one lay in the same direction as the wind and the visible part of the other was to lee'ard, the surf was pounding everywhere. The fact that whether the reef was to lee'ard or to wind'ard seemed to make no difference in that respect.

'Look out!' shrieked Ted warningly. 'Aren't we getting in too much?'

They were. Under the influence of an unseen current the *Sempione* was being carried towards the corner of the reef. Already she was feeling the effect of the rebound of the breakers.

Brian put the helm over still more. Although the ship answered, it was soon evident that he was 'pinching her' too much. The squaresail began to flap. It was no longer drawing. 'We'll have to let go and trust to luck!' he declared. 'If the wind shifts in the right direction we may be blown clear. Nip for'ard to drop the anchor.'

Had he but known it, the anchor was useless for the present position. The water was so deep to within a hundred yards of the reef, that the cable, when all out, would be practically 'up and down'. The anchor might even not touch the bottom.

Just as Ted was hurrying for'ard, Brian caught a glimpse of something that gave him a ray of hope. 'Hold on!' he shouted. 'There is a channel! Stand by with the sheets. We'll do it yet!'

Close to the angle of the reef—which on nearer acquaintance proved to be a bold curve—was a gap hitherto hidden from view by the wall of surf. It was deep water, as could be seen by its colour, and its width might be anything from thirty to fifty yards.

The success of the attempt depended on whether the ship would carry way—it would tax the trim of the square-sail to its uttermost—and whether she would be able to weather the extremity of the reef to lee'ard.

If she did, well and good; if she did not, then the ship would strike and either go down in deep water or else be pounded to pieces.

Another five minutes would decide her fate and that of her amateur crew.

XVI

BROUGHT UP

THE roar of the breakers was now deafening. At regular half-minute intervals showers of spray were hurled across the entrance, to baffle still more the young helmsman's vision. Brian had already put the rudder over to port. The *Sempione* answered. Ted trimmed the squaresail and waited, wondering whether the sail would spill. It was an anxious moment.

Now the ship was heading straight for the narrow channel; now too far to lee'ard. She'd hit the tail of the reef.

It did not seem practicable to put the helm over still further. Already the canvas was shaking, but the ship carried a fair amount of way. If she had enough to 'shoot' her own length she might run through. If her bows fell off, then the low-lying reef would claim its victims.

Brian gave her more helm.

A cloud of spray flying over the foredeck prevented his seeing what she was doing, but he knew that her bows were in the gap. Would the rest of the ship clear, or would the hazardous amount of helm swing her stern against the coral ledges to lee'ard?

The shower of spray subsided, leaving Ted drenched to the skin. Not that he cared! He waved his arm to his chum in a gesture of triumph. He did not know the actual facts. The bows were through, but would the rest of the ship shoot clear? He shouted some remark, but the roar of the surf drowned his voice.

Brian shook his head and gripped the spokes of the wheel harder. The rudder was almost kicking the wheel out of his hands. For the moment, blinded by the spray, he thought that the ship had struck and that the rudder was grinding against the rocks. Probably it did. He was conscious of a distinct shock; then, her quarter slapped by the backwash off the reef to lee'ard, the *Sempione* glided into the deeper water of the lagoon.

Quick to realize the danger of the ship being taken aback—in which case she would drift stern foremost or else broadside on upon the inner side of the reef, Brian put the helm over in the opposite direction. It was touch and go, since the *Sempione* had nearly lost way. She hung irresolute for several long-drawn seconds of anxiety, then slowly her head fell off and the now light breeze again filled the squaresail. Again she forged ahead on a diagonal course towards the island. She was safe!

Thankfully, Brian left the steering-wheel. The ship would keep on her course without attention to the helm. His muscles ached with the unaccustomed strain. The reaction parched his throat and made his limbs tremble. All he could do for the present was to lean over the guard-rails and peer in the direction of the land.

It was Ted, shouting to ask where he had to let go the anchor, that brought Brian back to present conditions. He it was who had to decide when and where to give the order that would bring the *Sempione* to rest. Hurrying to the wing of the bridge, he looked down through the clear water. The bottom could be distinctly seen at a depth of between five and six fathoms. It consisted of patches of bluish white sand and clumps of fantastically shaped coral over which brightly coloured fish swam lazily.

The ship was now about midway between the nearest part of the reef and the beach. She would be sheltered from winds and waves in all directions and have plenty of room to swing to her anchors.

'Let go!' shouted Brian in his best nautical manner.

A couple of blows released the slip. Then, thrusting back the lever of the compressor, Ted let the ten hundredweight anchor go. With a rush and a roar to the accompaniment of a cloud of rusty dust, the studded cable ran out through the hawsepipe to the bitter end. Slowly the *Sempione* lost way until, with a perceptible jerk, she snubbed at her cable.

The job was only half done. It was essential to let go another anchor to prevent the ship from swinging.

Again Ted wielded the maul. Out rushed the second cable, following the stockless anchor, until half its entire length was paid out.

It was not a properly executed task, since the chain might drop in coils upon the anchor; but fortunately the ship was gathering sternway owing to the strain on the stream anchor cable.

Leaving the fo'c'sle Ted started up the auxiliary motors that provided power to the capstan. But for that, the capstan was useless, since it required the manual efforts of a dozen men to work it independently of the engine.

Meanwhile Brian had gone for'ard, and when Ted rejoined him they brought the first cable to the capstan. Then slowly the vertical drum began to revolve. Foot by foot the cable, now washed clear of its rusty deposit obtained during the months of idleness, began to come home until half of its entire length was stowed in the manger.

The *Sempione* was almost properly moored but not quite. She was riding almost equidistant between her anchors and consequently she would swing on a radius of which her bows formed the focal point. With only one anchor down she would swing to the whole length of her cable.

There was a snag. If the ship remained riding at the two anchors for any length of time, the cables would get twisted. If the twists increased in number to any extent there was a risk of one of the chains parting.

In practice, to obviate this it is usual to introduce a mooring swivel, but the present crew of the *Sempione* were not capable of making use of one. As in the case of the capstan, they were insufficient in numbers and experience to complete their task properly.

'Well, that's that!' declared Ted in a satisfied tone, unaware of the deficiency of his work. 'Now what about going ashore?'

'As soon as we can,' agreed Brian, delighted at the prospect of being able to set foot on dry ground and to feast upon the obvious natural resources of the island. 'I suppose the place is uninhabited?'

'Bound to be,' replied Ted confidently. 'There'd be a crowd on the beach to watch us come in if'——

'Yes, but there may be a few people living on the other side of the island.'

'If so, we'll soon find out. We can explore the whole place in a day. Let's swing her out!'

'Her' referred to the sole remaining boat lying on chocks just abaft where once the funnel had been. It was a double-ended craft, eighteen feet in length, heavy to row but stiff and seaworthy. Owing to its weight, it was beyond the unaided strength of the two youths to drag it up the beach when once they arrived there. Before that came the task of swinging the boat out and lowering her.

They had seen this done during their voyage from England to Bolomaya. It was a two-man job lifting the bows by means of the for'ard davit. Then they had to belay and man the after falls. Once the boat was slung it was an easy matter to capsize the folding chocks and swing the boat out.

Then came the snag. The boat was now about twenty-five feet above the surface. It would take one youth at each davit and even then they would have to be very careful in case the boat took charge and, falling rapidly, should break her back. There was wanted a third person: someone in the boat to keep her from crashing into the ship's side as the *Sempione* rolled in the gentle undulations.

Since there were only two of them, that risk had to be run; so they hung a couple of cork life-belts over the boat's gunwale to mitigate any shocks, and hoped for the best.

'Ready?' asked Brian.

'Right!'

'Then together: lower away!'

Checking the boat's descent by means of a turn round a cleat with each of the falls, they succeeded in getting the boat into the water without any damage, having first put into her an old rifle belonging to the captain.

'I don't suppose we'll have to use it,' remarked Brian. 'But it seems the proper thing to do when fellows land on a desert island.' He sprang upon the rail capping, intending to swarm down the falls in professional style. One glance made him change his mind. The boat, twenty feet below, looked ridiculously small as she lifted and fell in the swell. 'We'd better rig the Jacob's ladder,' he suggested. 'Easier for getting on board again, you know!'

Ted nodded. He would have 'chipped' Brian on his timidity but for the fact that he felt that way inclined himself.

They fetched and unrolled the ladder. Then, just as Brian was about to descend, he gave an exclamation of astonishment. 'She's filling as fast as anything!' he announced.

He had not exaggerated. The boat had been so long out of water that, in spite of the awning, her planks had opened through the heat of the sun. She was leaking like a sieve.

'Let her soak alongside,' suggested Ted. She'll take up in a couple of hours.'

'A couple of hours?' echoed his companion. 'Why, we want to get ashore. Game to swim for it?'

Ted gave a cautious glance shorewards. The distance was not more than two hundred yards. There was no current. A piece of wood thrown overboard hardly moved. They were both good swimmers, but——Looking downward he caught sight of the fish. Some were almost six feet in length—ugly-looking creatures with nasty spines projecting from their backs. 'Better not,' he replied. 'Look at those. And there may be sharks. Look here; aren't there air-tanks in the boat? She can't sink. What matters if the gunwales are below water. We can bale her out when we land.'

'All right,' agreed Brian. 'I'll go first.'

Ascending a rope ladder is an awkward business, as Ted had already discovered; but descending one is still more so. So Brian found as he gingerly groped his way down, face to the now rusty sides of the ship.

Then he had to wait his chance to clear the gap between the ship and the boat; and that, too, was a difficult, not to say dangerous, business since the rung of the flexible ladder gave him little chance to make a spring. If he missed he might easily crack his head against the gunwale or, at best, get off with a ducking and a pair of barked shins.

He didn't miss! For a moment he poised precariously upon the side of the boat. She dipped but recovered herself. Brian jumped to one of the thwarts, balancing himself with his feet planted well apart. Even with the

quantity of water—it was nearly up to the thwarts—
and his weight in addition, the boat showed at least
nine inches of freeboard amidships.

'She'll take us easily!' he shouted. 'Come on down.
Sling a couple of buckets down first. We'll want them,
I reckon!'

In Ted's case the descent was much simpler owing
to the fact that Brian was holding the lower part of
the ladder and drawing the boat closer to the ship.

They placed the rowlocks in position and then
unhooked the lower blocks. Then, pushing the boat
clear, they manned the oars and commenced to pull
towards the shore.

Ted was quite right when he declared that the boat
was unsinkable; but he had overrated her capabilities
as a means of transport. In her semi-waterlogged
state she was a regular beast to pull. With each stroke
of the oars her bows dipped and the water surged
for'ard. Only while there was a strain on the heavy
ash oars did she move. She carried no way; at the end
of each stroke she stopped dead.

With the perspiration pouring from them they
laboured under the hot sun. Again and again they
paused to rub the moisture from their eyes—and the
shore didn't seem to be any nearer! To make matters
worse the boat was still taking in water through her
seams. The rifle was already immersed, while the
rowers were now nearly up to their hips in water.

'I believe the air-tanks aren't tight,' opined Brian
breathlessly. 'We may have to swim for it after all.'

'Hang it! We can't abandon the boat. We must have
one to get back to the ship.'

'A raft would be handled easier.'

'Stick it, man. She's still afloat!' urged Ted. 'If the
worst comes to the worst we can walk! See, the water's
only three feet deep, if that!'

'In that case, overboard we go!' declared Brian,

beating his oar. 'So here goes!' He jumped—not into three feet of water but well over his depth. The remarkable clearness of the sea had deceived them both. Hurriedly he scrambled back again and resumed his oar.

After another twenty strokes the boat's keel grounded about thirty yards from the edge of the beach. They jumped out. Relieved of their weight, the whaler lifted slightly. They were able to drag her another ten yards farther ashore.

There they left her, taking ashore the anchor, attached to the long painter, and planting it firmly in the sand. They had arrived at the island of their dreams!

XVII

BADLY SCARED

IT was a strange sensation to feel land under their feet, even if the land was soft sand. Apart from the usual difficulty of walking along the beach they found themselves reeling like drunken men as the ground apparently was moving up and down like a sullen ocean swell. It was merely the result of having spent weeks afloat—a result that, if experienced, proves one to be a good sailor!

When they reached the firm ground they took to their heels, running up and down in sheer exuberance until the weakness of the muscles of their calves made them desist.

'What's the tide doing?' asked Brian. 'We don't want the boat to be left high and dry.'

'It's the best thing to happen to her,' rejoined Ted. 'Then we can remove the bilge-plug and the water will drain out by itself. It'll save a frightful lot of baling. I suppose the plug wasn't out when we lowered her, by any chance?'

'No fear; I saw to that. Very well, we'll let her stop where she is. We won't be away more than an hour.'

They waded in and retrieved the rifle. Having emptied the water from the barrel they tried the mechanism. Although the weapon was already rather rusted as the result of neglect on the part of its recent owner it still seemed serviceable. As for ammunition they had about twenty rounds that, being well greased, ought to be proof against damp.

The coconut palms then demanded their attention. Enviously they looked up at the tempting green nuts growing in clusters amongst the leafy heads of the trees; but they were unable to climb and without means of felling them. The fruit was as safe as the Crown jewels!

Not so other fruits, most of which they were already familiar with. Bananas, guavas and melons were there for the taking; but knowing the risks of over-indulgence in tropical fruits, they ate sparingly.

'I vote we go right round the island before we venture inland,' suggested Brian. 'Then, if there is anybody living here we'll be bound to find traces of him . . . I say, doesn't the old *Sempione* look fine from here?'

They paused to take in the picture of the ship— their ship, in effect—riding easily to her two anchors in the lagoon. Distance lent deception to the appearance, for even the patches of rust on her side blended with the weather-worn paintwork. Even the loss of the funnel did not greatly detract, since its absence went to show what she actually was—a motor ship— even though her propeller shaft *was* fractured.

'I say; what about Bombardo's letter to General Sandano?' suddenly asked Ted. 'What are you going to do about it?'

'Freeze on to it, of course.'

'The war will be over by the time you can hand it over; so it won't be of any use. We can see what it's all about. It must be important or those Grossaguayans wouldn't be so frightfully keen on getting hold of it.'

'All the same, I was told not to let it out of our possession until I had handed it to Señor Madeira at La Serena.'

'There's precious little chance of either of us ever setting foot on shore there. Why not open the thing? And you have let it out of your possession. You're here, on the island, and the letter's on board.'

But Brian would not satisfy Ted's curiosity—or his own, if it came to that. He had been willing to destroy it rather than let it fall into the hands of the Captain of the *Chacal*; but while he could retain possession of it he would do so until he was able to forward it to its destination through the medium of the postal authorities at the first port he touched. That might be a matter of weeks, months, perhaps, years. They had only just arrived on the island and they were in no hurry to leave it, even if they had the means at their disposal.

'All right, freeze on to it,' rejoined Ted, unruffled by his chum's decision. 'Come on; we've a five-mile tramp in front of us. I bet we won't do it in an hour— or anything like it!'

They set off, devoting their attention mainly to the ground on their right, though not neglecting to scan the reef in case there were other channels than the one by which they had so fortunately succeeded in entering.

For the most part the going was good, as the gently sloping ground between the sand and the edge of the vegetation was remarkably hard and smooth. From the spot where they had landed the coast ran north and south. They were following the former direction, with the lagoon on their left, the wind blowing off shore, though in a slanting direction. The time being about midday, the sun was almost overhead, casting the shadows of the two lads no farther than the extremities of their shoes.

For the greater part of this side of the island the beach was bounded by a line of low cliffs varying in height from three to thirty feet and composed of hard rock. In many places the strata were violently disturbed, showing that volcanic action had been particularly active during some period of the island's existence.

'We ought to find some caves,' said Ted, looking up at the highest part of the cliffs. 'If we do, we ought to have some fun.'

They found none—at least on this side of the island —but presently they came across a narrow valley through which a stream of fresh water was flowing. It was not of sufficient volume to carve a channel through the beach into the lagoon. The water just disappeared in the thirsty sand.

Walking a few yards upstream, the lads plunged their cupped hands into the water and drank. How delicious they found it after having been dependent upon the ship's tanks! They appreciated the boon so much that they shut their eyes in grateful ecstasy as they drank.

'No more ship's water for me!' declared Brian. 'At the first opportunity we'll load the boat with those stone jars we found in the pantry and fill them up from here.'

Refreshed, they continued their tour of exploration, but before they had gone a hundred yards, Ted discovered that his finger was itching painfully. Examining it he was just in time to see a small black object drop upon the ground, leaving an angry mark on the tip of his middle finger.

Gingerly he stooped and picked the thing up. It was a leech already distended with his blood. 'Where did that come from?' he asked.

Brian made no reply. It was not that strange sensation of sympathy and suggestion that made him look at his own hands. Adhering firmly to the back of his right were two leeches while three more were satiating themselves on the back of his left hand! 'Ugh!' he ejaculated, after he had made a gory mess by hastily removing the parasites and squashing them into the bargain. 'We must have got them when we dipped our hands in the stream. I hope we haven't swallowed any!'

The mere suggestion was enough. For the next five minutes both lads were firmly convinced that they had leeches at work in their interiors! They imagined that the beastly things had been swallowed, but had not yet commenced active operations!

All thoughts of continuing their tour of discovery vanished. They had already discovered more than they had bargained for. Taking to their heels, they ran back to the spot where they had left the boat. The tide had receded about a foot, leaving about fifteen inches of gunwale above the surface. Using both buckets vigorously they soon emptied the boat of water and floated her off.

As they rowed off to the ship they hardly noticed that the boat was now making very little water; all their efforts were centred upon speedily getting on board and swallowing some raw spirits to settle the leeches that they imagined were being given food and lodging!

They made no attempt to hoist the boat. Merely taking the end of the painter with them, they swarmed up the rope-ladder, made the boat fast and then hurried to the captain's pantry.

On the shelf, secured in a rack, were a dozen bottles of rye whisky and a similar number of rum.

The inexperienced youths drank hurriedly, swallowing nearly half a glassful of raw spirits that made them gasp and splutter.

On their subsequent movements during the rest of the day it is better to draw a veil!

Awakening came just before sunrise, when they found themselves lying on the starlit deck and suffering from the worst headaches they had ever experienced.

It was extremely unlikely that they had swallowed any leeches; but there was now no doubt left in their muddled minds that the remedy was worse than the disease!

XVIII

ECHO HARBOUR

THEY made no effort to go ashore that day! They were hungry yet disinclined to eat. Their throats felt like lime-kilns in spite of frequent cups of coffee. Their heads throbbed, their tempers were frayed. They never mentioned the leeches!

Next morning they awoke in very chastened spirits. Headaches had vanished, but recollection remained.

'We've been drunk!' declared Ted.

'Three sheets in the wind is the seaman's term for that,' added Brian.

'Three sheets! It felt like three hundred blankets pressing on my head! No more of the horrible stuff for me. . . . Now, what's for brekker?'

The meal over and the things washed and stowed away, the lads resolved to resume their interrupted tour of the island. Fortunately the boat had remained quietly alongside during their 'indisposition'. To their satisfaction they found that the seams had taken up and that there was not more than half a dozen gallons of water in the bottom.

In spite of her heavy construction she now moved well under one pair of oars; so much so that the youths decided to row round the island, landing at whatever spot demanded their attentions.

'But why row when there's a breeze?' asked Ted. 'Isn't there a mast and sail somewhere?'

'I believe there is,' replied Brian. 'Right-o! Let's go back and get them.'

They rowed alongside and climbed aboard. After a search they discovered the boat's mast and yard—together with those of the other ship's boat—lashed to the booms; while the lugsail, dirty but in fair condition, they routed out from the sail room. It was the work of a few minutes to lace the sail—a loosed-fitted lug—and to drop the gear into the boat. There was no rudder, although there were pintles on the stern post, showing that the boat was fitted for one; but this deficiency they made good by steering with an oar.

'How about grub and water?' asked Ted.

'We aren't going outside the reef, and we can get stuff ashore,' explained Brian. 'The water will be all right if we strain it. I've been looking it up in the book. It says: "The water to be found on many of these islands must be treated with suspicion unless known to be sweet. Several streams have leeches in them. This is an infallible sign of the purity of the water, but special care must be taken when drinking or filling beakers to make use of efficient filters. Numerous cases have been recorded of animals being killed through these parasites being introduced into their stomachs——" So there you are, old son; leeches serve their purpose, besides being used for drawing blood.'

'I'll take jolly good care they don't draw mine again,' declared Ted stoutly. 'We've got all we want? Right! I'll cast off!'

The boat drew from under the *Sempione's* lee. The breeze filled the sail. She gathered way, heeling to Ted's evident alarm.

'We've no ballast and she's supposed to carry a dozen men,' explained Brian. 'There's nothing to worry about. She hasn't dipped her lee-gunwale and I haven't even had to ease the sheet.'

Brian had been used to small-boat sailing. His companion had not. Compared with the centre-board craft he sailed at home, this boat was awkward to handle. She would not point anything like so high and when it came to going about it required the assistance of an oar to get her round on to the other tack.

All the same, it was an enjoyable sensation skimming through the tranquil, wind-ruffled waters of the lagoon; and presently, having soon regained his confidence in Brian's helmsmanship, Ted declared that 'it wasn't bad fun—almost as thrilling as motor-bike racing!'

'Better, you mean,' rejoined Brian. 'If you're thrown out here you'll fall into something soft. A motor-bike smash doesn't let you off so easily.'

It was a series of 'long and short legs' past the east side of the island until they stood within half a cable's length of the entrance to the lagoon. Looking seaward they had a fairly 'close-up' view of the breakers, while the spray flung up from the reef drifted over the boat in clouds.

'My word! We were lucky to get the old *Sempione* in,' declared Brian. 'The gap doesn't seem more than twice her beam. . . . Lee-ho!'

He put the steering oar over to wind'ard. Slowly yet unhesitatingly the boat went about. On this course there was no tacking, but full-and-bye along the northern side of the island. It was a 'soldier's wind', so Brian had very little to do beyond an occasional touch to the steering oar, while Ted sat on the bottom-boards and watched the scenery glide past.

Here, unlike the western side, the coast appeared to be considerably indented. The cliffs were higher and bolder, while in some places considerable landslides had occurred, carrying masses of huge rocks down into the lagoon.

'I wouldn't like to have been there when that lot began to fall,' observed Ted. 'And it wasn't very long ago when that took place. The rocks look as if they've only just been thrown down.'

'There's been time for bushes to start growing,' said Brian. 'Of course, in the Tropics that doesn't take very long. . . . We'll stand in and have a look at that little harbour. It seems interesting.'

He pointed to a gap between the cliffs through which they could see a miniature sheet of water backed by steeply rising well-wooded ground.

'Is there enough water?' asked Ted cautiously.

'Enough for us. We'd better lower the sail and take her in under oars.'

The sail was stowed and the mast unstepped. Each lad took an oar and urged the boat towards the narrow entrance.

'I'll have a permanently twisted neck if this goes on much longer,' said Brian, who had to turn his head to see that they were keeping direction.

'Then why pull? Let's try pushing her like the native boatmen in Santa Teresa harbour.'

Accordingly they stood up, facing for'ard, and rowed by thrusting at the oars. This method had its advantages, especially as the lightly laden whaler had a high freeboard; but, as Brian observed, the strokes were less efficacious and it would be doubtful whether they could do much against a stiff breeze. Another advantage lay in the fact that they could look over the side and watch the coral-strewn bed of the lagoon as the boat glided only fifteen or sixteen feet above.

'Plenty of depth for us so far,' announced Brian. 'Yes, and it's getting deeper. We must have struck a channel of sorts.'

'Yes. I reckon it's thirty feet deep now,' agreed Ted. 'Deep water right up to the edge of the cliffs.'

'Easy with her! We don't want to hit a rock in the middle of the entradce.'

There was no rock. The depth was almost uniformly maintained right throught the gap, which was roughly twenty yards in width.

Then a surprise awaited them. The natural harbour was considerably larger than it appeared to be when seen from outside. It was nearly a quarter of a mile wide and protected by the two narrow ridges of rock that acted as a breakwater, each terminating on either side of the entrance. Although there was a five-knot breeze blowing the basin was so landlocked that, until the boat's way disturbed it, the surface was unruffled. Every detail of the cliffs was reflected in perfect reproduction upon the mirror-like surface.

With easy strokes the chums urged their little craft towards the shore opposite the entrance. Looking down, they could see that, although the bottom was remarkably clear, the depth was even more than at the entrance. There was, however, no trace of coral formation nor even of bright-hued marine vegetation —nothing but an expanse of sand.

'If we could get the old *Sempione* in here wouldn't it be a snug anchorage for her?' remarked Brian. 'Secure from all winds and so close to shore. We could moor her so that we could run out a gangway to the land.'

'And in the lagoon she'd roll quite a lot in an on-shore gale,' added Ted. 'We might be cut off from the island for days on end. We must have a shot at getting her in.'

'How? We'd never have a fair wind on two sides of the island.'

'We don't want a wind,' continued Ted. 'What we want is a flat calm.'

'And tow her with this?' rejoined Brian, indicating the boat. 'Simply couldn't be done!'

'Can't it? What are those auxiliary engines on board for? We can spare one, put it into the boat and fix up a shaft and propeller. Ten horse power will be enough, although I grant it'll take quite a time before the ship gathers way. Once she's on the move it'll take an anchor to stop her.'

'Might be done.'

'Might? It can,' declared Ted emphatically. 'And think of the advantages; no toe-stubbing on that Jacob's ladder, for one thing. Now we are here, and we may be here for months, we might just as well have things comfortable. . . . Going to land?'

Brian nodded. He was beginning to feel enthusiastic over Ted's extravagant notions but, being of a cautious nature, he was turning over in his mind the various problems that such an undertaking would set. The novelty of being in possession of a ship and an uninhabited island would take a long time to wear off. The only thing that worried him, as well as Ted, was their inability to let their parents and relations know that they were very much alive and kicking. If the *Sempione* were taken into this landlocked haven gone would be all chances of her being sighted by a passing ship.

They ran the boat ashore almost opposite the entrance. Here the water shoaled rather steeply, the beach consisting of a mixture of sand and clay, backed by rising ground covered with short grass resembling a lawn, as far as the edge of the palm groves. Beyond that the ground ascended in a series of terraces towards the twin peaks, which they judged to be about eight hundred feet above sea-level.

There seemed to be no lack of water, for they noticed at least half a dozen little streams falling over the cliffs in miniature waterfalls. In one instance the clear liquid dropped into a deep basin worn into the solid rock, forming a natural reservoir. A careful examination showed that there were no visible signs of animal life so that they could drink without fear of swallowing leeches.

'What a grand spot!' declared Ted, as they gained

the rising ground at the edge of the coco-palms.
'Everything's to hand, plenty of natural resources and
all that. What about cutting down a tree and getting
some nuts?'

It was not so much a wish to satisfy their hunger
as to commit an act of destruction, that took possession of them. Fetching their axes from the boat,
they attacked a tree on the edge of the grove. The
result of the first blow was remarkable. The thud
echoed and re-echoed round the little harbour as if
Nature was shouting a string of protests.

They dropped their axes and looked at each other.

'We could make a small fortune out of that from
trippers at sixpence a head!' declared Ted. 'I've never
heard such a perfect echo.' He drew himself up and
shouted.

The echo replied, first on the left side of the haven
and then on the right, like two comedians hurling
back-chat at each other. It was not until about thirty
seconds had elapsed that the sound died away.

'If that sort of thing goes on we'll be sorry for ourselves,' declared Brian in quite an ordinary voice.

'Sorry for ourselves!' came the mocking echo.

For several minutes they amused themselves by
hearing their voices coming back to them. Then they
discovered that if they moved more than half a dozen
paces away the echo was no longer audible. By some
strange acoustic freak the reverberations took effect
when the chums stood close to the trunk of the tree
they had picked out for destruction.

'I'm glad of that,' said Brian. 'We don't always
want to live with an echo. Now we're about it we'll
have the tree down.'

It took them five minutes of continual din before
the graceful palm tree came crashing to the ground.
Five green nuts filled with delicious milk rewarded
their efforts.

'And there's the first timber for our landing-stage,' declared Ted, indicating the felled trunk. 'So here's to the *Sempione*'s new berth!'

Brian took another drink of the coconut milk. 'And here's to Echo Harbour!' he added.

XIX

THE PERIL ON THE REEF

AFTER a bathe in the deliciously warm water, since there were no signs of sharks in the haven, the lads re-embarked, rowed out into the lagoon and hoisted sail. The breeze had freshened slightly and it did not take them long to round the north-western point of the island. Then came a dead run, and no easy task to keep the loose-footed lugsail from gybing. In less than five minutes Brian had accidentally gybed twice and on each occasion Ted's sun-hat went overboard!

'Clumsy blighter!' exclaimed Ted.

'Think yourself lucky we haven't a boom or you'd be holding your head and feeling a bump rising!'

'If so, there would have been trouble for someone!' rejoined Ted. 'Hello! What's that? There are people swimming!' He pointed to a long low-lying ledge with three or four outlying rocks about two hundred yards ahead. Swimming about were half a dozen dark forms, though only their heads were visible.

A pang of disappointment flashed across Brian's mind. 'So it isn't an uninhabited harbour after all!' he exclaimed. 'What are they—natives?'

'Looks like it. It's no use sheering off. They won't harm us, especially if we put on a bold front in the matter.'

So the boat held on her course while her crew waited for some sign from the swimmers.

Presently Ted began to laugh. 'Aren't we silly cuckoos!' he exclaimed. 'They're seals!'

As if to confirm his statement, one of the animals that had been basking on the rocks floundered awkwardly into the water. They were the first signs of animal life on the island. So unaccustomed were they to human beings that they made no attempt to dive when the boat glided past within a dozen yards of the nearest of them. On the contrary, a couple of inquisitive seals swam after the boat, keeping pace with it without apparent effort.

'They want a good clout,' declared Ted.

'Whatever for?' asked Brian in astonishment, and knowing that, like himself, Ted would not harm any animal unnecessarily.

'Because another time they'll pay dearly for their trustfulness. There are pleny of people about—including so-called civilized men—who, if they had the chance, would kill the seals out of sheer devilment. If we gave these creatures a fright they'd keep clear in future.'

'Yes—perhaps. They don't seem to have come across men before but it seems a pity to destroy their confidence in us. It would be rather a joke teaching a dozen of them to do squad-drill!'

'One would think you've made up your mind to serve a life-sentence here,' remarked Ted dryly. 'Be steady; you nearly gybed her again.'

The point off which the seals had been swimming was the easternmost and not the south-easternmost point of the island as they had supposed. Opposite it was another channel through the reef, while a little to the south'ard of it was an islet about two hundred yards in circumference, with steep sides and separated from the larger island by a narrow strait. To judge by the formation of the rocks on either side of this channel the smaller island had been detached by the action of the waves long before the protecting reef had raised itself to the level of the sea.

'Plenty of water, I think,' decided Brian. 'We'll go between them. Look out for foul puffs. I may have to gybe again.'

They hadn't sailed very far through the gap when they caught sight of a large cave on the main island. Its entrance was about twenty feet in height and ten in breadth, and was well above high-water mark. Undoubtedly it owed its formation to the action of the waves, but ages ago volcanic action must have raised the island several feet higher than before, without causing the cave to collapse when forming what geologists term a 'fault'. Slow-growing as was the coral-reef, it was quite youthful compared with the venerable age of the volcanic island.

'Exploring?' asked Ted laconically.

'Not now. We've to get back to the ship some time today. Once we've sailed round our domain we'll know something of what it's like.'

'Ah! I wonder!'

Presently the southern side of the island opened up. Here the coast was more regular, resembling that of the western side with which they were already acquainted.

There was a difference, however. The reef was considerably nearer to the shore, while in the centre of the lagoon was a small atoll on which grew a few palms. The reef itself was broader, with a number of patches about three feet above the general level. On these, too, vegetation was struggling for existence.

'I don't like the look of it,' declared Brian.

'Look of what?'

'That reef ahead. It looks as if it connects the other reef with the island. If so, we'll have to retrace our course—and we've only about another couple of miles to go before we reach the ship.'

9   (H 60)

Brian's fears were not altogether unfounded. Between the atoll and the reef the ripples on the surface of the lagoon hinted at shoal water. If the boat hit one of those sharp coral ledges that lurked just beneath the surface she would have her garboard planks stove-in as effectually as if they had been hit with a sledge-hammer. He decided to have the sail down. It was letting a good wind run to waste, but discretion was the order of things at this particular time. It might be the work of a moment to knock a hole in the boat; it would take hours to repair her, even if she could be brought ashore for that purpose.

Under oars they cautiously approached the 'bridge' or connecting reef, seeking for a possible deep channel over it. There was none. It was now high water—the rise and fall being but three feet at springs and only about nine inches at neaps—but nowhere was there a greater depth of more than a foot. They tried one or two possible gullies, only to find that they were blind alleys out of which they had to back the boat, conscious of a waste of time and energy.

The narrow stretch between the atoll and the island remained. It did not look promising; in fact, the crew of the boat came to the conclusion that it was impracticable.

'Yet I don't like being done,' declared Brian. 'We'll go in a bit closer.'

Cautiously they approached the barely submerged ledge which at low tide would be high and dry. Then the boat's forefoot grated on the coral.

'Hang it all, there's deeper water just ahead,' said Ted. 'Suppose we go overboard and try to drag her across?'

'If we stick we're here for twelve hours,' objected Brian.

'In that case we can wade ashore and camp out. We'll be able to get all the food we want.'

'All right, then,' conceded Brian. 'We'd better put on our sea-boots. The coral will cut our shoes to shreds.'

The sea-boots were of leather, heavily shod with iron nails in the soles. They were almost new, having been taken from the ship's slop-chest. With difficulty they put them on, the exertion making them perspire freely.

'We'll have to be jolly careful,' cautioned Brian. 'If we should slip into deep water these boots will take us down for good! They're too tight to kick off.'

'I'll look out for that, my dear old Bags!' rejoined Ted with a grin. 'Now, we had better go ahead and see what it's like. It's no use trying to shove the boat farther on if there's not enough water.'

Awkwardly they clambered over the gunwale. The water was just above their ankles. The boat, relieved of their weight, refloated, so they had to drag her another three or four yards before she grounded again.

'She's all right!' announced Ted. 'Come on!'

'I'm not going to risk that,' protested Brian. 'A fine old mess we'd be in if she drifted away while we're tramping about. Wait till I've put the anchor out.'

He leant over the bows and lifted out the twenty-pounds anchor. With this over his shoulder he floundered through the shallow water with the intention of dropping the 'hook' well clear of the boat's stem. Suddenly he uttered a loud yell and dropped the anchor with a splash.

Ted saw him trying to free his left foot from some obstruction. 'What's wrong?' he asked. 'Foot caught in a crack?'

'Be quick!' shouted Brian, without answering the question. 'I'll be down in a moment!'

Ted hurried to his comrade's assistance and grasped his arm. 'Now pull your foot out,' he said.

'Can't!' replied Brian. 'It's giving me gyp. There's something crushing the toe of my boot.'

'Hang on to me, then!' Ted, with Brian's arm round his shoulder, bent down to see what the cause of the trouble was. To his surprise and horror he discovered that Brian's boot, as far as the instep, was hidden by the upper shell of a large clam. Brian had incautiously put his foot into the cleverly camouflaged trap. The lips of the bivalve had closed, holding him as if in a vice. But for the tough, reinforced leather sea-boot, his toes and no doubt the rest of his foot would have been pulped.

'I'll get an oar and prise the shell open,' declared Ted.

'No, don't leave me,' protested Brian in a mild panic. 'I can't keep my balance if you do! Where's your knife?'

Out came the Welshman's sheath-knife, but he hesitated to plunge the short blade into the powerful muscles that controlled the hideous man-trap. If his hand were caught, their plight would be precarious. He put the blade back into the sheath. 'Hang on!' he exclaimed.

Brian did not want to be told that. He was hanging on like grim death already!

Stretching out his hand, Ted gripped the anchor. Then, raising the clumsy piece of iron and wielding it like a pickaxe, he began to rain heavy blows upon the bivalve's upper shell. Each blow, at first, increased the pressure on Brian's foot. He had not been trapped long enough for it to become numbed. Soon scaly splinters began to fly. Ted could hardly credit the toughness of the shell. He continued to hack close to the clam's 'hinges' until he had to rest to recover his breath. 'Easing?' he asked tersely.

'No, I don't think so!' spluttered Brian.

Ted resumed his efforts. He was striking wildly.

Sometimes the fluke of the anchor hit the coral. His blows were weakening. The shell seemed as tough as before, if not tougher. Again he desisted and while resting he thought of another way. Slowly he guided one fluke into the gap in the bivalve's jaws close to Brian's boot until one arm of the anchor was almost hidden. Then, applying his remaining strength to the stock, he levered for all he was worth.

There was a sinister sucking sound. The shells were wrenched apart, and Brian, freed from the vice-like hold, fell back into Ted's arms, nearly capsizing him before he could recover himself.

The short distance back to the boat was a nightmare. Brian could hardly put his foot to ground. Both boys were fearful lest they should stumble against a similar trap; and it was with feelings of relief that they flopped over the gunwale into the boat. For about five minutes they could not speak. They sat breathing heavily, with no thought but one of thankfulness for the safe ending to the adventure.

Then——

'Tide's falling,' announced Brian.

'We've got to get that anchor!'

'Yes!'

'All right. I'll fetch it!'

'Then be careful.'

'Won't I just?' rejoined Ted.

Armed with the iron-shod boathook, he went over the side and followed the line of warp up to the anchor. Close to it was the battered shell of the clam; just beyond it was a gully of fairly deep water. 'We can do it yet, I think,' he shouted. 'Think you can get out and shove?'

'Right-o!'

While Brian was painfully climbing over the gun-wale, Ted waded back with the anchor. Then, one on each side of the boat, they heaved and lifted.

'She's moving! Keep her going!' exclaimed Ted. 'If she can't go for'ard she can't go back, so it won't matter if she does stick!'

They could hear the metal keel-band rasping. Inch by inch, foot by foot, they urged her nearer their immediate goal. Then, with only a couple of yards to go, she stuck hard!

Forgetting about his bruised foot, Brian jumped back into the boat and began to push the oars, mast, yard and other gear to one side of her. 'That'll cant her,' he explained breathlessly. 'Now both of us on this side! Lift and heave ahead!'

'She's off!' shouted Ted.

She was. By giving a list the keel was raised slightly higher than the bilge, with a correspondingly reduced draught. Still grinding and scraping, the boat forged ahead until two-thirds of her length was in deep water. She was again held up, this time on her heel. That was an easy problem to solve. The lads jumped on board and, armed with oars, went right for'ard. Their weight depressed the bows slightly and gave a corresponding lift to the stern. By pushing with the oars the boat was made to slide into deep water.

While Brian was stowing the displaced gear, Ted stood on the thwart to assist him in restepping the mast. Happening to look shorewards he made the discovery that there was a narrow S-shaped channel through the ridge. If they had not been in such a hurry they might have spotted the way through and saved themselves a lot of hard work, to say nothing of their encounter with the giant clam!

'Next time we'll know better,' observed Brian, when Ted had told him of his discovery. 'Give me a hand to get this sea-boot off, old son; my foot's hurting like blue blazes!'

XX

THE MOTOR BOAT

'HURTING like blazes' may be a very indefinite term of comparison, but the fact remained that for the next two days Brian was virtually a prisoner on board the *Sempione*. Within a few minutes after Ted, with considerable difficulty, had removed the heavy leather boot the victim's leg had swollen to alarming proportions. Although only the foot had been gripped the limb was affected up to the knee.

Nor did Ted venture ashore. Between his spells of attendance upon his crippled friend—his remedy was the frequent application of hot salt water—he began to make the necessary parts for converting the whaler into a motor boat. He started on the propeller and shaft. The latter was made from a seven feet length of tubular steel with an exterior diameter of one inch. He would have liked to have it of gunmetal, but the resources of the ship did not supply that. Steel was less satisfactory, since it was very liable to corrosion, but as Ted philosophically remarked: 'The best you have is better than the best you can't have.' He found a pair of couplings in the engineers' stores, one of which he fitted to the 'filled' end of the tube, securing it by a steel pin passing through opposite sides of the shaft and filed flush to enable the shaft itself to enter the stern-gland. The propeller gave him a good deal of thought and trouble. This he fashioned on the anvil, using a piece of mild steel eighteen inches by four and bending it so that the ends were at right angles to each other. At the centre he bolted on another coupling after drilling a hole to take the shaft in an exact fit.

At the end of the second day Brian was able to hobble about, although Ted's drastic treatment, while it reduced the abnormal size, had well-nigh parboiled the leg. After that the patient tended himself, sub-stituting bandages soaked in olive oil for painful hot sea-water applications.

As soon as Brian was able to bear a hand—he was no slacker!—they unbolted one of the auxiliary motors from its bed and by means of a tackle whipped it up on deck. Fortunately it was of the water-cooled type with pump feed, and there was no lack of copper piping to make the necessary connections.

Then came the task of hoisting the boat.

First Ted swarmed down and secured the hooks of the lower blocks. Then he had to return on deck again and help Brian man the falls.

It was a slow business. With both of them tailing on to the end of one fall they lifted the boat's bows about two feet. Then they had to belay while they hoisted the stern twice that height. Then, working alternately at each davit they eventually hoisted the boat to the davit heads and swung her in.

'Gosh!' ejaculated Ted, sitting down on a bollard and mopping his forehead. 'That's that; but what about hoisting her out with the engine in her? The engine alone weighs about a quarter of a ton, I should imagine.'

Brian grinned. 'What's wrong with the mainmast derricks?' he asked. 'They're tested to well over a ton!'

'Splendid!' exclaimed Ted in genuine admiration. 'I never thought of that. Now what do we do? Put the motor in first and line the shaft to it or the other way about?'

They decided on the former way. Two days it took them to fit the engine beds, place the motor in position and bolt it down. Then when it came to boring the stern for the stern tube they discovered that the engine shaft and the propeller shaft were not in line. They made an angle of nearly ten degrees.

'And we haven't a universal joint,' complained Ted. 'If we raise the tail shaft the prop'll be out of water!'

They looked at each other, then at their unsatisfactory handiwork, then at each other again. They scratched their heads in perplexity.

'It'll mean lifting the engine again,' said Ted dolefully. 'Then we'll have to pack up the bearers, tilting the engine aft until the shafts are in line—a brute of a job.'

That took up the best part of four hours until sunset put an end to their day's labours in that respect. They had still a dozen other tasks to perform before they were able to turn in.

They were up by sunrise and returned to their task in the boat immediately after breakfast, working under awnings to shield them from the heat.

At last the motor was properly installed—or at least they hoped it was! With the plugs out in order to destroy compression, the propeller could be turned with very little effort, showing that the new alignment was practically true. Then came the fitting of the fuel tank and boring the hole for the water inlet.

'There will have to be no more cutting corners over coral rocks, my festive,' remarked Brian when the latter operation was being commenced. 'Look at these planks. They're scored half-way through.'

'So they are,' admitted Ted. 'It wouldn't take much more of that sort of thing to rip the bottom right away.'

'While we're about it we may as well do the job properly,' continued Brian. 'Once the boat's in the water she won't be out again in a hurry, so let's put copper sheathing on her. It will protect the planking and stop weeds and barnacles growing.'

There were plenty of sheets of that metal on board, so another day and a half were taken up with the sheathing operations.

At last—and by which time Brian had quite recovered from his painful experience—the motor boat, as she now was, was ready for her trials. One factor had to be taken into consideration: the limited supply of petrol, of which they had about two hundred gallons. When that was exhausted the motor boat would be useless as such unless they could devise some means of burning oil fuel, of which the *Sempione* carried an almost inexhaustible supply.

Ted then set to work to start the donkey-engine supplying power to the mainmast derricks. That was an easy task. The difficult part was how to control the lifting gear. He had seen the crew working cargo when they were waiting in Santa Teresa harbour for the ship to sail. The donkeyman—a rather stupid-looking fellow—did his job easily enough, so Ted decided that *he* ought to make quite as good a fist at it!

The boat was fitted with eye-bolts for slinging. The bow one was all right, but the stern one wasn't! The amateur engineers had run the shaft immediately over it; consequently they had to fix another sling under the keel and round the boat's quarters.

Next they found that the derrick head could not be brought immediately over the boat, so the latter had to be shifted on rollers—another arduous job—until the relative positions were correct. Then, when the purchase took up the strain the boat tilted. She had to be hurriedly lowered again until the lead of the slings could be altered. It took three attempts before this was done properly.

Then came the crucial test: to lift the now heavy boat clear of the rail and drop her gently into the sea.

While Brian tended a guy-rope attached to the boat Ted controlled the levers operating the donkey-engine.

Up leapt the boat almost to the derrick head. The amateur donkey-man had checked the ascent only just in time. Then, before either youth realized it, the massive inclined boom with its weighty burden at the outer end began to swing outboard.

'Check her!' yelled Ted.

Brian, tailing on to the guy-rope, did his best, but his best wasn't good enough! The swaying boat had gathered too much momentum. There wasn't even time to take a turn with the guy-rope round a convenient belaying-pin.

In spite of his effort, Brian found himself being carried obliquely across the deck. Either he must relinquish his hold or be dashed against the capping of the bulwarks.

'Hold her!' bawled Ted.

'Can't!' shouted Brian.

'Stand clear!' yelled Ted, visualizing a frightful smash.

With a tremendous jerk that made the massive mast creak and groan, the derrick brought up against the after shrouds, until the stout steel wires were bunched together with the strain.

Both lads fully expected either that the derrick would buckle and break or that the boat would be hurled from its slings as the derrick rebounded from the shrouds. In either case it would be 'good-bye' to their motor boat and their arduous labours of the past week.

Greatly to their relief and delight, neither accident happened. The boat, from which the guy-rope was now dangling uselessly, was swaying gently at the end of the derrick. Yet, should the *Sempione* roll to starboard, there was nothing to prevent the boom swinging inboard and right across to the other side of the ship.

Ted knew by this time what he should have done to prevent the derrick taking charge. It looked as if he would have to pay dearly for his inexperience and lack of foresight. Was it too late to save the situation?

'Bags, old man!' he shouted. 'Come here a minute, will you? Stand by this lever. See that it doesn't jump or the whole caboodle'll start winding! I won't be half a tick.'

With that he gathered up a small coil of two-inch rope and sprang into the rigging, making his way up until he was level with the part of the derrick now pressing against the shrouds. Working quickly yet methodically, he passed half a dozen turns of the rope round the spar and the shroud, finishing off with a reef-knot. 'She'll hold!' he declared triumphantly as he rejoined Brian. 'Now, then; I'm going to lower away. Get hold of the guy-rope if you can and steady her or she'll swing her nose or her stern against the ship's side.'

A breathless suspense followed as Ted slowly unwound the wire from the drum. Now the boat was level with the rail. She commenced to spin; brought up against the ship's side. 'Making any water?'

'Not a drop, as far as I can see,' replied Brian.

'Splendid! I'll switch off and then we'll get on board her.'

Descending by the Jacob's ladder, they boarded the converted boat. She was leaking slightly but nothing was coming in through the rough and ready stern-gland.

'We'll start her up and have a trial run,' declared Ted. 'Stand by the tiller. We've no reverse, remember!'

The motor started at the third swing. Waiting until he was satisfied that the water was circulating properly, Ted called to Brian to cast off. He let the clutch in.

With a decided jerk the boat leapt ahead. Quickly

she gathered way, throwing out a big wash and leaving a track of 'soapsuds' in her wake.

'By Jupiter! She does move!' bawled Ted excitedly. 'Ten knots, I guess!'

'She certainly is shifting,' agreed Brian with equal enthusiasm. 'We've made a thundering good job of it, old son!'

Then, as if in disagreement with these sentiments, the motor suddenly stopped. Quickly, owing to the drag of the propeller, the boat lost way.

They realized that they were about three hundred yards to lee'ard of the *Sempione* and that they had neither sails nor oars in the boat!

XXI

A HEAVY TOW

'IGNITION!' announced Ted laconically.

'Yes, it's not carburation, I think, or she wouldn't have stopped so suddenly. Get her going as soon as you can, or we'll drift on the reef.'

Ted set to work. Quickly he removed the plugs and tested them. Each showed quite a healthy spark, but from experience he knew that a plug functioning properly when laid on top of the cylinder head might not fire under compression.

'Any luck?' asked Brian anxiously. 'We're drifting pretty rapidly.'

'Then chuck the anchor overboard.'

'If I do we won't get it again,' objected Brian. 'It's bound to get foul of the coral.'

'Well, hang on half a tick. I'll dope her. Pass that can, will you?'

Brian handed him the tin containing about half a gallon of petrol and gave another anxious look to lee'ard. 'It's good-bye to your precious propeller if she hits,' he declared, helping Ted to screw home the 'doped' plugs.

Ted gripped the starting-handle and gave the motor a vigorous swing. Instantly the engine fired, and, since Brian had not declutched, the boat leapt ahead, nearly throwing her crew across the thwarts.

'Good business!' yelled Ted.

His triumph was short-lived. The engine stopped

again, but even that brief run had given them the advantage of another fifty yards farther from the reef.

'It's not ignition!' panted the Welshman. He tickled the carburettor. There was no sign of flooding. Then he removed the float chamber cover.

The float-chamber itself was bone-dry!

'Choke in the needle-valve—that's what it is. It'll mean taking down this pipe. Won't be more than five minutes!' He grasped a spanner with the intention of slacking back the pipe union; then he remembered that it would be as well if he turned the petrol off at the tank. 'I say; it's already off!' he announced.

'Well, I didn't do it!' protested Brian.

It was no time to commence an argument. The tap was turned on again, the carburettor flooded and once more the engine started and continued to run.

Then Ted, still mystified, tried to probe the problem. He soon discovered the cause: the tap turned too easily and the vibration of the pipe while the motor was running did the rest.

'She's all right now!' he declared, after tightening the small nut underneath the tap.

'Good enough! We'll run back to the ship and pick up the oars and mast,' said Brian. 'Then if she konks out again——'

'She won't. But we'd better get the gear, all the same.'

After all their labours it seemed fitting that they should have a joy-ride in their reconstructed boat; so Brian proposed a run to Echo Harbour.

'And we'll take a lead-line while we're about it and take soundings,' he added.

They fetched the lead-line—a twenty fathoms' length of plaited line with a seven-pound lead weight at one end. It was marked, unlike British ones, in metres, while the *Sempione* still adhered to her draught measurement in feet, since her subsequent foreign owners had not gone to the trouble of altering it.

Right aft the ship was drawing seventeen feet, so Brian tied a piece of white rag to the lead-line at the sixth metre mark so as to leave a fair margin.

Off they went with the motor at half throttle while Brian, standing up, swung the lead in a fair attempt to imitate the professional seaman's way.

The bottom of the lagoon was very uneven owing to the sandy holes between the intricate ridges of growing coral, but everywhere, until they were about a hundred yards from the entrance to the haven, the depth was not less than thirty feet on the line of direction the boat was taking.

Suddenly the lead sounded at seven metres.

'Stop her!' ordered Brian. 'We'll row her a bit 'cause it's getting shallower.'

Realizing the urgency of the task, Ted switched off the ignition and obligingly took both oars while Brian continued to take soundings.

There was never less than seven metres in the entrance and more inside. In fact at the eastern end of the landlocked haven there was a depth of twenty metres close to the shore.

'This will be the old ship's berth,' declared Brian. 'With a gangway we can step ashore from her. And look: those trees will do fine as mooring posts.'

'When shall we shift her?'

Brian glanced at the sun. 'Too late today,' he decided. 'High water tomorrow morning is at about nine. It'll take us a couple of hours to unmoor, I reckon. Start her up, old son! We'd better go back. We haven't any too much petrol to use unnecessarily.'

On returning to the ship they secured the motor boat alongside, placing large coir fenders in position to prevent her chafing.

Before they turned in that evening, they made a

careful examination of the barometer. It was high and steady, and promised a continuance of fine weather. By experience they had found that although the island was within the limits of sou'east Trades there was generally a calm spell for about a couple of hours after sunrise and another one around sunset. A calm was what they wanted, since even a light breeze might upset all their calculations when it came to towing the comparatively bulky *Sempione* with the puny motor boat.

Well before dawn they were out and about, preparing warps and getting the motor capstan ready to perform its task. Then, the moment the tropical dawn flashed across the sky, they commenced to unmoor.

It was a long, arduous business. First the cable of the stream anchor had to be paid out while the capstan heaved up the cable of the sheet anchor. Then they discovered that both chains had crossed in a double turn —which was the last thing they expected to find, although of very common occurrence.

'Now what's to be done?' asked Ted.

'I don't know,' confessed Brian. 'Consult the book of words, I suppose!'

This was a tattered copy of a Manual of Seamanship printed in Spanish and embellished with numerous technical diagrams. Although both lads could speak the language tolerably well there were several important words in the book that baffled them until they found that there was an explanatory glossary at the end of the volume. After about half an hour—and every minute counted—they found the procedure to be adopted. Then came the business of putting this into practice.

First they had to pass a wire twice round one cable in the opposite direction to the turns and bring one end fast to the second chain. Fortunately the 'mix-up' had

10

occurred close to a shackle. The latter was then opened, allowing the wire to take the strain, and then came the hazardous and exhausting task of untwisting the heavy cable and freeing it from the other.

Next the two ends of the unshackled parts had to be joined again—a job that meant paying out and heaving-in before it could be accomplished.

The straightforward part of weighing both anchors was then proceeded with until one—both were of the stockless type—was close up in the hawsepipe and the other was almost up and down and just sufficient to hold the ship.

It was now ten o'clock. Two and a half hours had been spent already and towing operations hadn't begun yet!

They just had to knock off for rest and refreshment! Anxiously Brian scanned the sky and sea for the expected though unwanted breeze. So far, the surface of the lagoon was unruffled although on the reef the surf was pounding in a long-drawn-out roar.

'Ready?'

'Quite!'

They went to their respective stations: Ted into the boat, where he had the triple task of running the engine, steering and tending the towing-wire; Brian to work at the power capstan until the anchor was home, and then to hurry to the bridge to take the wheel and keep the *Sempione* in the motor boat's wake.

Ted started up the engine, leaving the clutch out. Gazing up at the *Sempione's* bows, he wondered for the first time if they hadn't taken on too much of a task. She looked enormous!

The capstan commenced to revolve. Idly Ted watched the studded links come up one by one, dripping as they broke surface. Slowly the ship moved, until the massive chain was leading perpendicularly from the hawse-pipe. Then, like some huge submarine monster, the rusty stockless anchor came into view, clattering against the ship's bows until it was firmly housed.

Ted's spell of inaction was over. The ship was no longer tethered to the bed of the lagoon. Gently he let in the clutch until the towing hawser took up the strain. Then more throttle until the propeller was sending out a creamy slip-stream that rippled against the ship's bluff bows.

For quite five minutes the *Sempione* seemed to be immovable. The tautened wire rope made not the slightest visible impression upon her. Then——

'She's moving!' shouted Brian through a megaphone.

Ted raised one hand in acknowledgment and then devoted his attention to his job.

Yes, the old hooker was moving! There were ripples against her stem that were not solely due to the motor boat's wash. The *Sempione* was actually throwing out a bow wave of her own—slight but nevertheless clearly discernible as it spread fanwise across the surface of the lagoon.

Ted's doubts changed to a strange sense of elation. The little motor boat, for which he had been mainly responsible, had proved her worth. David was leading Goliath on the end of a wire rope!

The turn at the nor'west angle of the island was successfully accomplished, but the wide turning circle caused both lads a certain amount of apprehension. Could the *Sempione* make the more acute turn to starboard when she was about to enter the haven? If not, what would happen? She would probably pile herself upon the rocks guarding the entrance.

Realizing the risk, they took the ship as close to the reef as possible in order to make the most of her limited manœuvring capabilities. Then, at a signal from Ted, Brian put the ship's helm hard over, while the motor boat sheered hard to starboard so as to give additional swing to the *Sempione's* bows.

Now the ship was heading straight for the gap. Unless a sudden beam wind sprang up, she would shoot into Echo Harbour; yet she must not carry too much way or she would run her bows into the low cliffs.

Ted promptly threw out the clutch. Quickly the motor boat slowed down; but almost before he was aware of it, he found the towering bows of the ship on the point of crashing into the transom. Only by jamming in the clutch was he able to avoid being run down. Yet he dare not tauten the towing hawser—the ship was carrying far too much way already. He had no idea how far she would travel under her own momentum in still water.

On the *Sempione's* bridge Brian was almost as greatly apprehensive. The ship was gliding through the water at about one and a half knots. There was not sufficient room for her to turn and glide into her intended berth. Even with the helm hard over she was only just turning.

There was only one thing to be done to save the ship running almost head on against the rocky shore—and Brian did it. Abandoning the almost useless wheel, he rushed to the fo'c'sle deck. Then, after a hurried glance down over the bows to make sure that the boat was well clear, he released the compressor of the stream anchor cable. With a rush and a roar, the massive chain ran out until, judging that sufficient had been let go to enable the anchor to obtain a hold, he checked and stopped the surging cable. For about fifteen seconds the ship continued to carry way until Brian gripped the rail and awaited the seemingly inevitable crash. He could have jumped on to the top of the cliffs—at least he thought he could. Then the cable snubbed gently. The ship came to a standstill and then gathered sternway, finally bringing up almost dead in the centre of Echo Harbour!

'Near thing, that, Ted!' shouted Brian.

'Yes, indeed! We're in; but now what's to be done?' asked Ted, who was trying to keep the boat clear of the now sagging wire.

'Spell-ho,' replied Brian. 'And we want one! Come alongside!'

Ted steered the boat alongside the Jacob's ladder, switched off and ascended, taking the end of the painter with him. 'I was wondering how we were going to stop her,' he said in frank admiration. 'It was jolly smart of you to think of that anchor.'

'And we've got to heave it up again,' rejoined Brian.

'Is it necessary?'

'Of course it's necessary. What else? We don't want the ship anchored in the middle of the harbour; we want her alongside.'

'Quite. But why not pay out all the cable? There's plenty of it. Then we can warp her alongside when we want her. We must have something to keep her just clear of the bank.'

For a few moments Brian did not reply. Then: 'You have my permission to kick me hard, my bright lad! My error! That's a sound proposition. What's more, her bows will be pointing towards the entrance.'

They adjourned for lunch, after which they spent a busy couple of hours under a broiling sun in preparing and laying out ropes for warping the *Sempione* into her berth.

The ropes had to be carefully coiled—one for'ard, one aft—and a couple of light lines taken ashore with which to haul the heavier ropes from the ship and make the ends fast to two convenient tree-trunks. As soon as the ropes were secured the other ends were brought to the motor winches. Slowly yet surely, since the weight of the scope of the cable had to be overcome, the

Sempione moved shorewards until a gap of only twelve feet separated her from the grassy bank. Even then she had at least ten feet of water under her keel.

'Good enough!' declared Brian thankfully. 'By Jupiter! Know what the time is? It's five o'clock!'

'We've earned a free evening and a good night's rest,' rejoined Ted. 'Whose turn is it to get grub ready?'

XXII

TO THE SUMMIT

THEIR present task was by no means completed. Brian knew too much about the ways of the sea to trust to two 4-inch manila ropes. If a heavy on-shore wind blew up there was the danger of big rollers setting in over the reef, and across the lagoon. Even the sheltered haven might be considerably agitated by the scend of the sea and in consequence the ship would 'work' at her securing ropes.

Early next morning the lads recommenced their labours. Two stout flexible steel wires were substituted for the ropes, while two more were passed ashore to act as 'springs'. Then yet another wire hawser was laid out from the port quarter to the opposite side of the harbour. The *Sempione* was now moored 'all fours' in addition to the springs. It was impossible for her to move more than a few feet in either direction. She was there, as Brian expressed it, 'until the cows came home'.

It was all very hard work, but they were full of energy and enthusiasm. They had come to realize that, even as slackness breeds discontent, strenuous useful work is one of the highways to happiness.

Then came the business of building a bridge or gangway to the shore. It had to be at least twenty-one feet in length not only to span the intervening space but to allow for the rise and fall of the tide. This task took them three whole days.

Luckily there were several gang-planks, normally

used for taking in coal from barges alongside, which were stowed on the boat-booms. Each was about twenty-five feet in length, eleven inches wide and two inches thick. Four of these were run ashore side by side and secured by stout cross-pieces. The end on board was made fast by means of light chains while the shore-end ran on a roller so as to do away with unnecessary friction and consequent wear. They must also have two hand-rails. Ted insisted upon that on the ground that it gave a professional touch to their handiwork and not because they were afraid they would tumble off the broad and substantial gangway.

Then came the problem of how to moor the motor boat. Ted suggested a stage jutting out from the shore, but Brian pointed out that the little craft would be continually riding up and down the piles with the rise and fall of the tide.

'What's wrong with the accommodation-ladder?' he asked. 'We can lower that—it's better than stubbing our toes on the rope-ladder—and make the boat fast to it!'

'We'll tackle that tomorrow, then,' decided Ted. 'I vote we stretch our legs a bit. Game for a climb to the top of the hill?'

'Which one?'

'Either or both!'

'Right then.'

They set off, taking the rifle and ammunition with them, as well as a light felling-axe. For the first quarter of a mile the going was fairly easy, since the ground between the dense masses of coco-palms was almost free from scrub. The foliage overhead was so thick that it was only here and there that the sun's rays penetrated; otherwise it was like being in the aisle of a dimly-lighted cathedral.

But for the knowledge that they had to ascend a steady gradient the chums would have lost sense of direction, since they had no compass with them. The silence, too, was profound except for their footfalls upon the dry, crisp ground. They saw neither bird nor animal.

'Imagine a wood at home without birds singing in it,' observed Brian. 'There might, at least, be a few parrots and half a dozen monkeys to liven things up! Ha! what's that?'

They stopped and listened intently. Quietly Brian opened the breech of his rifle and inserted a cartridge.

Something was approaching—something big and ponderous, judging by the steadily increasing noise.

'It's coming towards us,' said Ted, in a low voice. 'Ssh!'

The tree trunks at this part of the wood formed a sort of slightly curving avenue giving, on account of the deep shade, an uncertain outlook of about thirty yards.

Presently and without undue haste a large white barrel-shaped form loomed up. There was a series of grunts and then the chums discovered what the moving objects were.

A huge cream-coloured sow with half a dozen piglets in attendance was ambling towards them. Presently the sow stopped and sniffed. Her little ones clustered round her. Then, seemingly utterly devoid of fear, she trotted past the motionless youths and disappeared amongst the trees on their left.

'No lack of fresh pork,' remarked Ted. 'But, hang it all! A fellow simply just couldn't! It would be as bad as taking pot-shots at those seals.'

'Quite!' agreed Brian, ejecting the cartridge and returning it to his pocket. 'It would be worse than shooting a sitting rabbit. Unless we're desperately hard up for food—which is unlikely—Madame and her brood will be safe as far as we are concerned.'

On emerging from the sombre palm forest into the brilliant sunshine the explorers discovered that before commencing the ascent of the first peak they had to cross a fairly deep valley, covered by a dense expanse of scrub. They had not taken this obstacle into their calculations since, when viewed from seaward, the approach to the culminating points appeared to be a steep, uniform gradient. Now they found they would have to descend almost to sea-level before making the final effort.

The vegetation in the valley consisted mainly of formidable-looking thorns interspersed with cacti, prickly pears and other varieties of tropical plants, all set so thickly together that a great deal of work with the axe would have to be done if this route were to be followed.

'Worth the fag?' asked Brian.

'We're climbing to the top somehow,' replied Ted resolutely.

'Quite! But what I mean is: is the shortest way the quickest? I vote we skirt this side of the valley. It's bound to diminish in width.'

They started off in the new direction, keeping to the steeply shelving side of the treeless belt. After they had covered about two hundred yards they were startled by a loud crash, the sound coming from the coconut palms on their left.

'Tree fallen down,' declared Ted.

'Yes, but why?' asked Brian.

'Anno domini, I expect. Trees can't be expected to stand indefinitely. Let's see what's happened.'

It did not take them long to reach the spot where a fine specimen of a palm tree, once measuring about fifty feet in height, now lay upon the ground.

There was no sign of decay, nor had the tree been uprooted. Its trunk had been almost eaten through at about a foot from the ground and its weight had done the rest.

As the boys stood contemplating the work of destruction and tried to find some explanation for the recent cutting through of the still-living trunk, they heard a peculiar rattling sound coming from the cluster of foliage that had formed the top of the tree. Going closer they saw that about a dozen large crabs were busily attacking the coconuts, breaking the tough green husks to get at the milk. The noise of their powerful nippers was a grim warning to any living creature that came within reach of those formidable claws.

'Crabs half a mile from the sea!' exclaimed Ted.

'Yes, land-crabs,' declared Brian. 'Look at that brute! He'd break a fellow's leg as easy as winking!'

'Then all I hope is that a crowd of them won't invade the *Sempione* in the middle of the night,' said Ted. 'Now if they are fit to eat——'

He made a swing with his axe at one of the nearest crustaceans. The blade missed one of the crab's pincers by the narrowest margin and buried itself in the soft ground. Before Ted could recover the axe the creature's nipper had closed upon the head.

In vain the Welsh lad wrenched and heaved. The crab, having obtained a hold, seemed determined to retain it even though it were lifted off the ground; while its companions, by some uncanny instinct, promptly left off attacking the nuts and advanced to its aid.

'Drop the axe!' shouted Brian. 'Look out!'

'I'm not going to lose a good axe!' declared Ted stubbornly. 'Put a bullet into the brute!'

Brian had already inserted a cartridge in the breech of his rifle. At almost point-blank range he pulled the trigger, blowing a large hole in the crab's shell. The claw relaxed its grip. Ted freed his axe and jumped back out of the path of the approaching crustaceans.

The deafening report had stopped them, but only for a brief moment. Again they came on with their characteristic sideways motion; but their object had

changed. Instead of attacking the slayer of their comrade they threw themselves upon the dead crab and
commenced to tear the flesh from the protecting shell
and to wrench off the still-quivering claws and legs.

Other crabs were approaching from the scrub,
spreading fanwise something like the famous encircling
movement of the Zulu *impis*.

Ted and Brian did not wait. They took to their
heels and were not ashamed of doing so!

'I always thought land-crabs were nocturnal in their
habits,' said Brian breathlessly when, the danger past,
the explorers slackened their pace.

'We've distinct evidence to the contrary,' rejoined
Ted grimly. 'And gosh! what a grip the brute had. It
quite numbed my muscles!'

'A jolly good thing we didn't try to force our way
through there,' said Brian, pointing to the valley.
'We'll give that place a jolly wide berth.'

Presently they reached the head of the valley, which
consisted of a semi-circular cliff of igneous rock over
which a small stream dropped. From this point they
had an uninterrupted view of their goal—the nearmost
of the twin peaks.

Again appearances at a distance were deceptive. The
peak consisted of a number of rocky terraces upon
which sun-dried grass struggled for existence. Here
and there were rifts, or 'chimneys', that afforded some
sort of foothold when it came to scaling the otherwise
almost perpendicular ledges. At last, after three-
quarters of an hour of strenuous endeavour, the lads
gained the summit, which they found to be a sort of
ring enclosing a shallow depression about fifty feet in
diameter.

Breathlessly they threw themselves flat to recover
from their exertions. After a while they sat up and
looked around. From their elevated position they had
an almost clear view of the horizon except where the

other peak—about four hundred yards away—cut the skyline. Away to the west'ard and showing above the horizon was a large island with two smaller ones to the north of it.

'How far away are they, do you think?' asked Ted.

'Allowing for the clearness of the atmosphere I should say thirty miles.'

'Then, if we get tired of this one there's no reason why we shouldn't go there in the motor boat. Thirty miles: she'd do that easily in three hours. . . . Look, there's a ship!'

The sun was now about half-way between its zenith and the horizon. Just emerging from the patch of dazzling reflected sunshine was a two-masted, single-funnelled, white-hulled steamer. She was about a mile outside the reef and perhaps twice that distance from the peak on which the chums stood. Apparently she was making no attempt to close the island but was standing on a southerly course.

'A Frenchman,' announced Ted. 'I can see the tri-colour aft.'

'Looks like it,' agreed Brian. 'There are three vertical stripes though I can't make out the colours. Shall we signal to her?'

The opportunity was there. It required only to make a smoke signal—and there was plenty of dry grass for that purpose—and the look-out on board the steamer could not fail to notice it. Binoculars would reveal the presence of two white men on what the Frenchman probably knew was otherwise an uninhabited island. In a couple of hours Ted and Brian might be on board, in two days they might be landed at Papeete. In a fortnight they might be at Panama en route for England!

Yet they had not fully enjoyed the fruits of their labours. The lure of a care-free existence upon a desert island, with many of the advantages of civilization at their disposal, had not begun to wane. It had not even reached its peak.

They read each other's unspoken thoughts.

'Keep down out of sight,' exclaimed Ted. 'They may spot us!'

So they let the French Government surveying sloop *Hirondelle* proceed, unsignalled, on her way.

XXIII

A FISHY TALE

IN silence they discreetly watched the steamship standing away until she was a mere speck upon the surface of the sea.

'Glad?' asked Brian.

'Rather!'

'So am I.'

'Why?'

'Blest if I can explain, only it seems like chucking up the sponge when there's no need.'

'And there's the *Sempione*,' added Ted. 'We've brought her so far, or rather she's brought us. There's a question of salvage. We'd be entitled to a good share of it if we didn't abandon her at the last lap.'

'What do you mean?'

'It's like this,' explained Ted. 'Supposing a vessel came here and took her in tow to the nearest port, we could strike a bargain for part of the salvage provided we remained on board until she arrived there. If we'd been taken off by that vessel we should have abandoned our claim.'

'What's she worth?'

'Haven't an earthly,' confessed Ted. 'But once the shaft is repaired she'll be perfectly seaworthy. Either her owners or the underwriters will pay up and look pleasant, and that's where we come in!'

'I thought when the crew left her the *Sempione* was ours,' confessed Brian.

'You thought wrong, old son,' replied his companion bluntly. 'She's not a wreck. We brought her here and moored her, but that doesn't mean she's ours.'

Brian pondered. He had never considered Ted as an authority on the question of *meum et teum* as applied to the peculiar laws of shipping. 'Then we've no right to use the ship's gear and stores?'

'Oh yes, we have! We're making use of them to ensure the safety of the ship. They can't even deduct those charges from our share of the salvage—when we get it! . . . I say! If we're to get on board before dark we'd better make a move!'

Except for the descent of the peak—and climbing down a steep declivity is a more risky business than scaling it—the journey back to the ship took far less time than the outward one. It wanted an hour before sunset when they reached the belt of grassland separating the palm groves from the shore of the haven.

'*Sempione* ahoy!' hailed Ted.

'*Sempione* ahoy . . . ahoy . . . hoy!' came the answering echoes.

'You'd think there were a hundred men over there,' said Brian, indicating the opposite shore of the sheltered anchorage. 'If anyone didn't know what it is they'd have a bit of a shock!'

'It rattled us the first time we heard it,' added Ted. 'Strange the echo only answers when we shout from this spot. Doesn't the old hooker look fine in the half-light?'

Brian merely grunted. He had not got over the shock of the knowledge that the *Sempione* was not wholly theirs: that they were but temporary occupiers of the ship they had saved.

After supper they fished from the ship's poop, using lines they had found in the bosun's store room and baiting them with pieces of tinned beef.

'Cheerful optimists, aren't we?' remarked Brian, after a few minutes of non-productive work. 'The fish don't

seem to like bully beef any more than we do! . . . Ha!
A bite!'

He hauled in his line with a six-pounder fish of all
colours of the rainbow that scintillated in the rays of
the electric lamp.

'Shouldn't fancy eating it,' said Ted.

'Neither would I,' admitted the successful fisher-
man.

For the next half hour they were hauling up fish
almost as fast as they could bait and lower their lines.
Some of the catch they set aside, since they were of a
familiar kind. Others, looking suspiciously as if they
were of a poisonous nature, were dumped back into
the sea.

'May as well pack up,' suggested Brian. 'We've
quite as many as we want.'

'Half a minute! I've a whopper!' exclaimed Ted
excitedly. 'Isn't it pulling!' He made no attempt to
play the fish but took a turn round a belaying-pin with
the line. Looking down over the side the chums could
see a large dark form struggling furiously and throwing
up showers of phosphorescent spray.

'It's a young shark!' declared Brian.

'No fear! . . . Here, we'll have to get a net under
it.'

The only net available was one used for handling
cargo. It was about five feet square and was enclosed
in an iron frame with slings fixed to each corner.

Leaving the line still fastened to the belaying-pin the
lads carefully lowered the net and adroitly manœuvring
it into position succeeded in holding the fish in the
bight. Then they commenced to haul in slowly while
the 'catch' redoubled its struggles and snapped furiously
at the meshes.

That was its undoing. Its hook-like teeth became
fixed in the wire strands. It had thrown away its last
chance of making a spring for liberty, for had the

11   (H 60)

youths attempted to get it on board solely by the line the fish's weight would either have broken the relatively weak cord or else the hook would have been torn from its hold.

After strenuous exertions they hove the net level with the taffrail. The chance of a direct haul was then over. The problem was how to get the net and its contents on board.

'We'll have to capsize the net,' declared Brian. 'The brute must weigh nearly half a hundredweight. I'll hang on to one side of the net to stop it from slipping, and you heave!'

This operation was successfully accomplished. The net and its occupant landed upon the deck, the fish struggling violently and lifting itself and the net three or four feet from the deck time after time by the muscular action of its powerful tail.

'Now it's here, what good is it?' asked Brian.

'No good at all, as far as I can see,' admitted Ted. 'It's only the fun of landing such a whopper. We can't throw it back so we'd better settle it.'

Fetching a handspike he dealt the fish four or five heavy blows across its head before its convulsive movements ceased.

'Dead as mutton!' he announced. 'I'll prise open its mouth and get the net clear. Then we can throw it overboard.'

He unshipped a wooden belaying-pin and proceeded to insert it into the fish's mouth, so that the mesh could be removed from the formidable hooked teeth. Suddenly the jaws closed, narrowly missing the startled youth's hand. The belaying-pin—made of ash and an inch in diameter—was bitten completely in two!

'And I thought the brute stone dead!' exclaimed Ted. 'It must be like an eel—that will keep alive after it's been skinned, so they say! We'd better leave it here till tomorrow. It's safer!'

'It won't attract the crabs, will it?' asked Brian, with the incident of the afternoon still vividly fresh in his mind.

'We'll barricade the entry port with another cargo-net,' decided his chum. 'That'll stop them!'

Next morning brought no evidence that the tree-felling crabs had attempted to board the ship. The fish —it measured five feet from its snout to the end of its tail—was stone dead; while, probably owing to its having been exposed to the moonlight, the flesh was already showing signs of decomposition.

'I say!' exclaimed Brian. 'I've heard of bulls and pigs wearing nose-rings, but I've never before seen a fish with a ring round its tail!'

Encircling the tail just above the fins was a flat band of grey metal. Even allowing for the present state of the fish it was evident that the ring had been placed there when it was much smaller.

Holding his nose and approaching from the wind'ard side, Ted made a closer examination. 'There's something written on it,' he announced. 'We'll have it off. Fetch a bucket of water and some pomegranates!'

'Permanganate, you mean.'

'Yes, I suppose that's it,' admitted Ted. Gingerly inserting a piece of flat wood between the tail and the deck, he raised his axe and with one blow severed the fish's extremity. Then detaching the ring he placed it in the bucket of crimson water.

'Let it soak!' he suggested. 'We'll heave the carcass overboard.'

It was no easy task and certainly an unpleasant one. To their disgust the dead fish floated and drifted slowly between the ship's quarter and the bank. Dozens of small fish, attracted by the—to them— tempting odour, nibbled at the bloated flesh.

'Dashed if I feel like eating fish again,' said Brian.

'Or swimming in the harbour, if it comes to that,' added Ted. 'Let's see what's on the ring.'

They removed the metal circle from the bucket. On it, in faint but discernible lettering, were the words: 'U.S. Fishery Board, San Diego, Cal. 18 . 5 . 19—'.

'That fish has certainly broken the *Sempione's* record,' said Brian.

'M'yes,' admitted Ted, looking over the side. 'But the *Sempione's* still afloat.'

'And isn't the fish?'

'No; it has been eaten by the others—beastly cannibals!'

XXIV

A CHAPTER OF MISHAPS

AFTER lunch they got the accommodation ladder out and lowered it into position, the lower platform about eighteen inches from the water. Ahead of it they moored the motor boat sufficiently near to enable them to jump from the bottom of the ladder to the boat's sternsheets. The arrangement was, as they were unanimous in declaring, a great improvement upon the rope ladder. It required less energy and no physical discomfort.

'What about a run out to the reef?' suggested Brian.

'Right-o; we'd better shove on our sea-boots,' rejoined Ted, mindful of their encounter with the big clam.

They donned the heavy leather footgear and embarked. The engine started without the slightest hitch. Brian took the tiller and adroitly steered the boat through the narrow gap between the ship and the shore, then headed for the entrance to the haven and thence across the lagoon to the inner side of the reef.

Here they found a convenient and fairly deep gully between the flat belt of dead coral. They took the anchor ashore, wedging one fluke securely in the crevice.

There was a stiffish wind blowing that sent the spray flying completely over the ledge like showers of driving rain. Not that they minded that. The only precaution they took was to put the cover over the motor and a piece of tarpaulin over the engine-case.

It was an exhilarating ramble. The constant shower of salt spray acted as a bracing tonic and tempered the heat of the sun, although walking—a tedious business in sea-boots—was only possible through the protection the iron-shod footgear provided.

There was no lack of submarine life. Crabs, lobsters and limpets abounded in the pools. There were oysters of various sizes, some large enough to form a dangerous trap for the unwary, but by this time both lads had a very wholesome respect for the larger bivalves. There were bones of larger fish bleaching in the sun alongside small specimens of tropical plants that were struggling for existence in the scanty soil.

Presently Brian stepped aside to avoid a dull greyish patch that looked like a flat heap of slime. He went on without giving it another glance, not knowing that it was a lump of ambergris and worth a king's ransom!

A few yards farther they spotted an oar. It was about fifteen feet in length, straight-bladed and coppered.

'Here's a find!' exclaimed Brian. 'Just what we want as a spare for the boat!' He floundered over a patch of kelp, stooped and picked up the oar by its loom. To his surprise the apparently stout oar snapped off close to his hands. As it fell the remaining portion broke into half a dozen pieces.

Closer examination showed that the apparently sound piece of wood was literally honeycombed with worm-holes so small as to be unnoticed by the eye of a casual observer.

The lads continued their walk until further progress was barred by the channel through which the *Sempione* had gained the lagoon.

'Did you notice the barometer this morning, Bags?' asked Ted.

'No, I didn't,' confessed Brian. 'Did you?'

'I forgot,' admitted Ted. 'But look out there!' He pointed to wind'ard. Low down on the horizon sombre, ragged clouds had appeared where a few minutes before had been clear blue sky.

'Another gale,' declared Brian. 'There's one thing, it can't possibly hurt us with the old hooker safe behind those headlands. We'd better be getting back.'

They had hardly gone more than half-way to the spot where they had landed on the reef, when Ted suddenly exclaimed: 'Look, the boat's adrift!'

Already, nearly one-third of the distance to the nearest part of the island, the errant motor boat was scudding before the now stiffish wind.

Ted started to run, but Brian restrained him. 'We'll want all our breath to swim across,' he declared. 'It's futile to run in sea-boots!'

'The sooner we start swimming the quicker we'll reach her.'

'My dear old son, she's drifting far quicker than we can ever hope to swim. She'll be ashore before we're half-way across.'

Arriving at the spot where they had left the motor boat, they found that the anchor was still where they had left it with about two fathoms of frayed painter made fast to the ring. Either the swaying of the boat had chafed the rope through on the sharp coral, or some shell-fish had bitten it through. It was of little use speculating upon the cause. The mischief was done. The anchor would have to be left until a more opportune time.

The boys kicked off their heavy boots that, for safety's sake, were two sizes too large. Then, without attempting to remove any of their clothing—they were wearing only shorts, singlets and hats—they dived off the rocks into the lagoon. Both were excellent swimmers. The distance meant little to them. It was only the fear of sharks that worried them.

Instinctively they started off, Brian on his left side

and Ted on his right. By taking up these positions, since they were back to back and only a few feet apart, they could command a view of the surface in practically all directions, each guarding one flank, as it were. They would thus be able to sight any shark that showed its dorsal fin above water and a combined vigorous splash ought to compel the brute to keep a safe distance.

Brian's surmise was a correct one. Even swimming their hardest, the chums stood no chance of overtaking the boat; so they slowed down to conserve their strength, thanking their lucky stars that they had not to make headway against the waves.

Although under the lee of the reef the water was only ruffled, there was quite a short steep sea running midway across the lagoon, while shorewards the waves were breaking angrily. It did not promise well for the motor boat. She would be pounding on the beach for some time before they reached her and were able to take her out into deep water before making for the ship.

Suddenly Brian gave a yell and disappeared. Before Ted could reach him he reappeared, spluttering. 'Something's bitten me!' he gasped.

'Kick, then. I'll stand by you!' exclaimed Ted encouragingly, thinking that his chum had been seized by cramp, and had attributed the loss of power in his legs to an attack by a fish.

Turning on his back, Brian lashed out. He had made no mistake. The calf of his left leg was discoloured with blood mingling with the salt water. The effort caused him acute pain. Whatever the cause, the effect had been to seriously cripple his legs. Although he had 'kicked out', Brian felt that it was the result of will-power over muscular action. He could not keep it up. A sort of numbness was affecting not only the bitten limb but the other. All he could do now was to keep floating on his back, with his legs slightly bent, and to propel himself with his hands.

Cramp, bite or whatever it might be, he could keep afloat for quite a considerable time provided he did not get into a state of panic.

'Hang on to me!' exclaimed Ted encouragingly. 'We'll do it easily!'

Turning over again, Brian grasped Ted's singlet by the hem of the neck. He was thus able to assist in their shoreward progress by paddling with his right hand.

Ted swam strongly, but before long he began to feel the strain. Even the comparatively light pressure of the neck-band round his throat made natural breathing difficult. 'Catch hold of my belt!' he spluttered. 'You're choking me.'

'I'll let go altogether. I can make progress.'

'No, you don't. Hang on when I tell you.'

For the next few minutes they continued in silence, each one obsessed by the dread—though neither mentioned it to the other—that he was being nibbled by some denizen of the lagoon! Ted was certain that he had been bitten more than once, while Brian, who had lost all sense of sensation in his legs, was equally sure that his toes had been badly nipped!

'Nearly there!' announced Ted.

Redoubling his efforts, in about twenty vigorous breast-strokes he found his feet touch the firm sand. With feelings of thankfulness and relief he stood up and grasped his companion by the arms. 'We can walk ashore now, old son!' he exclaimed.

Brian tried to do so, but promptly went under. 'Can't use my legs!' he spluttered, as his chum hoisted him up.

'Can't? All right. I'll drag you.'

This was a fairly easy task in spite of the breaking waves but only as long as Brian's body was water-borne. To drag him up the sandy beach out of the reach of the miniature breakers was a tedious business.

Ted's next act was to examine his chum's injuries.

There was a circular wound nearly an inch in diameter and perhaps a quarter of an inch deep in the back of his leg, midway between knee and ankle. It was still bleeding, although prolonged immersion in salt water had tended to reduce the flow. The bite, for such it undoubtedly was, was bad enough but it was little compared with the swollen and discoloured condition of the limb.

The only thing to be done in the circumstances was to bind Brian's soaked singlet round the calf of his leg.

'You'd better see to the boat,' he suggested. 'She won't do herself any good banging about on the beach.'

'She can take care of herself a bit longer,' declared Ted. 'My job is to get you back on board as soon as I jolly well can!'

'You can't unless you get the boat,' expostulated Brian. 'We'd never get up those cliffs and all the way round the side of the harbour. I'll be all right here for a bit. Lying in the sun's doing me good already.'

'All right, then,' conceded Ted. 'I'll be as quick as I can, look you!'

'There's no hurry now. While you're about it, you'd better fetch our boots and the anchor; only don't let the boat break adrift again!'

Ted ran along the beach for a distance of about eighty yards to the spot where the motor boat had come ashore. The exercise brought warmth and restored suppleness to his limbs. Fortunately the tide was rising so that the little but heavy craft had not been left high and dry. She had struck on a sandy patch between two ledges of rock, and was quite unharmed.

Pushing off, Ted jumped aboard and rowed her into deep water. Then, rather dubiously, since he did not know whether the propeller had been damaged or not, he started up the engine and let in the clutch. To his great satisfaction the boat leapt ahead with no more than the former amount of vibration. She had come through her ordeal unscathed.

In roughly one sixth of the time the chums had taken to get across the lagoon the motor boat made the run out to the reef. Then, recovering the missing gear, Ted steered for the part of the beach where Brian was lying.

It was no light task to get Brian into the boat, which was pitching considerably and showing a tendency to drive broadside on. Since the injured youth couldn't stand without assistance—and then only on one foot— Ted had to lift him bodily and wade in thigh-deep before he could dump him into the boat.

That done, it was a matter of a few minutes to run back to the *Sempione*.

Didn't they bless the thought that had prompted them to rig the accommodation ladder! But for that, Ted would have had a strenuous and exhausting struggle to get his companion on board, for the only alternative was to haul him up the low cliff and then carry him across the gangway.

As it was, Ted had to lift Brian on his back, step out of the boat upon the lower platform and then climb the twenty-odd steps of the swaying ladder.

'Good enough for the present!' he gasped, as he deposited his human burden on the deck. 'I'll have a breather and then I'll get you up to your bunk. How do you feel now?'

'Fine,' declared Brian mendaciously.

He was far from it. Now that he was on board the ship, he was beginning to feel faint, although he would not admit it. There were three more ladders to ascend before he reached their sleeping cabin. At the present time he didn't feel equal to it, even though the journey was to be accomplished on his companion's back.

'Now, then!' exclaimed Ted. 'Up with you!'

There was no response. Brian had fainted.

It took about a quarter of an hour before he recovered sufficiently to attempt the ascent. Since Ted wanted both hands and feet to climb the three steep ladders, Brian must have the use of his hands in order to cling to his friend's back.

At last the task was accomplished. Brian was placed in his bunk, while Ted fetched bandages from the medical store chest. Then, after taking a mild sleeping-draught, the patient fell into a slumber.

Then and only then did Ted discover that his fears of being bitten were not unfounded. There were at least two dozen marks upon his legs that had undoubtedly been caused by the mouths of small fish, although only in two cases had the skin actually been punctured. When he had finished treating the irritating spots with iodine his already sun-tanned legs looked as speckled as a leopard's skin.

His tasks for the day were by no means over. He had to secure the motor boat in her accustomed berth, to prepare his own supper, and then, in view of the approaching storm, to furl the sun-awnings and lash down or stow all loose gear.

By now the sky looked very menacing although at sunset there was not a breath of wind. In the stillness the roar of the surf sounded louder than he had ever before heard it. The glass stood at 29.2 and was still falling.

'Glad I'm not at sea tonight,' he soliloquized, as he prepared to turn-in. 'There's one thing: we're safe as houses here. Nothing can harm us.'

XXV

TED MAKES A DISCOVERY

A VIVID flash of lightning roused Ted from sleep. For a minute or so he lay still, listening to the moaning of the wind. He was dimly aware of a gentle movement as the ship responded to the rollers outside the haven. 'Blowing like blue blazes now,' he thought. 'Nothing for us to worry about.' He snuggled down between the sheets to recapture his disturbed slumbers.

Then another flash appeared to leap through the scuttles. A deafening crash of thunder followed.

'Old Bags is sleeping like a hog,' mused Ted. 'I'll draw the curtains or the glare is bound to wake him.' He tumbled out of his bunk, switched on the light and proceeded to draw the thick curtains over the scuttles.

Hardly had he got back into his bunk when, while the thunder now reverberated almost continuously, heavy rain began to patter down upon the deck-head only four feet above his face. It was 3.15 a.m.

Confident in the ship's immunity, Ted went to sleep again in spite of the din without. Again he awoke, imagining that he was at sea, until he realized that the *Sempione* was snugly moored in a sheltered haven.

But was she?

Apart from the usual noises of the storm there were other sounds—the crashing of broken wood and the unmistakable grinding of a vessel in collision with some large object. She was afloat all right. She was quite lively as she rolled; yet with each roll to port there was that disconcerting banging sound.

It had disturbed Brian, too, who had slept through most of the night without rousing from his slumber. 'You there, Ted? What's up?'

'Hanged if I know! I'll switch on the light. Don't you get up, with your leg in that state!'

It was now nearly 7 a.m. In a few minutes intense darkness would give way to daylight. The barometer stood at 28.5, a drop of seven-tenths of an inch in eight hours.

'She's aground, I believe,' said Brian as a heavier shock shook the ship. 'Surely her anchors can't have dragged?' He struggled to his feet.

Ted opened the sliding door, there to be greeted by a flash of lightning that left him peering with unseeing eyes. It was still raining heavily, but although the wind was howling furiously over the top of the protecting headland only a slight backdraught could be felt on deck.

Again a disconcerting bump.

Before his eyes could grow accustomed to the darkness again there was another blinding flash. The whole of the surrounding land and the forepart of the ship stood out in dazzling distinctness, and then everything was blotted out by the contrast following the glare.

'We're where we were,' announced Brian. 'She hasn't broken adrift, but something has! It's no use finding what's wrong until dawn.'

'She's bumping badly,' added Ted. 'I suppose she hasn't knocked a hole in her bottom.'

'If she has, she has! We can't do anything. If she sinks, her well-deck will be above water. . . . What a crash!'

'A tree blown down, I expect. It wasn't anything on

on board. . . . There's another. The coco-palms are getting it on the hill!'

They continued to talk in a desultory manner until, with the suddenness common to the Tropics, night became broad daylight within the space of three or four minutes.

They went on deck, Brian limping badly.

The rain had ceased, but the wind was blowing with terrific force overhead. Spray was flying completely over the lofty ridges guarding the haven, giving a good indication of the state of the sea inside the lagoon in spite of the protecting reef. Within Echo Harbour the surface was hardly ruffled except for a fan-shaped patch of ripples just inside the entrance. But although the surface was quiet there was a long swell setting in that broke into creamy froth as it surged against the steep-to shore.

'It's our gangway that's carried away!' declared Brian.

That structure, however, was still in position and apparently undamaged although the rollered end ashore was ploughing into the rain-soaked ground.

It was the accommodation ladder that had accounted for the bewildering and nerve-racking noises. The scend of the sea outside had been too much for the spring of the heaving cable. The ship had been driven several feet nearer the shore, while the continuous grinding had smashed the lower platform and about half a dozen of the lowermost treads of the accommodation ladder to splinters!

'Where's the boat?' gasped Ted.

She had vanished.

A part of her sternfast could be seen dangling over the ship's side. The bow-rope, having been made fast to the bottom of the accommodation ladder, had carried away when the platform had been pulverized. But where was the boat?

Ted hurried aft, hoping that the boat had been swept clear of the ship's side and was now floating somewhere within the haven.

Not a sign! Except for a few tree trunks that had been blown over from the top of the cliffs, the surface of the harbour was clear of floating objects.

'She's been nipped!' declared Ted dolefully, when he rejoined his waiting companion.

Assisted by Ted, Brian hobbled to the open entry port, and peered down. Here the surface was rippled by the gentle motion of the ship, which prevented them from seeing the bottom of the haven as they usually could.

Presently, as the *Sempione* temporarily increased her distance from the shore, the ripples died down. Then, only too clearly they saw what remained of the motor boat upon which they had spent so much time and energy and from which they were looking forward to such great things! She was lying over on her bilge with the greater part of her port side completely stove-in. Even if they succeeded in raising her she was beyond repair. Nipped between the ship's side and the cliffs, she had gone down like a stone.

Self-recrimination wouldn't help. It was of no use saying that they ought to have foreseen such a calamity. They hadn't. They had, as they thought, taken every reasonable precaution for her safety, but Nature, as she frequently does, had won in the contest between herself and human ingenuity.

Now they were virtually prisoners. Without the boat, they were confined to the limits of the island and the ship. Gone were their chances of making a voyage to the nearmost island should occasion or inclination demand it.

For the rest of the day they were too dispirited to say much. Ted prepared their meals, but felt disinclined to eat. The loss of the motor boat had hit them both pretty hard. Without it their outlook, as far as the island was concerned, had undergone a complete change. It was as if their liberty of action had been drastically cut down. They were prisoners as surely as if the island had been surrounded by a barbed-wire fence!

The storm continued to rage until about four o'clock in the afternoon. On the high ground palm trees on the wind'ard side of the grove were being felled like ninepins until the inclined trunks of those that had been thrown against the trees that were still standing resembled a sloping wall of rough timber.

Masses of rock, loosened by the heavy rains, came rolling down the slope, to crash into the haven, sending up tall columns of spray. Portions of the cliff, too, shaken by the terrific reverberations of the thunder, slipped into the water, one landslide occurring within fifty yards of the *Sempione's* bows.

Then the wind backed through four points and rapidly eased down. The sun once more shone from a cloudless sky, its heat causing clouds of vapour to rise both from the ground and from the *Sempione's* rain-swept decks.

With the return of sunshine the boys' spirits rose. They began to realize that things might have been far worse. Their floating home, for example, had suffered no harm. The gangway was intact, so they were still in easy communication with the land. The damage to the accommodation ladder was of slight consequence. As for the motor boat——

'We'll have a jolly good shot at building another one!' declared Brian.

'Rather!' agreed Ted. 'And we can use another of the auxiliary engines. When shall we make a start?'

'I can't do much, can I?' rejoined the injured lad. 'I hope I'll be all right within the next three days.'

Alas for these hopes! It was more than a week before

12   (H 60)

he could set his foot on the deck without feeling acute pain. The wound healed slowly, in spite of Ted's attention. Actually a fortnight elapsed before the swelling of the limb—due probably to the fact that the fish was a poisonous one—had gone down sufficiently to enable Brian to resume his share of their daily tasks.

Meanwhile Ted had not been idle. Far from it! Not only had he to act as nurse and cook—and how he detested the latter task!—but there were a score of odd jobs on board that could not be left.

During that fortnight he hardly left the ship to go ashore except to gather fruit and greenstuff to supplement their ordinary fare. That was on Brian's account, for although Ted laughed at his fears, Brian dreaded the idea of his going ashore alone lest some mishap should befall him. Dangers they were willing to face together. It was not on his own account that Brian was reluctant to be left alone; it was the fear that Ted might get into some difficulty and be unable to help himself, that prompted Brian's anxiety on his behalf.

One afternoon, just before Brian was able to resume his normal occupation, Ted thought he would explore Number two hold. A previous though cursory examination had revealed that there were several long planks stowed there that would be useful if they carried out their intention of building a boat to replace the one they had lost.

Armed with a portable electric lamp he descended by means of an iron ladder and found himself standing in a narrow alleyway between the securely stowed cargo. That on the port side consisted chiefly of rectangular crates; to starboard there were mostly barrels placed over a quantity of nitrates. Over the barrels and lashed down by ropes and chains were the objects Ted had taken to be planks.

A closer look showed that he was partly in error. They were crates, two of them, each about twenty feet in length and about eighteen inches square. The tops, bottoms and sides were made of two-inch planks each nine inches in width, secured at each end by heavy-gauge brass screws.

'Just what I want,' thought Ted. 'A bit on the heavy side, perhaps, but there's more than enough wood to knock up quite a decent flat-bottomed scow strong enough to take a motor. . . . I wonder what's inside them?'

He judged, from their position, that the crates had been part of the cargo taken on board at Santa Teresa. He was perfectly right in this surmise, for, after obtaining a large screw-driver and opening the top of one of the cases, he discovered that it contained something that at first sight he took to be the barrel of a large pump.

Another and longer look convinced him of his error; it was a quick-firing gun.

Or nearly so; in its present state it could not be discharged, since there were no mountings. Possibly these were in another crate.

So far it was complete with breech-block, telescope sights, and firing-pistol. Obviously it was intended for use and not for disposal as scrap metal, otherwise these would have been removed before shipment.

For the present Ted forgot about the planks that formed the crate. He went on deck and reported his find.

'It beats me why it should be on board,' he declared. 'It must have been shipped at Santa Teresa. Why? With the war on between Bolomaya and Grossaguay surely President Bombardo would want every gun he could lay his hands on? He wouldn't want to send them out of the country!'

'I wonder if there's any reference to it in the letter I have to deliver to Señor Madeira?' asked Brian.

'For General Sandano? Quite possibly. Well, there

doesn't seem much chance of it getting into his hands. Why not look and see?'

Brian shook his head. He was obdurate on this point; he must do his utmost to carry out his bargain with President Bombardo, little knowing to what base means the head of the Bolomayan Republic had descended to gain his own ends.

XXVI

A RELIC OF THE PAST

NEXT day—the first on which Brian was able to get about after his misadventure—the interest in the discovery of the quick-firer underwent an almost complete 'fade-out' in favour of the task of building a boat.

Obviously, one crate would not provide sufficient timber. Two would. Also, although it might be a fairly easy matter to remove the top and sides of one crate it was out of the question to get at the bottom planks without lifting the gun.

'We'll have to get both crates on deck,' decided Ted. 'The gun must weigh at least a ton.'

'What's wrong with the derrick?'

'All right! We'll want a clear space on deck. Let's see what's to be done.'

They removed tarpaulins and hatch-covers, started the engine operating the derricks and adjusted slings on the first packing-case. This last task was not an easy one, since the bottom of the case was almost flush with the top of the one underneath. They solved the difficulty by lifting one end by means of a sling, sufficiently high to allow a second sling to be slipped underneath and adjusted. Then, with Brian tending the guy-ropes, Ted commenced to hoist. After their previous experience in getting out the motor boat, the twenty-foot box was a fairly simple thing to tackle.

The crate with its contents was placed on the starboard side of the well-deck. The remaining board forming the cover was then removed and the gun lifted out. Carefully the remaining screws were taken out, with the result that the amateur boat-builders found themseves in possession of eight stout planks.

Next, the other crate, which also contained a rifled breech-loading gun, was hoisted on deck and similarly treated.

'What about these?' asked Ted, indicating the two weapons. 'They're in the way here.'

'We can't very well put them back into the hold. It would be a fearful swot. I say; are there any mountings? If so, why not set them up. It will be a lark pretending we're in an armed cruiser!' suggested Brian.

At first Ted demurred, urging that it was a waste of time. 'I'd sooner dump them overboard,' he added.

This suggestion, if acted on, would have saved a host of complications later on!

'We can't jettison cargo except for the purpose of safeguarding the ship,' declared Brian. 'All right. Let the things stop. If we break our necks over them in the dark, don't blame me!'

'Have it your own way, then,' rejoined Ted good-humouredly. 'You generally do! Let's see if we can find the things!'

It did not take them long to find the two mountings. Each was in a case, on which was stencilled: 'Piano, with care' in Spanish, although, from the shape of the crates, such a declaration would hardly have deceived anyone.

The mountings were then hoisted on deck, one on the port side, the other to starboard. Again the derrick was brought into operation and the guns were soon in position, facing fore and aft, yet sufficiently high to clear the capping of the bulwarks.

'Don't they look businesslike?' exclaimed Brian.

'Yes; but let's get down to business. I want the boat finished inside a week!'

Ted had already drawn the plans of the proposed craft. She was to be seventeen feet in length and with a beam of six feet; flat-bottomed with a slight camber. The task of building her would have been a fairly simple one but for the thickness of the planks, each of which, when supported at each end, would bear the chums' united weight without much appreciable bending.

How, then, would they be able to get the sides to meet at the stem-head and curve aft to the transom?

Then Brian remembered having been told how Dutch shipbuilders bend the stout oak planks of their *botters* and similar craft. 'They place the planks on trestles, one at each end, and dump weights in the centre,' he explained. 'Then they pour water on the upper side of the planks and gradually they get the right curve. I believe the process takes six months.'

'Six months!' snorted Ted. 'We aren't Methuselahs! Can't we cut notches in the planks to let them bend easier?'

'The planks wouldn't bend in a regular curve. We'd better make the bottom and then try the effect of boiling water.'

It took them three days to cut the bottom planks to shape and secure them by stout battens. The seams were caulked while the timber was dry, after which the completed bottom was suspended with weights placed towards the middle of it. For two days the galley fire worked overtime as the enthusiastic and indefatigable amateurs poured cans of boiling water upon the woodwork, until the desired camber was obtained.

The planks for the side were similarly treated, but in the end, short of the long and difficult job of 'halving' the woodwork, the two chums decided to notch the material and trust to luck!

At the end of five days the hull was almost complete.

The deadwood aft had been bolted on and bored for the propeller-shaft; knees, breasthook and other strengthening pieces had been fixed in position, and the final caulking carried out. All that remained to be done was to paint the boat inside and out, fix the engine bearers, build a light fore-deck and finish a few other small jobs before installing the motor.

'Tomorrow we'll give her the first coat of paint,' decided Ted, who seemed to have taken the initiative over the boat-building task. 'While the paint's drying —it won't take long in the sun—I vote we have half a day off.'

'I could do with it,' agreed Brian. 'A nice lazy time in a deck chair——'

'No, no! Couldn't think of it! A change is as good as a rest, they say, though I have my doubts! We'll make another trip inland. This time we'll climb the other peak.'

'What a hope!' exclaimed Brian.

'And you won the school cross-country race only three years ago!' rejoined Ted. 'Don't tell me you're getting soft, Bags!'

'I'm not,' declared Brian. 'Tell you what; I'll race you to the top! Start two hundred yards from it! What do you say?'

'You'll allow me fifty yards?' asked Ted.

'No, twenty-five yards start!'

'Done!'

After the painting job had been completed they set off, wearing shorts, singlets, hats, and leather sea-boots—the latter a necessary precaution in view of the previous excursion into the interior. In addition, for use in the arranged contest, each carried a pair of canvas shoes slung around his neck. Brian also took his rifle and a dozen rounds of ammunition, while Ted, as he had done on the earlier occasion, carried a long-handled felling-axe.

This time they skirted the shore to about the middle of the western shore of the island, where they had had their unpleasant experience with the leeches on their first landing. From this spot they followed the stream towards its source since it apparently rose in the slopes of the peak they proposed climbing. Presently they neared another belt of dense scrub which was interspersed with trees that met in a series of arches over the stream.

'Goodness knows what's lurking in that stuff,' said Brian. 'Shall we push on or work round it?'

'Let's push on, suggested Ted.' It can't be more than a quarter of a mile to the open country at the foot of the peak. We can wade along the stream. It's quite shallow here.'

This suggestion was agreed to. The streamlet—it was now only about a couple of yards in width—promised a fairly clear passage through the belt of tropical vegetation impassable unless the explorers laboriously hacked a way with the axe. It was pleasantly cool. Overhead, the foliage shaded them from the sun. The water, only a few inches deep, flowing over their boots as they trudged along, almost made them forget their heavy footgear.

In several places they had to bend to avoid the spiked branches. Once they had to use the axe to clear a barrier of pliant tendrils that completely obstructed their path. Otherwise the going was good and did not call for any great exertion.

Presently, just as they were expecting to emerge from the belt, they found themselves in a clearing about thirty yards in diameter. Except for the way by which they had entered, the place was surrounded by an impenetrable wall of dense vegetation. The peculiar thing was, however, that the clearing was covered by short grass, as rich as any lawn at home. Not a shrub occupied any part of the enclosed space, but right in the centre was a long ridge of rock partly covered by a greenish-brown moss.

It was under this rock that the stream had its source so, obviously, as a means of guiding them through the rest of the scrub belt, it had ceased to exist.

'We've struck a dead-end, Bags!' declared Ted disappointedly.

'Seems like it.' Brian moved a few yards to the left. 'This is jolly strange.'

'What is?'

'This rock: what do you make of it?'

Ted stepped over to his chum.

Viewed from that standpoint the ridge of rock looked something like a recumbent statue.

Actually it was!

There was something awesome about that huge monolith lying face to the sky in the centre of that eerie open space. The face was rudely carved. Even allowing for the ravages of time, the features retained a weird, repelling fierceness. The long straight nose, the massive, slightly protruding chin and the high straight forehead were obviously intended to portray the features of some once-powerful but long-forgotten potentate or, perhaps, heathen deity.

They examined their find. The statue was twelve paces in length and must have been thirty feet high when standing. Originally it had been set up on a wide circular pavement. This, buried to a depth of several inches by decaying leaves, had accounted for the absence of trees and shrubs. It had faced the rising sun; now it stared with unseeing eyes at the orb of day when the sun was at the zenith.

The huge dowels by which the feet had been secured to the base were almost intact, but the corresponding holes in the pavement had been long hidden. Evidently some tremendous force had been required to dislodge the statue.

'An earthquake, most likely,' observed Brian. 'But where did the stone come from? There's none like it here—at least we haven't come across any on the island. And how did they hoist it into position?'

'Goodness knows! I don't suppose they had many mechanical appliances. They might have used an inclined plane of earth. In any case it would take hundreds of men using brute force. Where have they gone?'

Perhaps this island is one of the few remains of a lost continent,' suggested Brian. 'At Easter Island there are similar statues—several of them—yet no one knows how they got there or who set them up. . . . Now, if we had a camera——'

'Unfortunately we haven't. What's more, we'll have to chuck the idea of climbing the peak today. There's nothing for it but to go back by the way we came.'

Brian gave a ready assent. He was grateful for at least the postponement of their race to the summit of the peak!

They retraced their steps until they were within sight of the lagoon; then Ted suggested that instead of walking along the shore they might cut off a corner by turning away to the right and reaching Echo Harbour by the route they had taken when they climbed the first of the two peaks.

Although they were now clear of the belt of scrub, they had yet to find their way through the coconut groves. They were hot and tired. The 'change is as good as a rest' theory hadn't worked in practice. They were looking forward with eagerness to a meal and a 'slack' on their return to the ship.

Fortunately, they found the path, although some distance farther inland than they had expected. In spite of this it had been a short cut and with renewed energy, they set out to complete their journey.

As they emerged from the grove and the whole

extent of the haven came into view, the lads stopped simultaneously.

Anchored in the centre of Echo Harbour was a schooner. Men from her were swarming over the deck of the *Sempione*!

XXVII

CAPITAINE THÉOPHILE CORBIÈRE

'WHAT a cheek!' exclaimed Brian. 'We'll have to drive them off!'

'Wait a moment!'

They stood watching the unwelcome scene. The schooner was flying the French tricolour. There were two Kanakas on her deck. The rest of her crew, including a white man, evidently the captain, and about a dozen natives, were on board the *Sempione*. Clearly they had not been there long, for although they were running about the well-deck and peering up to the bridge and massive superstructure, they had not ventured to invade these and other parts of the ship.

The boys were quick to notice this hesitation on the part of the intruders. Evidently the absence of an ensign on board the *Sempione*—and more than once the two lads had wished for a Red Ensign to display— had encouraged the crew of the schooner to conclude that she was abandoned. Actually she was, since none of the crew, amateurs or otherwise, not even a dog, remained on board.

'We're on the "echo" spot!' said Brian. 'Let's give them a warning shout. The echo will scare them stiff!'

'What shall we shout: *allez-vous-en* or *vamoose*?'

'Just "clear out of it",' replied Brian. 'Now: together!'

They shouted their hardest. Round the haven echoed and reechoed the warning until it seemed as if a platoon of leather-lunged men had given tongue.

The result more than fulfilled the chums' expectations. For a second or so the intruders stood stock still, bewildered by the rolling volume of sound that came to them from all sides. Then, almost simultaneously, the Kanakas ran to the entry port. Here they were out of sight, but judging by the shouts and other noises, they were either jumping into the boat or else, in their panic, were leaping overboard in their haste to get back to the schooner. Only the white man remained. He, too, was wavering, until he chanced to see Brian and Ted running down the slope towards the ship.

Rather breathless, for leather sea-boots, although an excellent protection in the scrub, are not to be compared with shoes when it comes to sprinting, the lads arrived at the gangway.

The captain of the schooner stepped forward 'just as if he owned the ship', Ted afterwards declared. He was about five feet six inches in height, fat, and bowed in the legs. His face reminded Brian somewhat of a full moon, since he was bald, with the exception of jet-black ringlets at the back of his head. Gold earrings adorned his protuberant ears. His 'rig' consisted of a pair of loose trousers of sky-blue colour, a checked shirt and a peaked cap, which he was holding in his left hand.

'*Bonjour, messieurs!*' he greeted them with a bow.

Politeness had to be met with politeness; but the lads realized that, if they replied in French—theirs wasn't too good—they would have to continue the conversation in that language. In all probability they would make a hash of things! Previous experience with their French master at school had taught them the fact that a partial knowledge of a language is very apt to be misunderstood, sometimes with dire results!

'Good afternoon, Captain!' replied Brian and waited for the Frenchman to open the main theme.

'Ah! You English? Dis English sheep?'

'Rather!' replied Brian.

'From La Serena, eh?'

That required some explanation. With the name *Sempione* and her port of registry—La Serena—painted on the ship's stern it would be a difficult matter to bluff the inquisitive and probably suspicious Frenchman.

Brian merely nodded.

'Sheepwreck you?'

'Far from it. We aren't shipwrecked mariners, if that's what you mean.'

'Vaire are de rest of de companie—de crew?'

'Over there,' answered Brian, airily waving his hand in a comprehensive sweep that embraced about a quarter of the island.

'Den why you here? Dis islan' eet belong to France.'

'Does it? We didn't know. There was no one to tell us,' said Ted, thinking it was about time he had a say in the matter. 'And your men had no right to come on board.'

The Captain shrugged his shoulders. Then he smiled broadly and tapped Brian on the chest. 'I onnerstan,' he continued. 'Now you listen; me, Théophile Corbière, Capitaine of ze *Fifine*, me make you offer: me take you two back to Papeete. No monnaie you pay. Me give ver' good food. At Papeete you take sheep to *Angleterre. Voyez-vous, messieurs?*'

The 'gentlemen' did see!

Without a doubt, Captain Corbière had got a pretty good hang of the situation and he was about to make full use of it—by force, if necessary, since his Kanakas were powerfully built men who would obey his command without hesitation. For the present he would try persuasion. Once he inveigled the two English youths on board the *Fifine* the game would be his. All he had to do would be to leave two of his crew on board the

Sempione and take the English youths to Papeete, there to hand them over to the French authorities on suspicion of being escaped criminals from some South American port. It would take weeks, perhaps months, for them to prove their innocence—if they ever did! Meanwhile Captain Théophile Corbière would charter a tug and tow the *Sempione* to Tahiti and then put in a joint claim for salvage with the tug master as part claimant.

'We're remaining on board—here,' replied Brian firmly. 'If we need assistance we can radio for it.'

Corbière muttered under his breath about *maudit radio*; at which the boys felt considerably bucked! The fact that they had bluffed him into a belief that the wireless was still in working order had told heavily in their favour.

Suddenly he changed his tune: 'Eet is forbidden to radio,' he declared.

'Who forbids?' demanded Brian, hardening his tone.

'Me, Capitaine Théophile Corbière,' replied the Frenchman, striking what he hoped was an intimidating attitude, although the chums with difficulty refrained from unseemly laughter at his ludicrous appearance.

'You have your written authority, I suppose?' asked Brian. 'We should like to see it.'

Corbière hesitated. He had no authority and he was trying to think how to extricate himself from the difficulty.

Brian gave him no opening. 'By the bye, Monsieur le Capitaine,' he continued, 'are you a government officer? One authorized by the French government?'

By now Brian knew that he had his man in a cleft stick. Captain Corbière had to declare truthfully that he was an accredited official of the French Colonial Government or that he was not. If he chose the first

The Relic of the Past

Page 186

alternative he was laying himself open to the grave charge of unlawfully purporting to be what he was not, with all its attendant penalties. He might have stuck to his guns had Brian been alone; but with two hostile witnesses the risk was too great. If he decided upon the second course and refused to admit that he was an authorized official, then Brian could tell him, more or less politely, to go to blazes!

In point of fact, Corbière was an ex-beachcomber who had more or less 'gone native' during his long sojourn amongst the Society Islands. By some shady means he had acquired a share in the *Fifine*, which traded amongst the islands in copra and in certain other commodities that did not meet with the approval of the authorities. Then, by more shady means, Corbière became the sole owner of the schooner. It was whispered on the beaches that his partner had been murdered. That might be, since he had died a violent death. Corbière, in spite of his physical condition, ruled his native crew with a rod of iron. Utterly unprincipled, he stopped at nothing in order to gain his ends—provided he was fairly safe from being brought to book for his delinquencies.

'My papers, zey are on board ze *Fifine*,' he replied.

'Then I should like to see them!' rejoined Brian cheerfully.

Corbière walked to the side and hailed the schooner. In spite of their fear, from which they had not recovered, half a dozen Kanakas dropped into the boat from the *Fifine's* deck. Brian noticed that each had a long knife in his waist-scarf.

'We are not letting any of those men come aboard!' he declared, as some of the natives were about to swarm up the ship's side.

For the first time the chums noticed that the Jacob's ladder had been lowered, no doubt for the use of Captain Corbière in coming aboard the *Sempione*.

'Zey assist me to make descend,' explained the Frenchman.

'Sorry! If you can't get down the ladder without help, there's the gangway,' rejoined Brian, indicating the wooden bridge to the shore. 'Your boat can pick you up from the beach. It will save you a lot of exertion!'

'I do not go!' decided Corbière. 'I tell my mans to bring papairs!' He gave instructions to the Kanakas in their native language. They pushed off at once and made towards the schooner.

Instinctively Brian realized that there was dirty work under way. Actually Corbière had ordered his crew to return armed, some to board the ship from the boat, others to land and then rush the *Sempione* by the gangway.

'I say, Ted!' he began. 'Do you mind entertaining Captain Corbière while I send off a wireless message? I won't be long!'

'Eet is forbidden!' reiterated Corbière, raising his voice.

'Not until you produce your authority,' rejoined Brian, and taking his rifle with him he went up the ladder to the boat-deck and thence to the wireless cabin.

Although the transmitter had been useless for quite a time there was enough juice in the batteries to produce a loud crackling noise. Brian gave a passable auricular demonstration for the benefit of his unwelcome and uninvited visitor. He remained in the wireless room until, through the scuttle, he could see about half a dozen Kanakas being landed from the schooner. Two of them were carrying rifles.

His suspicions now confirmed, Brian went down to where he had left Ted with Corbière. 'It's all right, Ted,' he reported mendaciously, 'I've got through to Suva. They're sending our protest on to the Governor.'

'Vat you say?' asked Corbière uneasily. He was beginning to wonder whether he hadn't made a bad mess of things. Perhaps the *Sempione* was a British government vessel, especially as she mounted two quick-firers. And, of course, the officers and crew might be ashore.

'I said,' replied Brian slowly and distinctly; 'I said that a certain Captain Théophile Corbière of the schooner *Fifine* was behaving in a suspicious manner on board the British ship *Sempione*, and requested the Governor of Fiji to communicate with the French authorities at Papeete, asking them to inquire into Captain Corbière's high-handed action. In view of the cordial relations existing between Great Britain and France, I think there will be no difficulty in getting the Papeete officials to take action.'

Corbière's bluff had been called. Owing to his genuine fear of wireless communication he dared not now use force. But for that he would not have hesitated to overpower the two youths and maroon them on another desolate island. He might even have thrown them overboard when out at sea and if his Kanakas should let the news leak out—which was very unlikely —he could declare that it was a case of double suicide.

Now he was done!

The natives, tall, muscular men, came running along the shore towards the gangway. Others in the schooner's boat were making for the ship.

Ted and Brian, not knowing what was in Corbière's mind, felt very uneasy. In fact, Brian was on the point of covering him with his rifle when he went to the gangway and shouted something to the menacing natives. Obediently they turned and went back.

Replacing his uniform cap, Corbière drew himself up to the full extent of his small stature and saluted. '*Messieurs!*' he exclaimed. 'I make regret that you have made mistake about ze situation. Eet is a pity we do not come to terms most advantageous to us both. I wish you good day!'

He turned and walked down the gangway and followed his departing crew.

XXVIII

THE ALARM

TED drew a long breath. 'Gosh! I thought we were in for it that time!'

'Yes,' agreed Brian. 'And if the echo hadn't scared those natives off the ship——'

'And you hadn't bluffed the blighters over that wireless——'

'We'd have been in the soup by now,' added Brian. 'I don't know whether we are out of it yet! It's just like it! Just as we are getting things going and having a jolly good time, that pestilential little worm turns up and spoils everything.'

'He may push off,' opined Ted.

Brian glanced towards the *Fifine*. The captain and his Kanakas had been on board nearly half an hour, but there were no signs to indicate that the schooner was getting under way.

'How did they know that the *Sempione* was here?' asked Ted. 'She's not visible from the lagoon.'

'No; but I wouldn't mind saying that the schooner's been here before. We, evidently, are not the first to discover Echo Harbour.'

'Supposing those blighters try to rush the ship while we're asleep?'

'I thought of that,' replied Brian. 'It's up to us to take all reasonable precautions.'

For the next hour there were sounds of great activity on board the *Sempione*, sounds that no doubt caused considerable curiosity, as far as Captain Théophile Corbière was concerned.

Obtaining several short lengths of half-inch wood from some of the packing-cases, Brian and Ted set to work to drive inch nails into them, so that the pointed ends of the nails projected in a formidable criss-cross. Some of the boards they placed with the spikes pointing upwards on the gangway. Others they laid in strategic positions at the foot of the ladders to the boat-deck. Any barefooted native attempting to rush the bridge would learn to his cost the penetrative properties of half an inch of pointed iron!

Not content with this, the lads rigged up a powerful cargo-lamp over the gangway and another over the Jacob's ladder, which they purposely left where it was, on the starboard or seaward side. When switched on, the sudden glare would temporarily blind any intruders.

Then they constructed a system of electric bell alarms, using the officers' cabins' bells for that purpose. One they placed at the foot of each ladder, with a switch covered by a light board supported by thin twine. Directly any heavy pressure was put upon the board the twine would break with the result that the switch would complete the circuit and the bell give out its shrill warning.

Even these precautions did not allay the lads' anxiety. Each, before he turned in, placed a loaded weapon ready to hand: Brian, the rifle; Ted, a revolver of ancient pattern that promised as much danger to the user as to the individual at whom it might be aimed.

'Think one of us ought to keep watch?' suggested Ted, stifling a yawn. 'Watch and watch, of course.'

'I don't know—suppose we ought to! . . . Any sign of them?'

They peered through the scuttles. The *Fifine* hadn't

weighed as soon as darkness had set in. She was showing no riding light, but there was a faint gleam from a skylight abaft the mainmast.

'Seems quiet,' remarked Brian. 'I'd rather they were kicking up a noise. This silence—it's suspicious.'

'What about switching on the cargo-lamps now and again just to show them——?'

'Better not. It's like an Irishman inviting people to tread on the tail of his coat! If they attempt to board, we're in the right if we wing some of them.'

'I suppose so,' agreed Ted. 'You'd better turn in. I'll keep watch for a couple of hours.'

Brian climbed into his bunk. Although he was bodily tired, sleep was denied him. He lay still, his eyes fixed on the back of his chum standing at the scuttle.

The allotted two hours passed slowly yet without any incident. It was now eleven o'clock.

'Time to change over!' announced Brian.

'I thought you were asleep. I wasn't going to rouse you. But, since you insist—there's nothing doing.'

Ted turned in, drew the single sheet over his head, and was soon breathing softly and regularly. Brian decidedly envied him as he stared through the darkness at the faint gleam—all that was visible of the *Fifine*.

Gradually the glimmer faded. Across the dark sky a huge profile spread. It was the face of the enormous image they had seen in the grove.

Brian's chin fell on his chest. He pulled himself up with a jerk. He'd been asleep. There wasn't an image; only that now distinctly visible rectangle of light on the *Fifine*'s deck. He wasn't at all sure that the position of the light hadn't moved. It had!

Surely the schooner wasn't under way? No! It was the *Fifine* swinging to her anchor as a change of wind caught her abeam.

Again his head drooped, to recover with a jerk that seemed to jolt his spinal column.

The next moment the electric bell at the gangway rent the air with its insistent warning. Seizing his rifle, Brian opened the sliding door of the cabin and switched on both cargo-lamps. For some moments the dazzling glare blinded him. The bell continued to ring.

'What is it?' asked Ted, coming to the doorway and nearly pushing the rifle out of Brian's grasp. 'Are they here?'

Then there was a deafening report that made them jump apart as if they'd accidentally touched the sparking plugs of a running engine.

It was Ted's revolver—on the involuntary pressure of the finger on the trigger—that had caused the latest alarm. The weapon, having a very easy pull, had gone off, though goodness only knew where the bullet went. The muzzle had been so close to Brian that the blast had singed his pyjama trousers!

Convinced that Ted had seen the Kanakas and had opened fire, Brian raised his rifle and pressed the trigger. The report was slight compared with the loud bang of the six-shooter but there was no doubt as to where the bullet had gone.

Still dazzled, Brian had taken a rough aim at the gangway. The bullet had shattered one of the cargo-lamps, putting the port side of the well-deck into darkness. It seemed seconds before the last tinkle of broken glass sounded on the metal deck twenty feet below.

Meanwhile the bell continued its tocsin. There were no cries of pain from the barefooted boarders as their feet came down upon the spiked nails.

'There's no one there!' exclaimed Ted after a pause.

'Then why the bell?'

'I don't know! Where's the torch?'

They found the required article and switched it on. The beam swept the gangway and thence along the shore. There was not a soul in sight!

Then they played it upon the schooner. Lining her

taffrail were a number of dark figures and one in white whom the chums recognized as Captain Théophile Corbière. They were doing nothing; they were merely standing and looking towards the *Sempione,* as they had every reason to do on account of the commotion on board her.

Descending the ladder and taking good care to avoid the spikes at its foot, Ted made his way to the spot where the electric bell had been placed. One look gave him the solution to the mystery. The thin cords supporting the board just above the switch had parted. The heavy dew had been responsible for that. The board was sufficiently heavy to set the bell off.

'Well, I'm dashed!' ejaculated Brian, when Ted, having silence the din, reported the cause of the false alarm. 'We've made fools of ourselves! That rotten Corbière will swear we fired at his vessel.'

'Let him!' rejoined Ted. 'I'm not sorry! It will let him know that we are keeping watch. What's the time? What, only a quarter past twelve? Let's turn in, both of us. They won't trouble us tonight, that's certain!'

They were not disturbed. So deep was their sleep that Corbière and his crew might have set the other alarm off without rousing the two dog-tired youths, who did not awake until the sun shining through the scuttles announced that the dawn was three hours past.

They were in the middle of a belated breakfast when they heard a hail that brought them on deck in double quick time. At the head of the gangway stood Captain Théophile Corbière, beaming like a philanthropist and public benefactor. He had taken the precaution of stepping over the spiked plank.

'Goot day, *Messieurs!*' he exclaimed with an elaborate salute. 'I haf called on a ver' friendly visit. Las' night: wizout doubt one of you make celebration of ze birthday, ah? Ring ze bells, make fire ze guns and you not make invite Capitaine Théophile Corbière for ze drinks!'

The lads could have kicked themselves! The Frenchman was treating them as if they were a pair of kids!

'We don't drink spirits,' announced Brian, which was true enough. They hadn't touched a drop since that unfortunate incident of the supposed leech-swallowing, and they didn't mean to!

'But ze wine?'

'Not keen,' replied Brian. 'We have some. You'd like a bottle, perhaps?'

'Assuredly, *Monsieur!*'

Brian led the way to the saloon, with Ted bringing up the rear. It was just as well, they thought, to humour the man after the fiasco of the previous night.

On the way aft they had to pass one of the ladders at the foot of which an array of spikes clamoured for attention.

'Oh, that!' explained Brian, noting the Frenchman's amused glance. 'You see, there are a lot of big crabs on the island, so we——'

'*Naturellement!*' interposed Corbière. 'I have myself seen them. You must haf no fears. For how? I tell you.' He went on to explain in broken English that the haven in which the *Sempione* was lying was heavily charged with sulphur. Although land crabs abounded in other parts of the island they gave this part a wide berth on that account. It was also the reason for the *Fifine's* appearance. Every few months she anchored here for a few days in order that the sulphur-impregnated water should rid her of barnacles and other marine growths. During that time the crew went ashore to obtain copra.

The boys presented Corbière with a bottle of wine. Instead of taking it away with him, as they expected him to do, he deftly knocked off the neck, and, heedless of the edges of the broken glass, took a deep drink.

The only effect, as far as Brian and Ted could see, was to make him affable and loquacious. He went on at length to declare what a good fellow he was and how anxious he was to help the two English youths. He gave his life history, which, according to his account, was one long succession of triumphs of virtue over adverse circumstances.

At last the lads managed to get him out of the saloon to the gangway, where he renewed his declarations of friendliness and gave them a cordial invitation to make a return visit to the *Fifine*.

'But we are very busy,' demurred Ted, indicating the almost completed boat.

'Nevertheless you will come,' rejoined Corbière, as he waddled down the gangway.

He still had hopes of making a considerable sum out of the *Sempione*!

XXIX

BLUFF!

ONE part of Corbière's story at least was true. The waters of Echo Harbour were charged with sulphur, only the boys hadn't noticed this peculiarity.

On looking over the ship's side they discovered that the long fringes of seaweed had entirely disappeared, leaving the anti-fouling paint almost as clear as on the day it had been applied.

'I think we'd better scrap these spiked boards,' suggested Brian. 'He knows about them, so they won't be of any use. We'll keep the electric bells ready, of course.'

'Rather! I shan't feel satisfied until we see the schooner hull-down,' rejoined Ted. 'Mind you, we're not going aboard her! We'd probably find ourselves clapped under hatches if we did!'

'And we'd better not leave the ship until she's gone. It's a thorough nuisance, but then, finishing off the new boat will keep us busy.'

That was certainly a foil to Captain Théophile Corbière's unwelcome presence. By dint of hard work they could shift a load off their minds—or nearly so. Always in their waking thoughts there was a dim suggestion that there were undesirable visitors within a cable's length of them; invisible except when the chums looked over the bulwarks to the *Fifine's* berth.

Fitting the motor was a simple task compared with their former one. Owing to the boat being almost flat-floored the difficulty of fitting the engine bearers hardly existed. But another problem presented itself.

'The propeller's going to be a tough proposition,' declared Ted, standing back and contemplating the squat and admittedly ugly hull.

'How's that?' asked Brian.

'With her shallow draught it will be almost out of the water. And what's worse, even if we trim her by the stern, the blades will be running in "dead" water. The transom will screen them, in a way.'

'In which case we must expect a speed of about two miles an hour!' remarked Brian. 'And we hoped to get a good twelve! Look here; suppose we rake the propeller-shaft still more—we can tilt the motor to ten degrees without upsetting the oil system—and run it through a chock aft.'

'Bolt on a deadwood? Yes, that should do. It will give a free run of water to the prop.'

They set to work. The motor had to be unbolted and removed. Then came the task of heaving the boat bottom upwards in order to fix the triangular block over the heel.

Then for the first time they realized how unnecessarily heavy their craft was. Built of two-inch planks with excessively heavy timbers, she took their united efforts, aided by tackles and levers, to capsize her. After that she had to be chocked up so that one of them could crawl underneath and 'hold on' while the other drove the copper spikes through the tough deadwood.

They were busily engaged upon this work when Brian, happening to hear a slight noise, turned and saw a grinning Kanaka standing at the head of the gangway.

This was a new departure. Except for the occasion when the *Fifine's* crew boarded the *Sempione* during Brian's and Ted's absence no native had set foot on deck. Corbière had made four visits and on each he had given the lads a most pressing invitation to inspect the schooner. 'Too jolly pressing,' Brian had declared, for no doubt Corbière, in his anxiety to get the two lads into his clutches, had rather overdone his part as a would-be host.

'Hello! What do you want?' asked Brian. 'Ted! Out you come!'

The Welsh youth emerged from his retreat, still holding the heavy hammer with which he had been working.

The Kanaka continued to smile. He of all the native crew could speak that form of English current amongst the islands of the Pacific.

'Cap, him tick-tick him slow stop!' he replied.

Ted and Brian looked at each other uncomprehendingly.

'Perhaps he means that Corbière's watch has gone wrong,' suggested Ted. 'What can we do? We aren't watchmakers and repairers.'

Evidently the native knew the meaning of the word 'watch'. He shook his head vigorously and still grinning placed his hand over his heart.

'Tick-tick him slow stop!' he reiterated. 'You come along me?'

'What does he mean?' asked Brian in perplexity. 'Surely he doesn't mean that Corbière has died of heart disease? Hi, Johnny; your Cap'n, him go topsides?' he asked pointing upwards.

'No, no,' replied the Kanaka. 'Tick-tick; him go slow. Most stop near it make!' In pantomimic display he clapped his hands to his stomach and uttered a groan.

'Cap'n him bad?' asked Brian.

The native grinned almost from ear to ear. 'Him bad,' he echoed. 'You make come?'

Obviously the situation was this: Captain Corbière was ill, seriously perhaps, and he had sent to ask the two lads to come to him. The dictates of humanity urged them to do so; caution, coupled with suspicion, prompted them to stay where they were.

'All right,' said Brian slowly and distinctly. 'We will not come to the schooner. Cap'n him ill. Get two, three mans and bring Cap'n here. Savvy?'

For a few seconds the Kanaka stared uncomprehendingly. Then, with a sudden movement he gripped Brian by his right arm and Ted by his left and began to drag them towards the head of the brow.

Both boys were fairly hefty fellows and physically strong and hard as nails; but in the grasp of the powerful native they were almost helpless, especially as the hammer had slipped from Ted's hand through the unexpected suddenness of the Kanaka's action. They struggled unavailingly. Held at arm's length they could not use their free hands with any effect. Almost before they knew what was happening they were on the gangway—Ted being pushed in front and Brian dragged behind their huge captor.

Like a flash a suggestion came to the Welsh youth. He had heard that negroes are particularly tender in the shins, almost their one vulnerable part. Was a Polynesian native's shin as susceptible?

Although the muscles of his legs had gone rather flabby since the days when he was considered a good footballer at school, Ted had not forgotten the tricks of many a hard-fought game. Not that he specialized in hacking. Far from it; but needs must if Brian and he were to regain their freedom. He lashed out hard with his left foot. Although he was wearing canvas shoes there was power behind that kick; and it was beautifully timed!

It caught the Kanaka midway between knee and ankle. With a roar of agony he released his hold of both his captives, and bending, commenced to rub his smarting shin with both hands. To rub effectually he had to stand on one leg.

That was Ted's second opportunity. He charged and at the same time hooked his instep against the native's uninjured ankle. There was another yell and a heavy splash.

Brian and Ted, alone on the gangway, looked down into the disturbed water.

Luckily for him, the Kanaka had missed the ship's side. He came to the surface but made no attempt to swim ashore. With a succession of powerful strokes, which Brian and Ted could not help envying and admiring, he made off to the schooner as if, as Brian remarked, 'Old Nick was after him!'

Apparently his hacked shin troubled him no more, for with very little effort, he clambered up the side and disappeared below.

For nearly an hour the lads awaited developments. In the circumstances, they dared not resume work. As a precautionary measure they brought the rifle and revolver from the cabin and placed them within easy reach.

So far nothing had happened. The Kanaka might not have given their message. The sick Frenchman was not brought to the ship nor was there any unfriendly demonstration on the part of the native crew on account of the treatment of the messenger.

'I wish we had cut away that gangway,' said Ted.

He had hardly uttered these words when Captain Corbière followed by a dozen armed Kanakas came hurrying along the shore towards the *Sempione*.

The boys realized that the visit of the native with the story of Corbière's illness was a 'put-up' job. Few men, especially those of Corbière's build, could have hurried in the tropical sunlight so soon after a heart attack! Obviously it had been another ruse to lure the lads aboard the *Fifine*.

Again foiled in that direction, Corbière was trying other tactics. He was attempting to obtain by force what he could not by pacific means, whether they be fair or foul. To make the situation more desperate, from Ted's and Brian's point of view, the schooner's boat with more armed Kanakas was approaching the ship. It meant that the attack, if forthcoming, would be delivered simultaneously on both sides of the ship.

'Quick!' exclaimed Brian. 'Swing that gun round! I'll get busy with this one!'

Fortunately Ted 'tumbled to it' without stopping to ask why or to raise objections—an awkward habit of his. He knew that the two quick-firers were not effective. There was no ammunition for them; but the crew of the *Fifine* were not to know that.

He sprang to his gun, swung it out and depressed the muzzle until it pointed straight at the approaching boat. Promptly the rowers backed the oars. Meanwhile Brian had trained his gun upon the pot-valiant ex-beachcomber and his men.

'Stop where you are!' he shouted.

'Ze island: does eet belong to you?' demanded Corbière angrily.

'No,' admitted Brian. 'But I'm going to stop you coming on board! Another two paces and I'll plank a shell into the lot of you!'

Although very drunk, Corbière had enough sense left to understand what had been said to him. For the same reason he was very much on his dignity.

'Listen!' he exclaimed. 'You have made assaults on one of my mans!'

'Have we? He was sent by you under false pretences. Is your heart still bad, Captain?'

Corbière ignored the question. Had he answered either 'yes' or 'no', it would have landed him in an awkward situation. 'You make assault on my man,' he continued. 'I come to demand ze satisfaction. I put you under arrest! If you make fire upon me, an officer of France, you are pirates. À la guillotine!'

'Your man tried to drag us off the ship,' declared Brian. 'Off a British ship, you understand. Now, listen! We've had quite enough of you! At this moment the gun on our starboard side is trained on your schooner's waterline. Since none of your crew is on board there will be no loss of life.'

Ted, taking his cue, swung the gun until it pointed to the *Fifine's* stern.

'I'm giving you five minutes,' continued Brian, noting with satisfaction that the threat had a marked effect upon the inebriated man. 'If by the end of that time you and your men are not on board the schooner again we'll open fire and send her to the bottom!'

There was a deadly silence. Brian's heart was thumping violently.

Would Théophile Corbière call his bluff?

Corbière's mind was working slowly. In his befuddled state he was beginning to ask himself what he was doing there. Things weren't shaping exactly as he had planned. Those confounded guns! He had forgotten all about them when he led his crew to board the *Sempione* and place the two English youths under arrest for assaulting one of his crew. And the curious part about it was that he had no recollection of having sent the Kanaka on a false errand until one of the boys had reminded him of it.

Then the threat to the schooner—his *Fifine*!

A retrograde movement on the part of his followers was the final argument. Quick to comprehend actions though they were ignorant of English, they realized that the schooner had been threatened. Apart from their few scanty belongings on board they had no personal interest in her. Provided they weren't in her when she was shelled they wouldn't worry. What did interest them was the promised spectacle of the *Fifine* being sunk by the 'big bangs' of the two white men. They simply must go closer to enjoy the unusual sight!

Captain Corbière followed his men, since, left alone, he felt decidedly uneasy with the muzzle of one of the quick-firers pointed at his moonlike face!

Then another difficulty confronted him. His boat was lying off, since her crew wanted to share the spectacle with the Kanakas ashore. In vain for quite a time he shouted to them to come to the beach and pick him and the others up. The stipulated five minutes was nearly gone!

Brian saw what was happening. Naturally he could do nothing after the time limit was exceeded, so the Frenchman might 'tumble to it' and with renewed confidence return to take forcible possession of the ship.

'Captain!' he hailed. 'I see I'll have to extend the time limit; but make haste and get your men on board!'

Corbière redoubled his shouts; but it was not until Ted had swung the gun until it trained abeam and away from the schooner that the Kanakas, after putting most of the boat's crew on board, rowed ashore for him and the rest of the *Fifine's* hands.

A few minutes later, to the lads' surprise and delight, the sound of the schooner's capstan was heard. The hands were heaving short prior to making sail.

'Good old quick-firers; they did the trick!' exclaimed Ted, with difficulty restraining himself from doing a hornpipe.

Fore and mainsail were set in quick time, and the headsails hoisted in stops ready to break out directly the anchor was apeak.

Although there was no wind in Echo Harbour there was a stiff nor'easterly breeze outside. In consequence, half a dozen Kanakas manned the boat and proceeded to tow the *Fifine* into the lagoon. The last the chums saw of her was when she glided past the headlands guarding the haven, where, her sails filling, the men in the boat had to scramble on board and pass the painter astern.

'Let's go to the top of the rise and see her safely through the reef,' suggested Ted.

Brian was about to fall in with his chum's suggestion when a sudden thought flashed across his mind. 'We'd better hang on here,' he objected.

'Why?'

'It may be a ruse on Corbière's part,' explained Brian. 'Supposing he's left half a dozen men ashore to take us unawares?'

'By Jupiter! I hope you're wrong!' exclaimed Ted.

'So do I. But we can't be too careful.'

For the next three days they remained on board, spending most of the hours of daylight in finishing off their motor boat. There were no signs of the danger that Brian had feared.

The *Fifine* was bowling along on her way back to Papeete. Captain Théophile Corbière had been foiled, but he had anticipated his planned departure only by about twenty-four hours. He had taken the statement quite seriously that the *Sempione* was in wireless communication with the British Crown Colony of the Fiji Islands and that a government surveying vessel, or perhaps an Australian gunboat, was on her way to the rescue. He had no desire to be involved in an argument with British naval officers. It was apt to be too one-sided an argument to suit him, even though he might claim the protection of the French flag.

He had not shot his last bolt. That, he decided, would be a most effective one, even though it meant sacrificing part of the large sum of money he had hoped to make out of the abandoned ship.

XXX

CUT OFF

IN happy ignorance of the rascally Corbière's latest
scheme, Ted and Brian continued their arduous
though engrossing task. The deadwood aft was secured
by a double row of bolts, leaving room between for the
boring of the hole for the propeller shelf. Then the boat
was up-ended once more and the engine replaced. Next
came the job of connecting water-pipes and other skin
fittings and securing the propeller, which, in design,
was a great advance upon their former effort.

After the final coat of paint had been applied they
decided that it was now safe to go ashore again. The
first excursion was to the top of one of the peaks,
whence a careful examination showed that the *Fifine*
was neither in the lagoon nor in the offing.

Next morning one of the derricks was brought into
service and the motor boat hoisted out into the water.
At first, as they had quite expected, considering the
time she had been lying on deck, the boat leaked freely.
They had to spend most of the forenoon armed with
buckets to cope with the inrush.

'It's a good thing we aren't professional East Coast
boat-builders,' observed Brian. 'East Coast of England,
I mean. There they have a custom—or they did have—
by which the builder has to give the owner as much beer
as the boat makes water when she's put afloat for the
first time! By tomorrow she should be as tight as a
bottle. What do you think of her?'

'Not much,' replied Ted with brutal candour. 'She's too heavy. She hasn't enough freeboard. She'll put her bows under in the first sea she meets!'

Brian had to admit the truth of these criticisms. The boat afloat looked a very different proposition from the boat lying on deck and even in the latter situation her lines were not impressive! 'We'll have a trial run to-morrow,' he rejoined. 'And then we can see what she will do. Where are we going to moor her? We don't want another mishap like the last.'

Having taken due precautions in this respect and also having baled the boat out just before sunset, they had an early supper and turned in. For the first time for more than a fortnight they slept undisturbed, now that they were free from the menace of Captain Corbière and his Kanaka crew.

Next morning came the trial run. In spite of Ted's destructive criticism they were greatly elated. Not only was it a new boat, but it was theirs both by construction and ownership.

In spite of her heavy build and ugly design the motor boat handled well and after a few trial runs round the sheltered expanse of Echo Harbour they decided to take her out into the lagoon.

'She's not doing so badly,' declared Brian. 'What do you think she's doing: nine knots?'

Ted looked over the side. They were so close to the surface of the water that it was hard to estimate their speed with any pretence at accuracy.

' 'Bout that!' he agreed. 'I say: we've four tins of petrol aboard. Suppose we make another round trip? Now we know the passage through the rocks, we'll be all right.'

'Good enough! Shall we put back for the rifle?'

'What's the use? We won't want it.'

'Grub then?' persisted Ted.

'We can run ashore for that,' declared Brian. 'Fresh

stuff will be a change. I don't believe in putting back unless it's absolutely necessary.'

They made for the western side of the island so as to tackle the rocky patch between it and the atoll while the tide was on the flood.

'What a difference it makes when you know a place,' remarked Ted, after the narrow, intricate passage had been successfully traversed. 'We were in a bit of a funk when we tried it the first time.'

'Yes, but we lose all the fun of being explorers. It's always the first time when a fellow gets a thrill!'

'Then let's explore that cave we saw last time. That's breaking new ground, if that's what you mean. When's high water?'

'Another three hours, perhaps four. It won't rise more than another couple of feet.'

A few minutes later they rounded the south-eastern corner of the island, off which, but inside the encircling reef, was a bold rock of about an acre in extent. Soon the cave came in sight, its low entrance being situated at the head of a fairly deep creek.

'I say: what about a light?' asked Ted, as he slowed the engine down until it was just ticking over.

'I put my torch in the after locker.'

'Thoughtful fellow, Bags! I believe you meant to have a look at this cave before we set out.'

'I didn't,' declared Brian. 'If you ask me, I can't say why I brought the torch along. Look! There's deep water right into the cave.'

There was. Owing to a sharp turn in the gully the floor of the cave appeared to be just above sea-level. Actually they found on sounding with an oar that there was a depth of about one fathom.

'Switch off the motor, Ted. We'd better row the boat in.'

'I'll row, then, and you stand by with the torch,' suggested Ted as he shipped the rowlocks.

Except for the plash of the oars and the murmur of the wavelets against the interior of the cave it seemed uncannily silent as the boat glided under the low archway.

'Light doesn't seem much good,' said Brian.

'For goodness' sake don't shine the beastly thing straight into my eyes,' protested Ted.

Brian promptly directed the beam upwards. To his surprise the cave, in spite of the low entrance, was quite lofty—probably forty feet in height.

Gradually their eyes grew accustomed to the relatively feeble light of the torch after coming straight in from the dazzling sunlight. Then they discovered that the cave was about forty feet in width, the waterway occupying about one-third. On either side were wide natural 'benches' or platforms composed of irregular slabs of igneous rock. They could form no idea of how far the cave extended; the rays of the torch failed to penetrate into the farthermost recesses.

'Jolly cold, isn't it?' remarked Ted.

It was. Even allowing for the fact that they were wearing only singlet and shorts, there was a distinct chilliness in the air. It was probably fifty or sixty degrees lower than the sun temperature, yet the walls above sea-level seemed to be perfectly dry and without any signs of condensation.

'Beastly cold,' agreed Brian, with chattering teeth. 'Let's get ashore. A little exercise will warm us up!'

The boat ran gently alongside one of the rocky platforms. Before stepping ashore, Brian sounded with the oar. He found no bottom at ten feet.

After a brief search Ted found a projection in the rocks, round which he was able to take a couple of hitches with the painter. 'She'll do!' he declared. 'Mind your step!'

The warning was hardly necessary. Except for the

narrow crevices between the blocks of rock the above-water floor was fairly level; while, contrary to their expectations, the surface was not slippery.

Slowly they made their way inward, shining the torch on the ground as they proceeded and playing it around when they paused to examine their surroundings.

For about a hundred paces the cave ran fairly straight. Then it branched into two passages, each about the same size.

'Which shall we take?' asked Ted.

'Trying to get to the very end?'

'Why not? It's exploring, anyway.'

They decided upon the right-hand branch. A few yards farther the waterway ended abruptly while the floor commenced to slope steeply upwards. The height, too, diminished, while here and there they had to clamber over slabs that, since the formation of this age-long cavern, had fallen from the roof.

'Going to risk it?' asked Ted, when they came to another partial obstruction, leaving a space of about three feet in height between the top of it and the roof of the cave. 'That bit of rock up there doesn't look any too happy!'

'It doesn't,' agreed Brian. 'But since it's been there for centuries it may hold on a bit longer. Give me a leg up, old son, and then hand me the torch.'

With Ted's assistance, Brian heaved himself on top of the rock. Then he directed the beam of the torch into the recess beyond. He gave a gasp of amazement.

'What's up?' asked Ted. 'Don't say we've found a pirate's secret treasure!'

Without replying, Brian carefully laid the torch on the rock. 'Up you come!' he exclaimed. 'I'll give you a hand up.'

At the third attempt Ted succeeded in rejoining his friend. They were then both lying at full length on a slab about seven feet in length and extending the full width of the now narrow passage.

Without another word Brian turned the torch until its beam was again directed into the cave beyond. Instantly the whole place seemed ablaze with sparkling lights. It seemed incredible that the reflected gleam of the electric torch could have met with such a response.

A hundred stalactites met or nearly met a hundred stalagmites. Some were as thick as a man's thigh. Others were as frail as a piece of string! Evidently in the midst of this island of undoubted volcanic action, there was a huge mass of limestone through which, for thousands of years, lime-impregnated water had dropped from some subterranean reservoir above the cave.

For nearly a minute the two boys gazed at the amazing spectacle without speaking a word.

The cave ended in this dome-shaped natural chamber, for its farthermost concave curved wall could be seen between the irregular avenue of stalactites.

They turned and retraced their steps, clambering over the rocky barrier that separated the inner from the outer cave.

'Look out where you're going!' called Brian.

They paused. Another half a dozen steps and they would have stepped into water. The torchlight showed that the flat rocks over which they had come were now covered. It was impossible to distinguish the platform from the deep water of the gully.

'What's happened?' asked Ted.

'Tide's risen.'

'Not good enough! The rise at springs is only about four feet. There'll be six feet above the place where we moored the boat.'

'And that means we're cut off,' added Brian. 'The mouth of the cave will be well under water.'

'I hope I gave the boat enough painter.'

At this alarming suggestion the peril of the situation became more apparent. Being trapped in the cave was bad enough although sooner or later the tide would recede. If, however, the painter was too short, the rising tide would have taken the boat under. The weight of the engine would sink her like a stone.

This, in itself, was a catastrophe—a swift and depressing end to all their labours—but that was not all. To get to dry land would entail a swim of nearly a mile through the shark-infested lagoon.

'We'll have to get to the boat somehow!' declared Brian. 'How much longer will the torch last? The refill must have been in for some time.'

'Then I hope it lasts out. It looks as if we're to be trapped here for several hours.'

'Yes, but when will that be?' rejoined Brian. 'It must be a tidal wave. Listen! That noise isn't the rollers on the reef. It's much nearer. There must be a storm raging and the breakers are sweeping across the lagoon on the shore.'

Faintly yet distinctly could be heard the regular boom of the waves. Even the previously quiet water inside the cave was affected by the undulations without.

Guided by the downward rays of the torch that enabled them to distinguish between the recently exposed rocks and the gully, Ted and Brian waded in. Soon the level was well above their knees and was deepening steadily. Curiously enough, although the air in the cave was piercingly cold, the water was warm.

No longer was there the light streaming in through the entrance to guide them. The arch was now a good way beneath the surface. Somewhere between it and the two youths was their motor boat—either afloat or lying on the bottom of the subterranean creek.

Pausing, Brian directed his torch towards the spot where they had left their craft. Thanks be! She was still there, looking, with her low freeboard, more like a floating log than a boat.

'We'll have to swim for it and be quick about it,' declared Brian. 'The painter is already pinning her bows down!'

Holding the torch above the surface, he began to swim, followed by his unencumbered companion. Before they had made more than a few strokes they were conscious of a distinct change in the temperature of the water. Near the surface it was warm since it was being fed by the sun-heated sea. Beneath, it was unpleasantly cold. For some reason, possibly because the salt and fresh water did not readily mingle, the former had formed a layer over the cold stream that had its source somewhere in the very recesses of this mysterious cave.

With feelings of relief the lads grasped the boat's side. Ted was about to climb in when Brian restrained him.

'Her bows are nearly under!' he announced. 'Our extra weight will sink her. Get your knife and cut the rope!'

Treading water, Ted drew his sheath knife. One hack was sufficient to sever the tautened painter, which was taking a big strain. The boat's bows, released from the tension, leapt six inches into the air and narrowly missed Ted's shoulder as they dropped back with a resounding splash that echoed along the cave like the roll of a drum.

Quickly the two lads hoisted themselves out of the water and into the boat. They were conscious of two things: that their wet scanty clothing was feeling unpleasantly cold, and that the boat was adrift.

'What headroom have we?' asked Ted.

Brian played the rays of the torch upon the roof. 'About ten feet, I should say.'

'Good enough. There's not much chance of the tide

rising and pinning us against the roof. Beastly cold, isn't it?'

'Cold isn't the word for it. If we could start the motor that would warm us up.'

'And we'd probably be gassed by the fumes. I tell you what: strip and wring out your togs. I'm going to do it.'

Wondering what Ted had in mind, Brian did so. Then, pouring a quantity of engine oil into the baler, the Welsh youth proceeded first to soak Brian's clothes and then his own in the viscous fluid. It had been in his mind to warm the oil-saturated things over the cylinder-block, but by this time the engine was stone-cold.

Before replacing their shirts and singlets they rubbed themselves down with the excess oil and derived considerable benefit from the vigorous exertion. Then when they had reclothed themselves they found that they were warmer than they had been since they had first entered the cave.

'The light is getting a bit down,' declared Ted.

It was. At most the battery would not last more than another half an hour. The prospect of spending perhaps the rest of the day in utter darkness was appalling.

'I'll switch it off, then,' decided Brian. 'We may want it badly later on.'

'Let's hope not. All right, let's see where we are first.'

The boat had drifted over the platform upon which the explorers had landed, and which was now six feet beneath the surface. She was rubbing gently against the wall of the cave, but the problem was how to secure her to prevent her drifting aimlessly into the recesses where, when the tide fell, she would be immovably stranded.

The feeble light showed a deep narrow fissure about three feet above the water level. Into this Ted pushed an oar and to the latter he bent the short end of the severed painter.

Then Brian switched off the lamp. The darkness was not only profound, it seemed to have weight and to press upon their now unseeing eyes. Their long, anxious and unpleasant vigil had fairly begun. They had lost all count of time. They felt too cold and miserable to talk, except to exchange a few more or less hopeful remarks upon the situation. At intervals they switched on the torch in order to examine the level of the water against the side of the cave. It was still rising, though slowly.

By now they were ravenously hungry, though Ted magnanimously refrained from reminding Brian that he had declined the suggestion to bring food with them. The fact remained that though coconuts and other fruits were growing perhaps within a hundred feet above them, they were as effectually cut off from food and drink as if they were shipwrecked mariners on a raft in the middle of the ocean!

It was too cold for them to seek solace in sleep. Like the Ancient Mariner, they had water everywhere but not a drop to drink. Even the walls of the cave above the abnormal sea-level were bone-dry.

Presently, hoping against hope, for the time of high water should have been hours ago, Brian switched on the light. 'Tide's falling!' he announced.

'Sure?'

'Certain of it!'

'Then we'll have to keep a sharp watch,' continued Ted. 'We don't want the boat left stuck on these rocks. She's too heavy for us to move if she gets left.'

At intervals they sounded. Presently they had to cast loose the painter and remove the oar. Already the level had dropped a little more than two feet.

About an hour later they had to shift the boat into deep water. By this time there was only about a foot over the platform, which meant that the entrance to the cave was open to the lagoon without.

A new situation now arose. The mouth of the cave being no longer submerged, the breakers without had a fairly unimpeded flow into the cavern. Instead of gently undulating, the surface was now considerably agitated. Great care had to be taken to keep the boat clear of the rocks, which, in spite of her massive construction, would smash her sides in if she were lifted by the waves and flung upon them. While these breakers were dashing shorewards it would have been foolhardy, even fatal, to attempt to take the motor boat out of the cave. The lads' term of detention was by no means over.

As the tide fell still farther, the mouth of the cave presented a perplexing problem. Through the darkness a constantly changing arc of pale light was visible at almost regular intervals, accompanied by the sound of foam sweeping against and receding from the cliffs.

Presently Brian 'tumbled to it'. It was now night. The sudden storm accompanying a big tidal wave was subsiding. The gleam they could see was the moonlight playing upon the white-capped breakers which, as they surged into the cave, momentarily eclipsed the segment of light. With the uncovering of the entrance the din increased, rising and falling in weird cadence and echoing distinctly through the pitch-black cavern.

There were now no moments of inaction for the two hungry and fugitive youths. For hours they had to remain alert, fending off with their oars in the darkness to prevent the now menacing rollers from hurling their craft upon the sides of the gully. The setting of the moon once more deprived them of even the faint reflected light. Their torch, when it was brought into use, gave only a feeble reddish glow.

'How much longer to daylight?' asked Ted.

'I don't know,' confessed Brian.

'Directly it's light outside we'll make a dash for it.'

'The boat would be swamped even if she escaped being dashed upon the rocks,' protested Brian.

'There's a chance she won't be,' persisted Ted. 'Anything's better than being cooped up in this horrible hole.'

Brian was almost inclined to agree with him. On the other hand, the motor boat, with her absurdly low freeboard, was ill-designed to punch into seas of any magnitude. Should she be swamped there was no shore for half a mile where the swimmers could land— nothing but sheer cliffs against which the breakers, unchecked by the now submerged reefs, were surging with impetuous fury.

At last the sudden tropical dawn. The welcome golden rays of the sun as it rose above the horizon seemed to floodlight the cave. Yet it had its disadvantages; the glare blinded the two lads as effectively as had the intense darkness.

In a few minutes the rays no longer poured directly into the cave. In the semi-gloom the companions waited for their eyes to grow accustomed to the new conditions. The sea had subsided with the dawn; probably owing to the calm usually preceding and immediately following the rising of the sun. Rollers instead of breakers were setting in, and definitely becoming smaller and slower.

'Now's our chance!' exclaimed Brian.

Ted required no urging. With visions of warmth and food awaiting him, he tackled the engine to discover for the first time that his benumbed hands were covered with broken and unbroken blisters after hours of fending off with one of the oars.

Being stone-cold, the motor did not fire until the dog-tired lads each gave half a dozen frantic swings with the starting-handle. When she did start, the motor fired with no uncertain voice, filling the cave with the deafening reports of her noisy exhaust.

Without the aid of the engine the boat could not have made her way out. Oars would have been useless in an attempt to make headway against the rollers.

Into the dazzling sunshine she dashed, although Ted had given her only quarter throttle. She rose to the first wave, dipped her bows to the second—luckily without shipping much water—and rode the rest like a duck.

Half an hour later the young adventurers, cheered by the prospect of food and rest, entered Echo Harbour.

XXXI

CHECKMATED

'FRIGHTFUL stench of sulphur, isn't there?' remarked Brian, as the motor boat glided across the harbour towards the *Sempione*.

Ted merely grunted uninterestedly. After their adventures of the last twenty hours he wasn't going to show any interest in sulphurous fumes; especially with satisfying grub within a hundred yards of the rapidly moving boat.

The next instant the centre of the sheltered haven was agitated by what looked like a huge bubble. It *was* one of sorts, rising like a balloon on the point of being inflated, to a height of about a foot above the surrounding surface.

Brian at the tiller promptly put the helm hard over. The boat swung round, missing the edge of the enormous bubble by about twice its own length. Her wash splashed against the thin air cushion. There was a faint though distinct *pop*. Up shot a cloud of yellowish vapour. The atmosphere reeked of sulphurous fumes that enveloped the boat and made the two youths gasp for breath and the stiff craft to rock violently.

'What was that? A submarine volcano?' asked Ted, as they eased down to come alongside the ship.

'Either that or something very like it,' replied Brian. 'Ugh! What a smell on an empty tummy! . . . Right-o; switch off! I've got her!'

Ted cut off the ignition as his companion grasped the

Jacob's ladder. Then the Welsh youth had to swarm up in order to fetch a rope to take the place of the cut painter. He returned with a startled look on his face. 'Someone's been on board, Bags!' he announced.

'How do you know?'

' 'Cause the gangway to the shore has been removed!'

'Removed? That blighter Corbière back?'

Fatigue temporarily banished, the lads climbed on board and went straight to the cabin. Nothing appeared to have been disturbed. They picked up their firearms and felt safer with the loaded weapons in their hands. 'Tween decks the smell of sulphur was even more pronounced than in the open.

Still they could find no traces of intruders. They went to the entry-port. Here they found that the gangway had been violently wrenched away, leaving only the twisted metal rod to which the end had been secured. The partly wrecked accommodation ladder, which had been left lowered, had been still further damaged. Going aft they discovered the gang planks, still secured side by side, floating under the ship's counter.

Then they 'tumbled to it'. The tidal wave that had kept them prisoners in the cave had swept round the island. Probably the result of some enormous disturbance of the ocean bed hundreds of miles away, the wall of water had advanced to upset the calculations in the *Nautical Almanac*. One of its effects was to lift the *Sempione* so high that the gangway was not long enough to span the increased distance between the ship and the shore, with the result that the shoreward end swung back with considerable violence against the ship's side. That, so far as could be seen, was the only damage.

'Thank goodness it's no worse!' exclaimed Brian. 'Come on; let's get our grub!'

In some respects Brian and Ted resembled a pair of

beavers. When any of their constructive works went wrong, they lost very little time in either renewing or repairing. So, next day, after a long and refreshing sleep, they began to re-establish communication with the shore. The accommodation ladder did not matter; they had no further use for it. The gangway was another proposition. Without it the only means they had of going to and from the ship was the boat, with all the attendant inconveniences of having to use the rope-ladder and to make the little craft fast to the tide-affected beach.

Incidentally they had discovered the secret of how to live happily on an uninhabited island. That is, to keep the body and mind active. As long as they had definite tasks on hand—so far there had been no lack of them—they had no cause for regret that circumstances had brought the disabled *Sempione* to the reef-encircled island. On the other hand, when they had moments for leisure and reflection they began to hanker after news of the outside world and wonder how events were shaping regarding the war between Bolomaya and Grossaguay, particularly as they affected Brian's father.

It took them three days to salvage the planks and rebuild the gangway. Profiting by their experience, they made it after the style of a drawbridge with stout ropes leading from the shore end to blocks secured to the edge of the boat-deck. If other abnormally high tides occurred, the bridge would lift with the ship instead of slipping from the bank and crashing against the *Sempione's* side.

All this time living on board was not a pleasant existence, on account of the strong sulphurous fumes that, owing to a lack of wind, hung persistently over Echo Harbour. There were, however, no more sub-marine eruptions—or if they took place, it was during the night—and on the next day, a gentle breeze spring-

ing up, the atmosphere regained its former state
of purity.

For the next three weeks they led an ideal existence.
The weather continued perfect, an almost constant
breeze from the sea tempering the tropical heat. They
worked, fed and slept, and also made several excursions
in the motor boat. But they gave the cave a wide berth.
One experience of being trapped by the tide in that
mysterious cavern, they decided, was enough for a
lifetime.

Meanwhile events were moving, thanks to the mis-
guided efforts of Captain Théophile Corbière.

On leaving Echo Harbour he had shaped a course
for Papeete. Under normal conditions the *Fifine*, which
had a clean pair of heels, should have made the voyage
in four days. Owing to a heavy gale that blew her out
of her course and a succession of calms it was seventeen days before the schooner dropped anchor in her
home port.

At the first opportunity Captain Corbière went
ashore with the intention of calling upon a Captain
Dubois, head of the *Société des Chantiers et Ateliers
de Papeete*, a firm that also specialized in salvage
operations. Unfortunately for his visitor, Captain
Dubois was away on a job on another of the Society
Islands, and was not expected back for a week. Corbière
spent a convivial evening with some of his beach-
combing pals and was carried on board the *Fifine* in a
helpless condition by some of his crew. There he remained for three days before he was able to think
coherently. Several of the Kanakas took advantage of
their employer's condition to slip ashore, which was
another unlucky thing, as far as Corbière was concerned.

Actually Dubois returned to Papeete four days
earlier than he had been expected, but it was not until

forty-eight hours later that Corbière, hearing that the salvage expert was back, called at the Company's offices.

'What brings you here, Théophile?' asked Dubois bluntly, for he had no great liking for the captain of the *Fifine*. 'Another loan? If so, it is impossible.'

'No,' replied Corbière with an ugly leer. 'It is business—mutual advantage—this time.'

'I have heard that story before.'

'Pardon. Not this one.'

'Proceed, *mon brave*,' invited Dubois, ostentatiously placing a bottle and a couple of glasses on the table. 'But be prepared if I think fit to decline what offer you may make.'

'Are we in danger of being overheard?' whispered his caller.

'It would be a bad day for them if any of my staff were caught listening to any conversation in this room. Now proceed, but be brief. I am, as you are aware, a busy man.'

'A month ago,' began Corbière, 'I put into Tula Ni, as the *Fifine* wanted her copper cleaned. There I found a ship—a British ship—moored fore and aft with only two boys on board.'

'And her name?'

'*Sempione*.'

A flash of recognition lighted up the salvage officer's eyes. 'Proceed, Théophile.'

'I offered them a passage here. They refused. That was, I think, because they imagined they would lose their chance of a share of the salvage.'

'That they certainly would,' agreed Dubois, adding sarcastically, 'And so you drugged them and took them on board the *Fifine*? Might I ask what became of them?'

'You misunderstand! They were as suspicious as a pair of Paris *gamins*. So I left and came here to put a proposition before you.'

'And the proposition is?'

'That you send one of your tugs to tow her to Papeete. An order from the Governor giving you authority will be sufficient to compel these two youths to submit. Then we share the salvage money, less your charges. Also you will deduct that trifling sum for which I am at present in your debt.' Having stated his terms, the Captain of the *Fifine* licked his lips and glanced meaningly at the bottle.

Dubois ignored the unspoken hint. Rising from his chair, he took down a book from a rack, opened it at the last written page and placed it on the desk in front of his visitor. 'Be so good as to read this,' he said calmly.

The Captain of the *Fifine* stared at the recently written lines with his bleared eyes. He wasn't quick at reading the sloping handwriting, with its elaborate flourishes.

'The firm's order book written up by me,' explained Dubois helpfully.

Corbière's jaw dropped as he read: 'To Capitaine Le Blanc, steam tug *Tityre*: you will proceed with all despatch to Tula Ni, there to pick up the disabled ship, name unknown, now lying there, and bring her in tow to Papeete.' This was followed by the hour and the day of the month. Dubois had written Le Blanc's instructions only forty minutes before Corbière arrived!

'So you see, Théophile——' he continued.

'But yes!' interrupted Corbière. 'Surely you will agree to my proposition?'

Dubois, who had good cause to remember certain unsavoury incidents in his visitor's past, shook his head. 'I do not pay for useless information,' he replied. 'Although, unhappily, I have done so twice before on your account. You have, however, imparted one item of news for which I am prepared to recompense you. Until a few minutes ago I was unaware of the ship's name. For that information I am agreeable to remit your debt to us.'

It was cheap at the price, especially as there was little likelihood of Captain Corbière settling the debt otherwise.

After unavailing protests Corbière broke into a torrent of curses and threats. Up jumped the wiry little Dubois. Without troubling to call upon his clerks to eject his unwelcome and abusive visitor, he gripped his still spluttering compatriot by the ears, swung him round and planted a splendid kick right between his shoulder-blades.

Corbière stood not upon the order of his going.

Little did he guess that he had been forestalled, not by the skipper of some other craft, as he thought, but by one of his crew. The Kanaka had given Dubois the information, except that he did not know the name of the disabled ship, with sufficient accuracy to show that the job promised to be a paying proposition. The native had gone off very well satisfied with the sum that the head of the Salvage Company had given him.

Taking down a Mercantile Shipping List, Dubois looked up the *Sempione*. There he discovered that she was not under the British flag—Corbière had mis-informed him on that point—but was owned by a Catamarcan firm. That made him sit up and take notice. He wasn't exactly sure but——

He touched a bell. 'Bring me the latest list of ships overdue and missing,' he said to the half-caste clerk who answered the summons.

It was quite a short list, but it gave him the infor-mation he desired. The *Sempione* was given as 'missing, believed lost' on a voyage between Santa Teresa and La Serena. Her insured value was also given.

Dubois was an honest man and strict in his financial dealings. He began calculating his firm's profits after all expenses had been paid—presuming that the towage to Papeete was successfully accomplished. Then there were also the charges for repairs, although he did not know to what extent the *Sempione* had sustained damage. Undoubtedly the work would be entrusted to the firm.

Then he remembered that there were two British subjects on board her. They must have a fair share of the salvage receipts. That was just, but he must first ascertain what part they played in navigating the ship to Tula Ni. Also, there was the question of what had happened to the officers and crew. Surely these two *garçons* who had resisted the ruffianly Corbière's efforts to remove them were not young desperadoes who by some means had overcome the ship's company and had seized the Catamarcan vessel?

Dubois recalled similar instances, but these had involved small trading schooners manned by natives under brutal white officers. Again there was the case of a large steamship whose entire crew succumbed to a virulent tropical disease. The only survivors were two English passengers—and they were boys, he remembered—who managed to get the ship ashore on the island of Kilba which is only three hundred miles nor'east of Tula Ni. Was the *Sempione* a parallel case?

Captain Dubois sat down and wrote a letter in English, addressing the envelope to 'Les Messieurs in charge, S.S. *Sempione*.' Then he summoned his tug-master, Captain Le Blanc. 'You will be ready to depart this evening?'

'Assuredly, sir!'

'Good! Take this letter and hand it to the two English youths you will find on board the vessel. Her name is the *Sempione*, I have discovered. These boys must be treated with every consideration. They may either remain in the *Sempione* or join the *Tityre*, whichever they prefer. *Bon voyage*, Capitaine Le Blanc. I shall expect to see you back within ten days.'

XXXII

THE *TITYRE* ARRIVES

'WHAT do you make of her, Bags?'
Brian lowered his binoculars and handed them
to his companion. 'Dashed if I know,' he replied. 'She's
not a sailing craft, so she's not the *Fifine*.'

'She's a steamer—not a motor craft,' decided Ted.
'I can make out the smoke. There's not much of it;
Welsh coal, perhaps, from Cardiff.'

The lads had climbed to the summit of the higher
peak—actually it was not more than twenty feet above
that of the other—and having taken a pair of glasses
with them, had been amusing themselves by examining
their domain and its surroundings from their elevated
position. Then away to the sou'west'ard they had
spotted a small object that presently resolved itself
into a moving vessel. At first they could neither determine her direction nor her speed, even through the
binoculars. A few minutes later she was appreciably
nearer, but the watchers were still under the impression
that on her present course she would pass some miles
to the south'ard of the island.

'Yes, she's a steamship,' agreed Brian, after taking
the glasses again. 'She's almost bows-on. She's making
for the island. Botheration! She's flying the French
flag, too!'

'Pals of that outsider Corbière, I don't doubt,' declared Ted. 'She'll be inside the reefs in less than an

hour. We'd better get a move on, if we don't want them to find a deserted ship!'

They hurried down the peak until they reached the spot where they had left their sea-boots. Although this heavy footgear was invaluable in crossing the swampy ground it had been discarded in favour of rope-soled canvas shoes—known on both sides of the North American continent as 'sneakers'—when it came to the actual ascent and descent of the peak.

From this point, although for the most part of the way there was a gentle down gradient, the lads' speed was decidedly reduced, not only on account of the cumbersome boots, but of the rough nature of the ground.

Hot and tired, they crossed the gangway and gained the *Sempione's* deck. Here they waited in momentary expectation of seeing the strange vessel's bows gliding between the bluffs that guarded the entrance to Echo Harbour. Now that she was approaching the island and might well be inside the reefs, they seemed to take it for granted that her objective was the *Sempione*.

'What's to be our course of action when she arrives?' asked Ted.

'We'll have to see what their attitude is towards us first,' replied Brian. 'We're not going to be made to abandon the *Sempione*, if we can avoid it, though!'

'Rather not! Doing anything with these?' Ted pointed to each of the quick-firers, useless except for purposes of intimidation.

Brian shook his head. 'Nothing doing!' he replied. 'If the Frenchman is a government vessel there'll be a most unholy row if we start any monkey tricks like that. They may take us for lineal descendants of the Buccaneers of Boya, and they vanished from the Pacific some years after the First World War. No! Discretion and a hint in due season concerning our dud wireless are our trump cards! Hello!'

A long blast from a ship's siren seemed to shatter the sultry air.

'She evidently means to let us know she's here,' remarked Ted.

The lads relapsed into silence, their hearts beating a little more rapidly than usual. Their eyes were fixed upon the gap that formed the entrance to the natural harbour. Metaphorically, was it a wolf or a sheep that was about to thrust its head into their room?

'Here she is!' exclaimed Brian.

The bluff, grey-painted bows bearing the name *Tityre* glided into view. Then a stumpy foremast with three empty lamp holders arranged vertically; next the bridge, on which were two white uniformed officers; the two funnels, each bearing the design in blue of the Gallic cock; a boat in davits; the mainmast, displaying a rather frayed tricolour; and finally the rounded stern with its double-arched towing horse.

There was no mistaking her nationality and her occupation. She was a powerful ocean-going tug. Although her engines were running at 'slow' as she swung her bows to starboard, the effect of her displacement was soon apparent. The *Sempione*, although by far the larger craft, surged forward to the full extent of her wire hawsers as if to greet the new arrival.

Now she was almost bows-on. Some of her native crew hurried for'ard. One of them held aloft a heavage line. Possibly others were doing the same thing aft, although hidden from sight by the 'midship super-structure.

'She's coming alongside us!' exclaimed Ted.

'We can't stop her. We'd better get the boat out of her way.'

'She is,' explained Ted. 'I shifted her under our counter. I suppose we'd better take her wires?'

The *Tityre's* engine-room telegraph bell clanged.

Simultaneously the blue, white and red ensign was dipped from her mainmast head.

'She's saluting!' said Brian. 'Pity we haven't an ensign to dip in return. Stand by! I'll go aft and take her bow rope.'

On glided the *Tityre*, engines now stopped, but carrying a considerable amount of way. Although she had a big 'pudding' fender over her bows and a thick plaited rope fender extending from stem to stern, her crew were placing 'faggot' fenders in position along her starboard side.

'She's going too fast,' thought Brian. 'She'll give us a frightful biff!'

His fears were groundless. The bell tinkled sharply again. Two streams of creamy froth leapt from under the tug's quarter, surging far ahead of her bows. The tug seemed to stop dead with less than a yard separating her from the relatively towering sides of the ship. Another clang and the powerful twin engines became silent.

Brian caught the heaving line thrown him and thanked his lucky stars that he had sufficient knowledge of seamanship to know what to do with it. A landlubber would probably take a turn with it, thinking that it was sufficient to secure the other craft alongside! He heaved away until the bowlined wire rope came inboard. The loop he passed over a bollard and then he raised his hand to signify 'All fast!'

He hoped that Ted was equally successful at his end. As it happened, Ted hadn't disgraced himself under the critical eyes of the Second Mate of the *Tityre*.

His task completed, Brian hurried amidships where he was almost on a level with the wing of the tug's bridge. On it was the French skipper, a tall, thin-faced man with blue eyes and a closely trimmed auburn beard. To Brian's surprise, he saluted and handed him a sealed letter, but made no attempt to send either his Kanaka crew or his subordinate officer on board.

'This is for us, old son!' Brian announced as Ted rejoined him.

'Then why not see what it says?' was Ted's practical suggestion.

Brian opened the envelope and withdrew a sheet of paper with the printed heading: *Société des Chantiers et Ateliers de Papeete—*

Dear Sirs,

I am the director of the above-mentioned establishment and tender you my respectful salutations.

I am dispatching the Capitaine Le Blanc with the tugboat *Tityre* for the purpose of taking the disabled ship named *Sempione* to our works at Papeete for repairs and for delivery to her owners. Mindful of the services you have rendered, although I have received no particulars, I offer you (*a*) a free passage either in the *Sempione* or the *Tityre* to Papeete (*b*) a free passage either to London or any other part you desire (*c*) a share of the salvage money later to be decided, but not less than fifteen per centum (*d*) an immediate advance of cash upon your arrival at Papeete, which amount will be deducted from your share of the salvage money decided upon by the Court.

I trust this arrangement is to your entire satisfaction.

Accept, gentlemen, the assurance of my perfect consideration.

JEAN DUBOIS,
Directeur.

'That seems quite a decent proposition,' observed Ted. 'You can't see any flaw in it, can you?'

'Not on the face of it,' replied Brian cautiously. 'It gives us a title, so to speak. No one would risk contesting it in a court of law.'

'So we'll accept?'

'It means leaving the island.'

'The place would be pretty hopeless without the *Sempione*. Apparently this Dubois has authority to take her away.'

'I suppose so. We'd better tell the skipper of the tug to get on with it!'

They went to the side and addressed Captain Le Blanc, who was patiently waiting on the bridge of the *Tityre*.

'It's all right, sir!' announced Brian. 'You can start as soon as you like. We'll remain on board here.'

'I no spik *anglais*, monsieur,' declared Le Blanc with a despairing wave of his hands. 'You spik *français, peut-être?*'

'*Un peu*, monsieur,' replied Brian diffidently.

The skipper of the *Tityre* rapped out a question Brian couldn't make head nor tail of. There wasn't one word that sounded at all familiar to him.

'Perhaps I put my oar in!' exclaimed the mate of the tug, who had been keeping in the background. 'Ah, yes, I speak your language—me, I sell onion in England five-six year past!'

Brian thankfully expressed his gratitude. The mate, who introduced himself as Monsieur Paul Babord, had started his career as a deck-hand on a Brittany onion-boat plying between Concarneau and Southampton, whence he had graduated by means of a berth in a Messageries liner to the post of mate in the service of the admirable Captain Dubois.

'When you ready to make start?' he asked, prompted by the now voluble Le Blanc.

'As soon as you like,' replied Brian.

Now that they had decided to go, there seemed little object in delaying their departure. A few hours ago they were serenely contemplating an indefinite stay on this lonely Pacific island. Now, civilization called them. They were all agog to hear and see for themselves what the world was doing.

'Ver' good!' exclaimed Babord. 'I send some of my mans to take in warps. Then they heave up anchors and off we go!'

At his bidding four natives put off in a boat to unbend the hawser that held the *Sempione* to the shore.

'I say! What about our boat?' asked Ted.

That was a problem. After having built it and installed an engine, they were reluctant to leave it behind. On the other hand, it was not going to be of any use to them, since they were leaving Papeete by the first available vessel. They explained the situation to Paul Babord.

He consulted Le Blanc, who went aft to examine the amateur-built craft. She wasn't much to look at, he decided. Yet she was strongly-built—most decidedly so. And that engine—it looked a powerful motor. He would offer these young Englishmen a small sum. Surely, in the circumstances, they would accept. Then in Papeete, he could easily sell the boat at a very handsome profit.

He sauntered back. Experience had taught him that if you wish to drive a good bargain haste or even the slightest display of eagerness was a mistake.

The plan of campaign was then explained to Monsieur Babord. Of course there would be a handsome *douceur* for him.

The Breton was not satisfied. He, too, came from a race that acquired modest riches by dint of haggling over sales and purchases.

The return of the unmooring party prompted the two Frenchmen to come to an arrangement. The mate approached the two lads and smiled disarmingly.

'She is a ver' old tub,' he began.

'No; quite new!'

'Possibly. You yourselves knock her together?'

In his English conversation the Breton had picked up numerous sea terms which he introduced, often with comical results.

Brian agreed that he and Ted were the naval

architects, builders and marine engineers responsible for the craft under discussion.

'Capitaine Le Blanc offers to buy her from you,' announced Monsieur Babord.

'Dash it all! She's not ours to sell,' rejoined Brian. 'We took the motor out of the ship and——'

'Ah, *bien*! It is impossible to make a deal. I tell ze Capitaine.'

Le Blanc had retired into the wheelhouse to await his subordinate's report. That exceeded his expectations. Excellent. The boat was legally part of the *Sempione's* equipment. He'd have her hoisted on board the *Tityre*. There was no necessity to explain her presence to his employer. A little arrangement with Babord and the craft could be conveniently sold after the English boys had left Papeete. He was quite a bit of money to the good already.

He whisked out of the wheelhouse, issued a string of orders with pantomimic accompaniment. The motor boat was brought alongside the tug, slings were adjusted in remarkably quick time, and within five minutes the boys' masterpiece was reposing on the tug's fore hatch.

Meanwhile the Kanakas had unshipped the gangway. Others in the *Sempione's* fo'c'sle were preparing to weigh the anchor by hand.

'Let them,' said Brian. 'They're running the show, not us. Why should we start the donkey engine?'

'They look beefy enough for the job,' rejoined Ted. 'Bit spindly about the legs, but they've got chests and arms on them!'

The capstan bars were inserted and manned. A native with a sort of ukelele perched himself upon the top of the capstan. Probably he had acquired this habit from his father whose father had seen the crews of British old-time sailing craft heaving up the anchor to the accompaniment of fiddle and sea-chanty.

16

'*Allez!*' shouted the mate, and the naked feet began to patter on the deck. A dozen voices broke into song, almost drowning the lilt of the stringed instrument and the slow rumble of the stud-linked cable.

Ted and Brian had been so intent upon watching the operation that they had not noticed the tug cast off until they saw her glide ahead and take up the strain of the wire towing hawser. Almost before they were aware of it, the *Sempione* gathered way.

They were leaving the island, no doubt for good.

XXXIII

FAREWELL TO THE ISLAND

THERE was no doubt about Captain Le Blanc's knowledge of the island's approaches. He did not attempt the narrow passage through the reefs by which the *Sempione*, more by good luck than anything else, had arrived. Instead, he skirted the nor'eastern end of the island and took the channel opposite the point where Brian and Ted had once seen seals fearlessly disporting themselves.

'Look! They're still there!' exclaimed Ted, pointing to the gently shelving ledge.

There must have been hundreds of seals either sunning themselves on the rocks or gambolling in the water, without paying the slightest attention to the squat tug and her much larger tow until the skipper tugged the siren lanyard.

The raucous bellow blared out in a farewell salute to Tula Ni. Instantly there was a terrific commotion ashore. The basking seals, frightened as they had never been before, floundered to the edge of the rocks and dived awkwardly into the lagoon, whose waters were already agitated by the almost simultaneous disappearance of the amphibian swimmers. In half a minute a hundred, perhaps more, seals had sought a secure refuge amongst the coral forests on the bed of the lagoon.

Round swung the tug, pivoting on the huge towing-hook just abaft the mainmast. The *Sempione* followed, taking a wider sweep as the French mate, who had remained with part of the tug's crew, put the helm hard over.

Seaward they headed until the almost forgotten lift of the *Sempione* to the ocean rollers reminded the lads that they were actually at sea. The *Tityre* slowed down. The towing hawser was shackled to a length of cable, to the other end of which another span of wire was made fast. Then the tug forged ahead again with thrice her original length of towing gear between her and the ship—the chain acting as a spring to ease any heavy jerks in a seaway.

'We must make the most of it,' declared Brian. 'It's our last trip in the old *Sempione*. Babord says we'll be in Papeete Harbour in three days.'

They had left the island without regrets. These would come, but would be retrospective. Nor did they bother themselves about the immediate future. They were indeed fortunate in being able to live in the present and make the most of it.

It was a strange experience to them—who had known so many. Instead of moving sluggishly through the water under the pressure of the wind upon a few square feet of canvas, the *Sempione* was slipping along at a steady nine knots in the wake of the powerful twin-screw tug. But the thing that impressed them was the almost complete silence. There was no rumble of machinery, with its accompanying vibrations—nothing but the plash of the waves against the bows and the high-pitched, cheerfully sounding voices of the Kanakas. The one thing that mattered, as far as Brian and Ted were concerned, was their forced inaction. Hitherto they had been responsible, to the best of their ability, for the navigation of the ship. Now they were mere passengers, warned by the amiable Babord not to take the wheel, since that would be 'losing face' in the eyes of the natives.

No longer had they to obtain their own meals. They 'messed' with the mate in the saloon, attended by a native and provided with dishes that lost none of their savour by having been prepared by a Kanaka cook.

In the evening they paced the deck with the mate, trying to pick up the severed threads of news. Babord could tell them plenty about his visits to England, of his life in Brittany and of his probably grossly exaggerated adventures amongst the islands of the Pacific.

'How's the war between Bolomaya and Grossaguay getting on?' asked Ted.

The Frenchman shrugged his shoulders. 'I tink *c'est la guerre* but it is a ver' little one,' he remarked. 'It is too far to be of advantage to us. No salvage, understand!'

That was all the information on that subject that he was able to give. Unless there was money to be made out of it—he would not object to taking a few risks as a gunrunner—a war in South America simply didn't interest him.

Just before sunset on the third day the bold ranges of Tahiti showed above the horizon. At four o'clock in the morning, while it was yet dark, the rumble of the *Sempione's* cable announced that the voyage, as far as Brian Steele and Ted Evans were concerned, was over.

They had packed most of their belongings overnight. President Bombardo's letter to General Sandano, still intact in the covering envelope to Señor Madeira, was safely under lock and key in Brian's suitcase. They were taking away from the ship nothing more than they had brought in material things, but they had collected a wealth of practical experience that would stand them in good stead in the future.

Captain Dubois was on board early and brimming over with good humour. He had already informed the Catamarcan owners, greatly to their delighted surprise, of the *Sempione's* impending arrival, and had secured a provisional contract for the necessary refit and repairs. One of his first acts on greeting Brian and Ted was to hand them the agreed sum on account of their share in the salving of the ship.

'There is a mail boat leaving for Panama on Monday,' he announced. 'From there you can easily return to England.'

'Can you tell us what has happened in the war between Bolomaya and Grossaguay, sir?' asked Brian.

'*Mais oui!* It is finished! Bombardo has fled. It would seem as if the Bolomayans have had enough of him and now General Sandano is head of the new government.'

Brian thought for a few moments. 'Can one telegraph to Bolomaya from here?' he inquired.

'Assuredly—by cable. I myself cabled to La Serena, which, as you know, is on that part of the coast, and I had a reply within eight hours.'

'Good! When we go ashore, Ted, I'll send a message to Dad. Of course, he may have left the Estancia Miraflores and be on his way home by this time.'

'What do you propose to do until Monday?' asked Dubois. 'You can either remain here or, if you desire, you can be my guests in my small house.'

The boys unhesitatingly decided to accept the Frenchman's hospitality. It was good to be in civilization again and Papeete was a flourishing outpost of France's colonial empire.

Then they had a shock! Dubois' little house was quite an extensive building, beautifully furnished and fitted with almost every modern convenience. And what a luxury it was to recline in a large porcelain bath nearly filled with hot *fresh* water!

Brian sent off his cable. It cost him a lot of money and he wondered whether he'd get that back if the cable could not be delivered.

Just before sunset came the reply, sent off from

Camata—so Mr. Steele hadn't left the Estancia Mira-flores!—via Santa Teresa and Panama.

'*Awaitu here.*'

That was all, but what a lot it meant! Brian's father had compressed his reply into two words which conveyed more than his son had done in a dozen!

Next morning Ted and Brian went for a stroll along het waterfront. They had not gone very far when they noticed a familiar figure rolling towards them. It was Captain Théophile Corbière returning to the *Fifine* after an all-night carouse ashore. He was almost upon them before his bleared eyes recognized the *gamins* who had baulked him of a small fortune. He scowled, then as the lads went by he saluted them with a gesture that would have flung any of his compatriots into a white-hot fury.

Ted and Brian burst out laughing. They just couldn't help it. Then they passed on, leaving Corbière to realize slowly that his final act of contempt had fallen very, very flat.

At last the eventful Monday arrived. Escorted by their jovial host, the boys boarded the steamer, dubbed by courtesy the mail boat, that was to take them to Panama.

There, after a tedious forty-eight hour wait they took passages to Santa Teresa in a vessel bound for Valparaiso.

Actually from Papeete the chums were travelling along two sides of an enormous triangle and covering more than twice the direct distance between that place and Santa Teresa. How they—especially Brian—chafed at the tedious voyage, even though it was performed at eighteen knots compared with the *Sempione's* three-knot drift half-way across the Pacific!

When at length the S.S. *Esquilino* was secured to the wharf at Santa Teresa they thought that their adventures were at an end.

They weren't!

XXXIV

PEACE!

TRUE to their resolution to maintain a discreet silence over certain facts concerning the *Sempione*, Brian and Ted had refrained from giving their version of what had happened to the crew. At Papeete, Captain Dubois had not pressed the point, thereby saving Brian and Ted the unpleasant task of having to refuse him. Panama had produced a knot of reporters to question and cross-question the two survivors of the long-missing ship; and it was here for the first time that they heard that none of the officers and crew had been seen or heard of since the ship left Santa Teresa.

So far, the Captain of the Grossaguayan cruiser *Chacal* had 'got away with it'!

The general idea was that the *Sempione* had been abandoned in heavy weather; but, for some unexplained reason, the two young English passengers had been left behind. Now, speculation was rife as to the reason for their abandonment, coupled with suspicions that grew with the lads' refusal to discuss the subject with representatives of the American Press.

The mob that awaited the S.S. *Esquilino* to berth at Santa Teresa almost petrified Ted and Brian. Obviously this strange crowd hadn't foregathered merely to see the usual fortnightly steamer make fast. There were Bolomayan soldiers and gauchos, policemen and *peons*, Indians and half-castes, swarms of women and children and a big leavening of reporters and cameramen—all waiting to greet the only two passengers who had booked to disembark at Santa Teresa.

Short of remaining on board, there was no way of escape. The customs officials would see to that!

The friends stood on the boat-deck waving to the mob, not because they wanted to but it seemed just as well to appear pleased with their boisterous welcome.

Just as the brow was being run out, Ted touched Brian on the shoulder. 'Look, there's your governor!' he exclaimed.

Mr. Steele, instead of keeping to his original intention to 'Awaitu here' at the Estancia Miraflores, had come down to the coast to welcome his son and his friend, whom he had never expected to see again.

Brian commenced to wave, although his eyes were so misty that he could not see his father's enthusiastic reply.

The end of the gangplank clattered on the wharf. Brian and Ted shook hands with the *Esquilino's* captain and the purser and then, carrying their battered and weather-worn suitcases, made their way down the inclined brow.

Cameras clicked and turned, according to their kind; people cheered and flung excited questions, Pressmen surged forward, eager to catch the first words that fell from the new arrivals' lips. But for the prompt action of the troops—who seemed to have smartened up considerably since the days of Bombardo's régime— the two youths might have had a very rough time, finishing with a dip in the harbour through the ill-advised though well-meant attentions of the crowd.

'We are sorry but we cannot say anything about the *Sempione* until we have delivered a most important letter to His Excellency President Sandano,' announced Brian.

It was a bit of bluff, although he did have the document safe in his possession. It worked. The soldiers and police cleared a way to the customs shed, where the officials with many bows waved them inside for the examination of their scanty belongings.

Escorted by two military officers, Mr. Steele was brought through the throng. Father and son shook hands and then Mr. Steele greeted Ted with a few words of welcome, words that were hardly audible above the clamour of the baulked but indefatigable army of Pressmen.

Somehow the trio reached a waiting car. Then, to the lads' surprise, Mr. Steele took the wheel. Evidently fortune had once more favoured the impoverished owner of the Estancia Miraflores!

'We must see the President, Dad!' announced Brian.

'Right!' Ambrose Steele was one of those men who, taking things for granted, rarely ask for an explanation. His son apparently had business with President Sandano; that was good enough.

The car glided on its way. The boys had had so many surprises that the fact that the car was escorted by a dozen mounted troopers of the Presidential bodyguard hardly excited their interest.

In half an hour—how long had it taken them to make the journey by train!—they entered the courtyard of Sandano's official residence at Ligna Salta. What a difference from their last visit under Bombardo's rudely interrupted term of office! Then a solitary surly soldier had curtly inquired their business and had put obstacles in their way. Now the guard, smart in well-fitting uniforms, had turned out and were standing at the salute. The President, informed by telephone of the impending visit of the two survivors from the *Sempione*, had given orders for them to be received with proper respect.

Without delay they were shown into Sandano's presence, Mr. Steele remaining in the car. The President was in a large, luxuriously furnished room and

with him were half a dozen of his ministers. He rose
and extended his hand to his callers.

'It is good that you have taken such an early opportunity to visit me,' he began. 'I await with great
interest the story of your adventures from your own
lips.'

'But, your Excellency, it is not with that intention
that we came,' rejoined Brian. 'Just before the *Sempione* left Santa Teresa, ex-President Bombardo entrusted this letter to me. Here it is: you will observe
that it is under cover addressed to Señor Madeira of
La Serena.'

'Señor Madeira of La Serena?' echoed Sandano,
taking the envelope. 'I do not know any person of that
name. Nevertheless you say that the enclosure is for
me?' He picked up a silver paper-knife and slowly slit
the flap of an outer envelope. Then, glancing at the
address on the enclosure, he smiled. 'It would seem as
if I have changed my *locale* since this was written,' he
remarked.'It is a far cry from Carabaya to Ligna Salta.'

He sat down at the table. His ministers discreetly
looked in front of them. None saw the flush on his
face as he read. He placed the folded letter on the table
and remained in deep thought for some moments.

Then, 'Señores!' he exclaimed. 'You have my confidence, and I know I have yours. Here and now, and
in the presence of these English gentlemen, I make
this solemn statement: Had this document reached
me on the plateau of Carabaya, as the villainous
Bombardo meant it to do, I should not be holding
my present position as President of the Bolomayan
Republic. I will explain.'

Amidst dead silence on the part of his audience,
Sandano told of Bombardo's duplicity; how that by
means of this letter he hoped to lure General Sandano,
as he then was, from his fortified position on the
plateau into making a sortie with the idea of joining

forces with the main Bolomayan army. Had Sandano done so, he and his men would have been surrounded and cut to pieces by superior Grossaguayan forces, because Bombardo had no intention of co-operating with his compatriot.

'And by the accident to the *Sempione*—fortunate as far as I was concerned—this treachery was frustrated,' Sandano continued. 'But for the good offices of these two Englishmen in going to great pains to preserve and deliver this document, I should have remained in ignorance of Bombardo's perfidy. And now,' he continued, addressing Brian, who seemed to be the spokesman, 'I shall be interested to hear of what befell the ship after she sailed from Santa Teresa.'

Brian came to the holding up of the *Sempione* by the *Chacal* and the peremptory orders of the latter's captain that the letter addressed to General Sandano must be surrendered to the Grossaguayan Government.

'There you see, gentlemen, another aspect of Bombardo's treachery,' interrupted the President. 'He meant that letter to fall into the hands of Bolomaya's enemies in order to make sure of my defeat and death, to the undoing of our beloved country. Now proceed, please.'

Soon Sandano was in possession of the most important fact: that the *Chacal* had caused the abandonment of the Catamarcan ship, and had been responsible for the loss of her officers and crew, whose disappearance had hitherto been put down solely to the violence of a storm.

'Have you mentioned this to anyone else?' he asked anxiously.

'No, Excellency. We thought it best not to,' replied Brian, and Ted nodded in confirmation.

'Then please continue not to do so,' resumed Sandano. 'I do not ask you to take an oath; I have good reason to believe that the word of an Englishman is his bond. You, gentlemen,'—addressing his ministers— 'will realize the utmost importance of secrecy.'

'Might I remind you, Excellency,' interposed one of them, 'that Admiral Perez—he was promoted by his government for his services during the late war—was in command of the *Chacal*. He is now Naval Attaché at Ligna Salta.'

'So he is!' exclaimed Sandano. 'I had forgotten. That complicates matters. However, these English gentlemen should know certain facts in order that they may be able the better to appreciate the urgency for their secrecy.'

He went on to explain that at the conclusion of the war between Bolomaya and Grossaguay, a solemn pact of non-aggression had been signed by the former enemies, with the important proviso that should either be attacked by the Republic of Catamarca the other should go to its assistance.

Consequently, if Catamarca ever learnt of the circumstances under which the *Sempione*—which sailed under that republic's flag—was attacked and her crew sent to their death, the chances were that there would be a war between her and Grossaguay. By virtue of her pact Bolomaya would have to join in and that republic would again experience all the horrors of a devastating war.

'So now, gentlemen,' Sandano concluded, 'in the interests of all parties concerned it would be well to let the fate of the *Sempione's* crew fade into oblivion. It is, of course, quite within the rights of these English gentlemen to lodge a claim for damages against the Grossaguayan Government, but in the circumstances I trust they will not proceed in that direction, in view of the dangerous situation I have already mentioned. We should be prepared to offer them a substantial sum to recompense them for the inconveniences to which they have been put.'

'But, your Excellency, we don't want to be—to be

rewarded for that,' interrupted Brian. He had very nearly said the Spanish equivalent for 'bribe', but had checked himself just in time.

President Sandano waved his hand in deprecation of such a suggestion. 'It is the duty of the Republic to reward its benefactors,' he declared grandly. 'In your case it shall be done!'

Next day the chums found themselves back at the Estancia Miraflores. They talked freely of their adventures to Ambrose Steele except on one subject upon which they preserved a difficult silence—the fate of the *Sempione's* crew.

Then they heard Mr. Steele's story. On top of his straitened existence on the fringe of the war area came the report of the loss of the *Sempione*, with all on board. The end of hostilities and the election of the national hero—for General Sandano had held out magnificently and by so doing had saved Bolomaya from humiliating terms—had helped Mr. Steele's financial position, since the new President was a friend of his. The prompt payment of compensation long overdue, more than tided him over his monetary difficulties, hence the car that had taken the place of the sorry horses that had lately been his means of transport.

A few days after the return of his son and Ted Evans —the new government seemed to have abandoned its policy of *mañana*—as a complete surprise came a deed conferring the Estancia Miraflores upon Ambrose Steele in perpetuity, while the boys received a munificent sum from the grateful Sandano.

These gifts, followed by a surprisingly large sum in respect of salvage money, put the Steeles and Ted Evans above further pecuniary anxiety, while, with conditions becoming stabilized in the remodelled Republic, the prospects at the Estancia Miraflores were very rosy indeed.